TRIBAL LAW

REVELATION

By Dave H Jordan

DEDICATIONS

TO GOD BE THE GLORY FOR THIS ENDEAVOR AND MAY EVERY WORD HONOR HIM AND HIS KINGDOM.

THIS BOOK IS DEDICATED TO MY REMARKABLE WIFE, AND HER UNRIVALLED STRENGTH: MENTAL, PHYSICAL AND SPIRITUAL STRENGTH, AS WELL AS HER UNPARALLELED STRENGTH OF CHARACTER, AND HER UNFAILING AND UNWAVERING LOVE. I WOULD BE LOST WITHOUT YOU AND I AM WHO I AM BECAUSE OF YOU. I LIKE YOU, I LOVE YOU AND I'M IN LOVE WITH YOU. YOU ARE MY BEST FRIEND AND MY INSPIRATION.

AND TO MY BELOVED GRANDMOTHER, EURIKA FAIRFAX HALL (1918-2013). I WILL MISS OUR LONG CONVERSATIONS, PEOPLE WATCHING, YOUR ENCOURAGEMENT AND YOUR CONFIDENCE IN ME. THANK YOU FOR YOUR WISDOM, ADVICE IN FAITH, ENDURING LOVE AND INFECTIOUS LAUGHTER. I LOVE YOU ALWAYS.

CONTENTS

Page

Prologue 1

Part 1: The Truth Shall Set You Free 4

- Chapter I 5
- Chapter II..15
- Chapter III 25
- Chapter IV 40
- Chapter V..57
- Chapter VI..76
- Chapter VII...91

Part 2: The Seeds of Change 97

- Chapter VIII 98
- Chapter IX 112
- Chapter X..125
- Chapter XI 137
- Chapter XII...149
- Chapter XIII 165

Part 3: Necessary Predicaments 182

- Chapter XIV 183
- Chapter XV 189
- Chapter XVI 195
- Chapter XVII...206
- Chapter XVIII 212
- Chapter XIX 221

Part 4: Until the End of Time 235

- **Chapter XX**...236
- **Chapter XXI** 241
- **Chapter XXII**...255
- **Chapter XXIII** 272
- **Chapter XXIV** 277
- **Chapter XXV**...286
- **Chapter XXVI** 300
- **Chapter XXVII**...305
- **Chapter XXVIII** 314

PROLOGUE

Life offers no one any guarantees. All anyone can do is be the best you can be, live well, stand for something bigger than yourself, and do not compromise your beliefs for anything. Along the way on this journey called life, a daily voyage into the unknown, you can only hope to work in a profession you love, prayerfully find someone you can love with all your heart and have the faith to believe that person will love you back as fervently as you have chosen to love him/her. That is an earnest pursuit for happiness and fulfillment and a privilege for everyone who seeks it.

For the most part, Marcus has lived his life this way. He has given his best effort in anything and everything he put his mind to accomplish. Years ago he surrendered to God, made Christ his Lord and Savior and chose to put God first in his life. He always prays and asks God for guidance before making his choices. The Word of God is his road map through life whether it comes from the Bible or from the various ways God chooses to communicate with Marcus based on Marcus' profound relationship with Him. It is the Word that guides Marcus' heart to love, to give and to mentor others; and, it is the Word that led Marcus to his beloved Zephora, the love of his life.

Zephora is Marcus' equal, and the half that makes him whole. Since they first met more than a year ago, they have gone from being friends, to becoming best friends, to being engaged to being almost married and to having their wedding thwarted twice by the would be African tyrant, Kwazan, who attempted to take Zephora as his queen and have Marcus killed. Marcus was able to meet that threat head on and come out on the other side victorious but not without scars, both physical and psychological.

The ordeal brought Marcus to the brink of death three times and the third brush with death has him still in the hospital fighting for his life. However, it seemingly hasn't prevented Marcus and Zephora from getting married and it would seem that the same love and marriage bug that bit them has also taken a bite out of their respective best friends, Angelo and Veronica, as well.

The two sets of friends are in Marcus' hospital room preparing to lovingly share an incredible moment together. The two couples are about to exchange vows as soon as Pastor Chappell finishes his trademark wedding speech that always precedes the exchanging of vows between every couple he marries. Surrounded by Zephora's parents, Zuri and Saphera, as well as Marcus' sister Charlie, joy has settled in the room as Marcus finds the strength to get out of the bed and sits in a wheel chair with his betrothed on his right, and Angelo and Veronica on his left. The door has been locked to keep out any unwanted elements that might unsuspectingly attempt to interrupt the pending nuptials; and, it would appear the wait is finally over for the two best of friends, Marcus and Angelo, as they are about to marry the two respective women of their dreams, Zephora and Veronica.

PART 1

The Truth Will Set You Free

CHAPTER I

As Pastor Chappell begins the hospital room marriage ceremony for the two couples, Marcus and Zephora for their third attempt and Angelo and Veronica in their first, he chooses to skip ahead of his normal introduction and get right to it in hopes of avoiding any interruptions. He loves Marcus and Zephora, but one more failed attempt at getting married is enough to cause even the Pastor to doubt the validity of their claim that God said they are made for one another.

"Dearly beloved, we are gathered here today to join Marcus and Zephora, and Angelo and Veronica in Holy matrimony. These two couples understand that marriage should not be entered into lightly and it is a pledge of commitment between themselves and God." He pauses, and chooses his next words wisely as they have ended his last two wedding ceremonies with Marcus and Zephora. He clears his throat and with faith and God's blessings clearly states, "If there are any objections to these unions, speak now or forever hold your peace."

All eight in attendance begin to look around at one another and then at the door of Marcus' room which has been locked to insure there would be no interruptions, not even from Marcus' doctor or nurses. While everyone is looking around,

Pastor Chappell begins a countdown in his head, "One one thousand, two one thousand, three one thousand four one thousand, five one thousand, six one thousand, seven one thousand, eight one thousand, nine one thousand;" until he reaches, "ten one thousand." Immediately after reaching ten, Pastor Chappell breathes a sigh of relief, smiles and continues with the ceremonies. "Let us pray. *Father God, we come before You today to first thank You. We thank You for life and life in abundance; we thank You for blessing us all with opportunities that others may not be fortunate enough to have. We thank You Father God for food, shelter and clothing. We thank You for keeping Brother Marcus safe through the night and for continuing in his healing process. We pray Father God that he make a full recovery and we thank You in advance for it. Next Heavenly Father, we ask and pray for Your forgiveness of our sins; the sins we are aware of and those we are not. Please make known to us all of our sins that we may repent and move forward covered by You. Now Father God, I pray for Your blessings over these young people as they enter into this next phase of their lives together. Marriage is the true test of friendship, love and commitment between a man and woman. I ask that You anoint them with Your Holy Spirit this day Father God and protect them all the days of their lives from the devourer. I pray Father God that You guide these four young* *people's lives so that they may guide others; and help them to be fruitful and multiply. Bless the parents of these young people and all other members of their families. Father God these young ones are about to embark on a life journey they do not yet understand; help them to remember to pray, remember to be humble, and to remember You are in control of all. We praise You Father God, we thank You Father God, and may our lives always be used for the honor and glory of Your Holy Kingdom; for You who began a work in us, is faithful to complete it. We ask all these prayers in Jesus Christ Holy name; Amen.* And all in attendance followed with a resounding "In Jesus Christ Holy name; Amen."*

With the prayer done, Pastor Chappell moves on to the next part of the ceremony hoping and praying this time he will actually be able to complete it. "Who here supports these couples in marriage today?" In a single resounding unified voice, Charlie, Saphera and Zuri look at one another and loudly say, "We do!" The three are holding hands and their smiles cannot be contained. For Charlie and Saphera, they have been waiting for this moment between Marcus and Zephora for what seems like an eternity; and having Angelo and Veronica joining them is a bonus that helps to widen their smiles. Zuri is overwhelmed. He hasn't had a reason to smile this big and feel so proud in such a long time. A year ago, he couldn't have imagined being there to see his babygirl get married, and now that he is, his smile is only matched by the joyous tears that stream down his face. He was not able to see his babygirl grow up, to hold her when she cried or to celebrate her accomplishments; and, not to mention, he has grown to love and respect Marcus, and cannot imagine anyone better for his daughter.

The moment is overwhelming for the two brides as well. They both begin to cry as the intensity of the moment takes its toll on their nerves. Marcus, sensing the passion of the moment, finds the strength to push himself up from his wheel chair, and his determination to stand is met by the solidarity of Angelo who simultaneously reaches down to help pull Marcus to his feet. Marcus feels blessed to be alive and even more blessed to have Zephora as his bride; and to have Angelo as his friend. Now standing next to his bride, Marcus gently uses his thumbs to wipe the tears from Zephora's eyes. Zephora thought she lost Marcus in Africa; and then, he took two bullets from Kwazan in order to save her life. How can she ever repay him for that? Is her love enough? She hopes so.

Pastor Chappell continues with the vows. "Marcus, do you take Zephora whose hand you now hold to be your lawful, wedded wife? Do you promise to love and cherish her, in sickness and in health, for richer or poorer, for better or worse, forsaking all others, keeping yourself only unto her, for so long as you both shall live?" Marcus takes his time, turns and looks into Zephora's weeping brown eyes, reaches up with his left hand and wipes her tears. He has waited for what seems like a lifetime to respond to this question. He went halfway around the world to be able to answer the pastor. He made the ultimate sacrifice by diving in front of a bullet to save the life of his betrothed and would do it again just to reply to this line of questioning. Smiling and staring into Zephora's eyes, Marcus takes a deep breath and proudly articulates "with all my heart I do!"

Again Pastor Chappell speaks, this time turning to Angelo. "Angelo, do you take Veronica whose hand you now hold to be your lawful, wedded wife? Do you promise to love and cherish her, in sickness and in health, for richer or poorer, for better or worse, forsaking all others, keeping yourself only unto her, for so long as you both shall live?" Until recently, Angelo could not have conceived of being in this position, but six months ago, upon being introduced to Veronica, he knew she was different and it didn't take long for her to capture his heart and stimulate his mind. Now Angelo, who is using his left hand to help hold Marcus up, first leans over, whispers in Marcus' ear "Together we stand," and then moves his left arm slowly from around Marcus' back, giving Marcus the opportunity to place his hand on Angelo's shoulder for balance. Angelo turns to his bride, holds both of Veronica's hands, stares genuinely into her eyes, and in a deep voice states "I most certainly do!" After which, Marcus whispers to Angelo "divided never," and they both smile.

The two best friends have done it, they have committed themselves to their beautiful respective lady loves, and now stand awaiting the responses of their brides to the same love committing question. Zephora has been waiting for what seems like a lifetime to say I do to Marcus and with the biggest smile on her face she is beginning to get impatient with the waiting process. Veronica on the other hand, is starting to get nervous. There is no doubt that she loves Angelo more than any man she has ever met; however, is this the way she wants to get married to him? Things have progressed so fast she hasn't had a chance to let her parents know. "Wow" she thinks to herself "my mother has never even met Angelo, how can I marry him without my mother meeting him?" Her thoughts and her nerves are all over the place and her right leg begins to shake, her face tenses up and furrows form between her eyebrows. "Is this my moment, is this the way I want to become a wife to this man I love so dearly? My God, what am I going to do, what am I going to say?" Angelo notices the tension in her face and gently begins to rub the top of her hand with his thumb and

Veronica raises her eyes to meet his and instantaneously she realizes that she has been waiting for this man her whole life and he will love her forever. She is no longer nervous and the furrows melt away from between her eyes, and are replaced with a smile and she tightly holds on to Angelo's hand.

Pastor Chappell first turns his attention to Zephora. "Zephora, do you take Marcus whose hand you now hold to be your lawful, wedded husband? Do you promise to love and cherish him, in sickness and in health, for richer or poorer, for better or worse, and forsaking all others, keeping yourself only unto him, for so long as you both shall live?" Unlike Marcus, Zephora doesn't take her time, and without hesitation answers. "I do, to the depths of my soul, I do!" Marcus is overcome with joy; "it is actually happening," he thinks to himself and his heart is beating extremely fast, almost too fast. He starts to get weak and instinctively Angelo reaches over to hold up his friend. Long ago the two friends promised to be there for one another, no matter what. That type of loyalty produces bonds in men that instill responsibility, empowerment, accountability and the love of true friendship and brotherhood.

Pastor Chappell then turns his attention towards Veronica. She is more confident now but still shaking in her shoes. "Veronica, do you take Angelo whose hand you now hold to be your lawful, wedded husband? Do you promise to love and cherish him, in sickness and in health, for richer or poorer, for better or worse, forsaking all others, keeping yourself only unto him, for so long as you both shall live?" Veronica takes her time, clears the frog out of her throat and carefully begins to speak with all eyes on her. "I do, I really, really do!"

Pastor Chappell takes a sigh of relief and continues. "Do you have rings?" Zuri steps in and hands Marcus his ring and Zephora hers and kisses her on the cheek as he steps back. Angelo reaches in his pocket and pulls out the ring box he retrieved from Marcus' home the night before and places one band in Veronica's hand and he holds on to the other.

"Gentlemen, repeat after me and in doing so slide the rings onto your brides' fingers: with this ring, I thee wed." It is at this moment that Angelo must allow Marcus to stand on his own, and it is this moment that Marcus has been waiting on for a long time and has been saving his strength for. The two friends standing side by side glance at one another and then face their perspective brides. Each takes the left hand of his bride and while sliding the rings of their lady's ring finger simultaneously state: "with this ring, I thee wed." Zephora bursts into tears of joy while thinking to herself, "Oh my God, it's finally happening."

Pastor Chappell turns to the brides, "ladies repeat after me and in doing so slide the ring on your groom's finger: with this ring, I thee wed." Zephora is crying but through her tears she is able to get the words out concurrently with Veronica, whose voice is trembling while they slide the rings on each groom's hand: "with this ring, I thee wed." The two couples turn now to face Pastor Chappell who begins to speak. "Now by the authority vested in me by the state of Georgia, and witnessed by your family and friends, I pronounce you husbands and wives; you may kiss your brides." Marcus places his hands on Zephora's face, pulls her in close, and softly lets his lips touch Zephora's lips before embracing her and passionately engaging in a real kiss. Angelo, overjoyed, is not so deliberate. He takes his new wife in his arms and the two of them engage in a long, wet and passionate kiss. Zuri, Saphera and Charlie begin clapping and shouting cheers and congratulations. Pastor Chappell makes his final decree of the quaint ceremony. "Ladies and gentlemen, it is my pleasure to introduce to you Mr. and Mrs. Marcus Howard, and Mr. and Mrs. Angelo Henson. Let us pray." Just as Pastor Chappell prepares to bless them with prayer, a mobile phone starts to ring. "Whoever has a phone ringing, please, shut it off!"

Everyone searches for the phone when Zephora notices it is Angelo's phone in his coat pocket on the chair in the corner where he slept in the early morning hours after Marcus had been revived. Zephora turns to Angelo and says, "It's your phone Angelo! Angelo, it's your phone ringing, Angelo your phone is ringing, Angelo!" At that moment, Angelo wakes up and Zephora is shaking him screaming at him that his phone is ringing; but, before he can gather himself and answer it, it abruptly stops ringing. Angelo then realizes he is sitting in the corner of Marcus' room and it was all just a dream. He drops his head into his hands in disbelief and murmurs: "my God, that felt so real."

CHAPTER II

Angelo's phone begins to ring again. This time he catches it on the second ring and instantly leaves the room in an attempt to not wake Marcus, and Zephora follows Angelo out.

"Angelo, who is blowing up your phone," Zephora sharply asks.

"Hold on," Angelo whispers and then answers his phone, "Hello." On the other end of the line, a man with a soft voice responds to Angelo's whisper.

"Good morning, is this Mr. Angelo Henson?"

"Yes it is," responds Angelo, "who is this and how can I help you?"

"My name is Matthew Hillberg, and I am the attorney of your grandmother, Ms. Ellanor Henson."

"What's wrong, what happened to my grandmother?" Angelo snaps.

"What's wrong Angelo?" Zephora chimes in.

"Shhh Zephora I'm trying to hear," Angelo replies.

"Mr. Henson," Matthew softly urges, "I'm sorry to tell you that your grandmother has suffered a massive heart attack and is in ICU here at Tampa Memorial." Angelo doesn't speak, he falls back against the wall and drops his head as Matthew continues. "Her doctors have stabilized her, but…"

"But what!" Angelo shouts, "What are you saying?"

Matthew's voice pierces through the phone as he softly continues, "they have her stable for now but the prognosis doesn't look good. It is imperative that you get here as quickly as you can."

Angelo taps the end call button on his phone as he slides down the wall and sits on the floor with his head in his hands and tears begin to stream down his face. Zephora kneels down beside him with a look of distress on her face.

"Angelo what's wrong, what has happened, tell me what's going on?"

"He said my grandmother is in ICU, she had a massive heart attack and they don't expect her to make it." Angelo's voice is shaky as he gets the words out.

Zephora has never seen Angelo so paralyzed before. "Angelo, get up, we have to get you a flight out of here. Come on I'll help you." The door to Marcus' room is partially open and lying there awake, Marcus has heard everything and calls out to Zephora.

"Zephora," Marcus calls out, his voice barely over a whisper and parched because he hasn't had anything to drink in a while, "Zephora, I need you."

"I'm here Marcus, I'm right here." Zephora helps Angelo up and they both walk in the room and stand next to Marcus' bed. Zephora leans over to better hear Marcus and Angelo stands there for moral support still with the tears streaming down his face.

"Tell Angelo to take the royal jet," Marcus whispers while grabbing Angelo's hand, "he should take the royal jet."

Zephora turns and looks at Angelo who is now seriously crying from the pain of the news and the gratitude from Marcus' gesture. And now the rest of the troop (Veronica, Charlie, Zuri and Saphera) enter Marcus' room. Saphera instantly heads over to give her daughter a hug. Charlie stops at Marcus' bed and leans over to kiss her brother on the forehead; Veronica immediately notices the pain Angelo is in, even though he tries to hide it.

"Angelo, what's wrong baby, what has happened?" Angelo turns and fades into her arms unable to control his tears, and Zuri is fixated on the passion of their interaction. "Baby what's wrong?" Veronica asks again her voice filled with compassion. Angelo's grandmother is everything to him; she is all the family he has. Since he left her to come here and be Marcus' best man, he has not missed an opportunity to call her every week, like clockwork, and her health has always been remarkably outstanding. The sudden and unexpected news of

17

his grandmother's hospitalization, coupled with the gratitude of Marcus, has revealed a more sensitive side to this normally strong man, a man's man. Angelo is barely able to talk through his tears so Zephora fills everyone in on what has transpired. Zuri offers to act as the liaison for the tribal counsel in the use of the royal jet which is needed in order for someone outside the counsel to use the jet. After a long hug from Veronica, Angelo returns to Marcus' bedside and leans over to give his best friend a hug.

"Thank you Marcus, I really appreciate this."

Marcus' voice is still raspy and he is still a little groggy, "I only wish I was going with you. Give your grandmother my love and tell her I miss her dearly."

"I will brother, I will." Angelo and Zuri are about to leave when Veronica steps in the way.

"Angelo, you are not going anywhere without me."

"I wouldn't have it any other way my darling," Angelo remarks as he has gathered himself and is now able to muster up a smile. Just as they are about to leave Marcus' room, Zephora calls out for them to wait.

"First father, how could you leave without even wanting to know how Marcus is doing, isn't that the reason you came here? Second, I'm fine too by the way; however, more important than that, is you doing what Marcus would do if he had the strength to do it, pray. As the elder gentleman here father, the duty is yours."

"My daughter, forgive me for neglecting to acknowledge you, I am still trying to get used to having you near me. My first impulse is always to help those who need me and I got caught up in that moment. However, when it comes to praying, it has been a long time since I even thought about praying. I cannot and should not be the one who prays for us all." At that moment Saphera steps in.

"Zuri my love, it only takes love to know how to pray. You of all people are full of love. You risked everything for love. You stayed away from your family for love. God is love and just like the rest of us, you are a child of the Almighty and thus an extension of love. I have trusted you since the first time we met and I trust you now to pray for your family, so please, believe as much as we all do."

Speechless for a moment, Zuri drops his head and then requests that they all hold hands. They all surround Marcus' bed; Zephora takes hold of Marcus' right hand and Zuri standing on the other side of the bed takes hold of his left hand. Marcus' doctor and nurses are on their way in and choose to join the circle as well.

"Gracious Master, Heavenly Father, and Trusted Friend, we stand here today first and foremost thanking You

for waking us today and giving us this unique opportunity to try and be better *today than we were yesterday. We thank You for restoring families, revitalizing friendships and reassuring our faith in You. We thank You for the continued healing of our young brother Marcus, for being with him through the night as he experienced a rough time and fought off death, and for surrounding him with a talented team of doctors and nurses. We pray that all his wounds will heal: mental, physical, and emotional. Father God we intercede this morning for Angelo's grandmother. We pray You send the Comforter to be with her at this time of need. Put her at peace and allow her to rest; be with the doctors and nurses as they care for her. Allow us traveling mercies as we take flight to be with her. And while we are gone Father God, protect our families and friends. Keep Your Angels encamped around us all and protect us from the powers and principalities that wish to steal, kill, and destroy; hold the devourer at bay on our behalf. Forgive us Master for our transgressions and we also forgive those who have trespassed and transgressed against us now and our families in the past. Lord, we love You and thank You for loving us despite our lapses in faith and neglect of our relationship with You. Father God we ask that You bless us and shower us with a fresh anointing of Your Holy Spirit. One that cleanses, purifies and restores a right spirit within us. Father we praise You and worship You with our words, our actions, our deeds, and thereby our very lives. It is in Jesus Christ Holy name we pray. Amen.* Everyone else in attendance follows with a resounding Amen.

Angelo, Veronica and Zuri spread hugs and kisses around the room. Zephora apologizes to her father for thinking he had forgotten about her and Marcus, which his prayer clearly showed he hadn't.

Saphera pulls her husband away from everyone with tears of sadness and joy in her eyes. "Zuri, I am so proud of you my husband and I am equally upset with you for choosing to leave me and your daughter alone again so soon."

"Wife, I am not leaving you, I am helping a trusted family friend. I do not have to stay; I just need to get Angelo and Veronica there and I will return immediately. Helping others is what I do; what I have always done." With that, the two embrace as if no one else is in the room. As they release from their embrace, Saphera turns to her daughter Zephora, who is sitting next to a barely coherent Marcus and smiles.

"Zephora baby, do you need me here for the next couple of days?"

"No mother, Marcus and I are fine. He is out of any immediate danger and all we can do is wait for him to start feeling better."

"Okay then, I'm going with your father, and together with Veronica, we will support Angelo in this difficult time." Marcus, who is drifting in and out of consciousness, is able to smile at Saphera and squeeze out a gratifying thank you.

Angelo makes his way over to Marcus' bed, grabs Marcus' hand and whispers in his ear, "United we stand." Marcus, who in this moment is nearly out of it, is unable to verbally respond, but manages to tighten the grip on the bonding shake he and Angelo are engaged in. The morning has been difficult on Marcus and the fact that most everyone is about to leave makes his doctor extremely happy as he ushers all of Marcus' guests except for Zephora out of the room. Charlie walks everyone out and gives Angelo one final hug and insures him that she and Marcus' prayers are with him. Afterwards, she walks back through the hospital and takes her all too familiar post in the family waiting area with a big frustrating sigh followed by, "I'm so sick of this place." Charlie has not been home since she came to Atlanta months ago, to what she thought was going to be her brother's wedding. She had amassed what she thought what was going to be the perfect wedding gift for Marcus and ended up on the journey of a lifetime. Now she is here for the second time in three months and about to become part of the upholstery again.

Meanwhile, Angelo, Veronica, Zuri and Saphera have made their way to the jet and are on their way to see Angelo's grandmother, praying the whole time that she will be alright. The flight will take at least an hour and Angelo uses the time to reflect back on all the lessons his grandmother had lovingly taught him. Some of these lessons he enjoyed and others he did not; either way, the lessons have not been forgotten. It was Angelo's grandmother who first insisted that he befriend Marcus, which has turned out to be the best lesson of them all: a lesson in patience.

The plane touches down on the airfield and it marks the first time Angelo has ever been anxious to be home. During the flight, Zuri called for a limo to pick them up. The plane has barely had time to reach the tarmac and Angelo is ready to get off. He is extremely nervous; his mind is racing and he is erratic, visibly shaken up and ready to go. Angelo and Veronica are already sitting in the car when Zuri and Saphera catch up and get in the car, and Angelo's right leg just won't stop shaking. Veronica places her hand gently on his knee and strokes it slowly to calm Angelo down. The driver spares no tread on the tires as he peels off to get his four passengers to the hospital. Angelo calls the hospital and there has been no change in his grandmother's condition. Because of her vivaciousness and vigor, no one would have ever suspected that Angelo's grandmother is ninety-six; she has always moved and acted like someone twenty-five to thirty years younger. Maybe it was the responsibility of raising a young boy alone that kept her looking and feeling so young up to now. Depending on Angelo's outlook of life, this is possibly either the end of a chapter in his life or the beginning of another; ironically it is both, but his perception of the situation will determine how he enters this next chapter without her. His grandmother, his only family, is dying and her eventual passing is destined to change his life forever.

CHAPTER III

Now that all the commotion has died down around Marcus, his new doctor, Dr. Lott, is able to give Marcus and Zephora the prognosis of his condition.

"Mr. Howard you were extremely lucky. The bullet that penetrated your chest cavity missed major arteries and grazed your right lung which we were able to easily, well maybe not so easily, repair. There should be no long-term physical damage because of your injuries; however, all that being said, we are going to be keeping you here for at least a couple of weeks to insure you don't contract pneumonia or retain any fluid in your chest, as well as making sure you do not reopen your wounds or begin to hemorrhage." Dr. Lott finishes with, "do you have any questions?"

Marcus is motivated by how thorough his doctor is in explaining his situation. He chimes in with his questions and remarks. "Doc, I first want to thank you for taking such good care of my body. I would like to ask, when can I get rid of this IV, oxygen apparatus and pain pump, well maybe we keep the pain pump a while; but the other two, when can I be rid of them?"

Zephora sits calmly next to Marcus caringly holding his hand the whole time and shaking her head at the silliness of her man as Dr. Lott gives Marcus his rebuttal.

"Well Mr. Howard, these devices are here to help us monitor you and make sure we are maintaining the proper amount of fluids and antibiotics required to precipitate your recovery; and of course, the pain pump will help you be more comfortable and hopefully we can disconnect it later this week as your condition improves."

With all the medical news out of the way, the four chat a few moments more before Dr. Lott leaves Marcus' room. Finally Marcus and Zephora are alone, but Marcus is exhausted after a day filled with an onslaught of emotions. Zephora reaches into the bed and presses the button for Marcus' pain pump and watches him slowly drift away to la la land, then presses it one more time for good measure and tenderly kisses Marcus on the forehead and then lets her lips softly and lovingly touch his. Now that Marcus is resting, she takes the time to go and talk with Charlie who is half asleep in the family waiting area.

Meanwhile at Tampa Memorial, Angelo finally gets to talk to his grandmother whose condition is stable for the moment.

"Granny what happened, how did this happen?" asks Angelo with tears in his eyes and a tremble in his voice.

In a very low toned whisper, his grandmother attempts to speak. "Listen baby, what happened is not important. What is important is what I have to tell you."

"I'm listening Granny, what is it?"

"When you were young, your parents died in a plane crash."

"I know Granny, you told me this before."

"Yes, but what I did not tell you is that they were killed because of who they were." At that moment she begins to cough, has a hard time breathing and her monitors begin to beep erratically.

"Shhh Granny, please stop talking now. We can talk about this later when you're feeling better."

"No son listen, I must tell you now, you need to know who your parents were and who you are. There isn't much time to..." In an instant, she begins breathing extremely fast and nurses rush into the room, in an attempt to stabilize her again. Zuri, who came down the hall looking for Angelo, finds him just as the doctors and nurses are doing their best to stabilize

Angelo's grandmother and keep her from going into full cardiac arrest. Zuri pulls Angelo back to allow the doctors to work and as he does, he catches a glimpse of the elder lady's face and is astonished; her face bears a familiarity of someone from his past. He faces Angelo and places his hands on his shoulders in an effort to help Angelo get control of his emotions. "Angelo I know this is tough, but you have got to pull yourself together, you cannot help her like this! Now listen, your grandmother looks familiar to me; tell me, what is her name?"

Still overcome with emotion and with tears in his eyes, Angelo takes a couple of deep breaths to pull himself together and says, "Her name is Ellanor, Ellanor Henson."

Not recognizing the name, Zuri turns and places his right hand on Angelo's right shoulder and walks him down the hall. "C'mon son, let the doctors do their job," and they proceed to the waiting room where Veronica and Saphera are waiting. Once there, Veronica takes over the duties of consoling Angelo and Zuri takes a seat next to Saphera still reeling from what he saw. Saphera notices his dismay and asks him what is wrong. "There is something familiar about Angelo's grandmother. I only got a glimpse of her but she looks like someone I used to know, but I must be mistaken, because she died a long time ago." Saphera can see the pain the memory is causing Zuri and decides not to pry any further.

Angelo is still having a hard time coping even with the beautiful Veronica soothing him. He whispers to her, "She's all I've got, my only family." She softly whispers back, "not anymore, you've got me too." Angelo gently tightens his grip on the embrace the two of them are sharing and is now enveloped by her warmth and her love, and returns her whisper with another of his own. "Thank you for being here, I love you Veronica Dawson;" and she, strokes the back of his head, leans in really close and with her lips almost touching Angelo's ear responds with a whisper that is softer than the softest cotton, "I love you back Angelo Henson," and Angelo's body melts into her satisfying and comforting embrace, and the truth of her words grip him tighter than the hug they are sharing.

Angelo's grandmother's doctor enters the waiting area, pulls off his head gear and begins to fumble with it in his hands like he is wringing out a face towel and holding his head down. His arrival hastens both couples to spring to their feet and approach him with anticipation of the news he comes to share.

———————————————————

Zephora sits in the chair next to the couch Charlie is lying on and is careful to not wake her; however, Charlie, who only just lying there, sits up and addresses Zephora.

"What's up sis, is my little brother doing better or what? I have tried not to interfere, but just sit back and let you do your thing; and I have to say, you're doing a great job of holding everything together."

"Thank you," Zephora interjects.

"However, right now, I need you to tell me the truth; how is my little brother?"

"He is well," responds Zephora, "there is no permanent physical damage from his wounds; he's getting the best care from Dr. Lott; and right now, he's resting comfortably. Now, how are you? You haven't been home in a while and spent way too many hours in this waiting room."

Charlie takes a breath and answers. "I'm doing well. So much has happened since I first came here to see you guys get married, and I've been living out of my suitcases for so long, it's starting to feel normal. But overall, life is good; my brother is recovering, he has you, and I can just sit back and be here as your supporting cast."

The two share a smile and a brief hug, and then Zephora asks a request of her future sister-in-law. "You know Charlie, I have everything under control here and I'm sure

Marcus is going to be out for a while. Why don't you take my car and go to Marcus' house, shower, get some food, and sleep in a bed for a while?"

Charlie graciously accepts Zephora's offer. "I think that is a great idea sis, thanks."

"And I wonder," Zephora remarks, "if you can do us a favor on your way back; no rush, no need to hurry back, but when you do come back; can you do it, the favor?"

"Of course I can Ze, anything, just name it."

"Thanks Charlie," and with that Zephora gives Charlie another hug. The two sit down and go over Zephora's request; after which, she gives Charlie her car keys and shows her which key is for Marcus' house. The two engage in one final hug before Charlie makes her way through the sliding doors of the hospital, and Zephora heads back down the hall to Marcus' room and pulls her chair up next to Marcus' bed. She presses the button to his pain pump again, reaches across his body, takes hold of his hand, kisses it, smiles, then lays her head on his stomach and whispers, "I love you Marcus Howard;" and, to her surprise, receives a soft whisper back, "Ditto Zephora Sherman, ditto."

Along with Angelo and Veronica, who are holding hands, Zuri and Saphera, who are doing the same, both staring directly into his mouth, Dr. Samuels, still twisting his hat, looks up and addresses his anxious audience. "Mr. Henson, your grandmother is relaxing comfortably for the moment, but she is not out of danger. We are monitoring her carefully; however, in my opinion, she does not have long to live. Her heart is simply giving out.

"Thank you doctor," Angelo calmly blurts out; followed by, "can I see her now?"

"Of course you can," replies the doctor, "right this way." As Dr. Samuels and Angelo head down the hall to his grandmother's room, Angelo reaches out for Veronica's hand to accompany him and Zuri stops them and suggests he also join Angelo for moral support and Veronica stay with Saphera until they are sure she is up to meeting Veronica. Reluctantly Angelo agrees and with the doc, they make their way down the hall to the room.

Once in the room, Zuri stands back and to the left of the bed out of Mrs. Henson's field of view, but at a good angle to see her when she turns her head his way. Angelo pulls a chair next to his grandmother's bed and places her hand in his and gently strokes it with his other hand, almost petting it ever so softly and tries to wake her. "Granny, can you hear me, it's me

Angelo, I'm here Granny, I'm here, everything's going to be okay Granny, and I'm here now."

Mrs. Henson is a tough old lady; she has always been this way, which is how she has survived this long. Even Angelo has no idea of the hardships she had to face and overcome to make it this far. As she lay there quiet and still, the deep wrinkle lines across her forehead, the crow's feet wrinkles at the corners of her eyes and the dark brown wrinkled skin hanging from her neck and chin read like an old scroll telling tales of ancient times. Her hair used to be jet black and soft as cotton is now gray but still soft complimenting her ageless features. Her lips are full, the top one dark almost like her skin and the bottom one still naturally rosy and pink. Her nose is wide and comes to a point at the tip, her eyes, though they are closed, set back in her face and slant upward exotically, helping to make her cheeks plump and full. She has always been a slender lady, and now in her nineties, her five foot eight inch frame has held up well over the years. She was a formidable lady in her day, and besides being in the hospital with heart troubles, not much has changed in that respect.

Everyone's heart has an expiration date, but only God knows when that date is; which makes each tick extremely valuable. However, most people don't realize this fact until it is almost too late to do anything about it.

Staring at his grandmother, Angelo is thinking about all the times he should have been spending with her, instead of wasting it doing God knows what. Whatever it might have been doesn't seem important anymore. Zuri recognizes the look of regret on Angelo's face and steps closer to him, places his hand on his shoulder and gently squeezes it and whispers in his ear, "no regrets Angelo, she wouldn't appreciate that," while attempting to get a closer look at the old lady's face.

Mrs. Henson opens her eyes, turns her head towards Angelo and smiles, out of the corner of her eye she catches a glimpse of Zuri and their eyes meet for the first time. Her eyes and his eyes grow to the sizes of marbles and simultaneously they both speak.

"TELEZA NUSHUMBA, oh my God!"

"ZURI NETUMBA, oh my Lord!"

Her heart skips a beat; then, beats erratically again setting off her monitors causing the nurse to rush in and inject a sedative into her IV to calm her down. Angelo's head is moving back and forth on swivel, as he is trying to figure out what is going on. "Who did you call her, how do you know him, what is going on?"

Zuri is somewhat in shock and mumbling to himself. "How can this be, I thought she was dead, I thought she was dead; oh my God, I can't believe this, oh my God."

Angelo is the only sane one in the room now and request the nurse to escort Zuri out of the room until his grandmother is calm again. After, he returns to his grandmother's side and takes hold of her hand. "I'm here Granny, I'm here." The medication starts to work and her heart rate slows to a normal pace and she motions to Angelo to come closer.

"Angelo baby, listen to me carefully."

"Don't speak Granny, you need your rest, we can talk later."

"No son, listen to me please, I'm okay just listen please" Angelo nods and sits back down to listen.

Meanwhile down the hall, Zuri is beside himself as he rejoins Veronica and Saphera. The ladies jump up and meet him mid-stride and Saphera addresses her husband, "Zuri, what's wrong, is she okay, what the hell is going on?"

Veronica wastes no time running down the hall to find Angelo to make sure he is alright. When she reaches the room and opens the door, Angelo rises from his chair, grabs her hand and pulls her over to meet his grandmother.

"Veronica, this is my granny; Granny, this is the woman of my dreams, and if she will have me," he turns towards Veronica, catching her totally by surprise and kneels on one knee, "I would love to make you my wife, that is of course, if you will have me." He takes Veronica by the hand and exposes a two carat brilliantly clear princess cut solitaire diamond ring ready to place on her finger. "Will you Veronica, have me that is?"

Veronica is stunned. Coming down the hall she did not know what to expect, but it definitely wasn't this. Mrs. Henson is smiling, a little loopy but still lucid and happy. Veronica looks over at her and Mrs. Henson is smiling with droopy eyes and nods ever so slightly. Then Veronica turns to Angelo, stretches out her left hand and says, "of course I will have you silly man." And with that Angelo slides the ring onto Veronica's finger, stands up, embraces her, then softly and passionately lets his lips rest on hers, and embraces her once more, this time he lifts her off the floor and whispers tenderly in her ear, "I will love you forever Roni, forever."

The two sit together next to Mrs. Henson's bed who then looks at Angelo and says, "Congratulation son, she is a lovely young lady. Now may I suggest you tell her?"

Veronica turns to Angelo and says, "Tell me what?"

Angelo turns to Veronica, smiles and begins to tell her what his grandmother had just told him and Mrs. Henson drifts off to sleep.

In the waiting room, Zuri has taken the time to tell Saphera who Angelo's grandmother really is and explains how he must get back down the hall to question her. Saphera is understanding of his predicament, but assures him that Angelo's situation is far more fragile and vital than anything he has to offer at the moment. "Give the boy a minute to visit with his grandmother without you interrupting and asking her all kinds of questions Zuri. She saw you just like you saw her, so I'm sure she wants to talk to you as well."

"Okay darling, I'll do it your way for now, but I do want to talk to her preferably before she dies."

"You will sweetheart, you will."

Back in the room, Mrs. Henson is awake again and getting to know her future granddaughter-in-law, and she can see why Angelo is so fond of her. In this moment she is filled with overwhelming joy, the kind she hasn't felt in a long while. The feeling reminds her that Zuri is out there and she must deal with him before her time is up. "Angelo" she says, "go out there and ask Zuri in here please."

"Yes ma'am, I'll be right back Granny. Roni, please keep her smiling until our return."

"We're fine, go on and hurry back my fiancé." Angelo looks back; the three of them share in a playful laugh and Angelo is out the door and down the hall to the waiting room. When he reaches the waiting room, Zuri is pacing and waiting with anticipation to both talk to Mrs. Henson and to talk to Angelo.

"Boy," Zuri says sharply, "don't move and don't talk." Angelo complies, though he does not understand Zuri's tone or agitation. Zuri looks at Angelo as if it is the first time he has ever laid eyes on him. He walks around him and examines his posture, his hands, and his head right down to his earlobes. "How could I have missed it?" Zuri thinks to himself while examining Angelo like a lab specimen, "but there it is, now I see it; oh my God." He is deep in thought when Angelo breaks the silence.

"She requests your presence Zuri; and when you get there can you please send Veronica out here to me sir?"

Zuri is overcome with emotion, and as he circles around in front of Angelo again, he stops and embraces Angelo like he is his long lost son; then releases him abruptly and, proceeds down the hall to Mrs. Henson's room. When Zuri enters the room, he motions his head to the left for Veronica to leave them.

"Now Mrs. Henson if you need me, I'll be right down the hall okay," Veronica states with the love and respect of a granddaughter.

"Thank you sweetie," Mrs. Henson replies, "and I'll see you later new fiancée." The two laugh as Veronica leaves the room.

"Zuri, come over here please so I can get a good look at you." Zuri slowly walks over to her bed trembling the entire way with tears running down his face unable to control his intense emotions. This man of strength, incredible stature and nobility has been reduced to the emotional state of a crying boy by the mere sight of this unassuming elderly lady. What secrets does she hold that enable her to reduce a world class federal agent, who has infiltrated governments and helped to remove leaders from power to tears and such humility? Sitting in the chair next to her bed now, the two just sit there staring at one another, neither one moving. Mrs. Henson focuses on controlling her breathing to keep from getting too excited and for now at least, it's working; however, she too begins to well up with tears the longer Zuri sits there.

Without advance notice, Zuri reaches across the bed and hugs her so tight she can hardly breathe. "Teleza, I have missed you so much and for so long. I thought you were dead. What about brother, where is he? Is Angelo his son, does he have any more children, where is he? How did you, and have you survived all this time"

Teleza can only say a few words. "I thought you were dead too," then she just continues to hug Zuri back like he is her long lost child with tears streaming down her face and the sounds of a crying mother coming from her voice. The pair is extremely happy to see one another, as if their entire existence has been for a moment like this one; and they don't want it to end.

CHAPTER IV

It's quiet, Marcus is asleep and Zephora is curled up in the recliner in the corner of the room. She takes this opportunity to send Veronica a text:

> *Hey girlie how's everything going? How's Angelo's granny doing? Everything here is quiet. Marcus is out cold & I keep pushing that pain pump button to make sure he stays that way (lol) it's for his own good. Girl, Chris Caldon texted me & said he is just checking on me. I hate I ever called him, this is the last thing I need. Call me when you can. Love u girl, take care.*

Chris Caldon is the one blemish Zephora lied to Marcus about. Before Marcus and Zephora met, Chris was her boyfriend; however she told Marcus he was just a friend from school. They dated for a couple of years and Chris actually proposed to Zephora, but she said no. Chris didn't take it very well and for six months, he stalked her. She had not talked to him since then until the period when Marcus was in Africa defending her honor. Not being able to talk to Marcus for that period of time took a toll on Zephora. In a moment of weakness, she reached out to someone she thought she could talk to: Chris. During their conversation, Chris comforted and helped her cope through that difficult time. However, hearing her voice lit the pilot light on the flame in his heart for her. The more they talked, the higher the flames grew. After receiving a text from Angelo that Marcus was okay, Zephora didn't call Chris again. This upset Chris and made him feel used all over again. Unbeknown to Zephora, Chris' heart had not healed from their previous relationship. When she called upon him, she inadvertently reopened that wound and turned up the flames on the torch he has been continuously carrying for her.

While Zephora is resting in her chair, Marcus' phone rings and Zephora reaches to answer it before it wakes Marcus. On the other end of the phone is Ruth, Marcus' grandmother, calling to check in on her precious Marcus. No one means more to her than he. Zephora is pleased to hear from her, she has grown extremely fond of Ruth and Ruth of her. The two have a pleasant conversation and Ruth is even more delighted to learn that her beloved Marcus is going to be just fine. She demands that Zephora have Marcus call her when he is up and around, and Zephora responds with a respectful, "Yes ma'am," after which, the two exchange I love you's and then hang up, both with smiles on their faces.

Just as Zephora presses the end call button and places the phone on the light oak round table beside her, it began to vibrate and the ring tone screams out, "I heard it through the grapevine." She catches it before the song could repeat. She checks to see who is texting Marcus and is surprised to see that it is Esther, Marcus' mother. Before looking to see what the message says, Zephora has warm feelings inside thinking how wonderful it is that Marcus' family is reaching out to check on him. Then she reads the message:

> *Marcus this is your mama. I need you to send me some money son. I wouldn't ask if it wasn't important. I need $500 before Monday morning if you can. I thank God in advance.*

The text ends there and Zephora is mortified at her audacity. There is no mention of even asking how Marcus is doing; only what she wanted. Zephora knows that Marcus and his mother's relationship is dysfunctional, but she never really understood all the reasons why, mostly because Marcus tries hard not to talk about it. When he does talk about it, he becomes completely enraged at her antics and it takes hours for her to calm him. Zephora thinks about not responding but, thinks it prudent to give some sort of answer to her and does so carefully:

> *Mrs. Howard, this is Zephora. Marcus is asleep in his hospital bed trying to recover from the multiple gunshot wounds he received saving my life. I know this information is not new to you, because I talked to you and told you myself. When he wakes up in a couple of days, I will let him know you texted him with little regard for*

his health. It may be Monday, it may not be but,
I'll let him know.

Zephora receives a quick return text:

Oh baby, how you doing? And how is Marcus
doing? It slipped my mind he is in the hospital. I
just know they are taking real good care of him.
Have him call me when he wakes up. Thank you
baby

Zephora laughs, is shocked and utterly disgusted, and chooses not to respond to anymore of her texts. She lays the phone back on the table and goes back to reading her magazine, trying to erase the memory of the two text messages from her mind. Zephora cannot understand how a mother can be so cold, callus and calculating towards her own child. She takes the time to say a quick prayer: *God help me to always treat my children with the upmost love, concern and understanding. Keep my heart free from darkness, open to love and Your glorious light; in Jesus Holy name, amen.*

Zephora has only just finished her prayer when Marcus' phone chimes in again, this time singing, "Papa was a rolling stone, wherever lay his hat was his home." Zephora answers it quickly and as she does, she can't help but wonder what is going on, why is Marcus' phone so popular this evening. This time on the other end is Jackson Howard, Marcus' father.

"Hello," Zephora whispers.

"Hello Zephora, how are you and how is my son doing?

"I'm fine Mr. Howard and Marcus is resting comfortably and his doctor says he is going to make a full recovery, thank God"

"That is good news Zephora, just what I've been praying for; and you my dear how are you really holding up through all the challenges the two of you are facing?"

"To be honest sir, I simply take it one moment at a time and try not to worry about the things I can't control."

"That's a good policy young lady. I won't waste your time, just wanted to check on you and Marcus and make sure you guys are okay. I know Marcus doesn't believe it but, he's my guy, always has been, always will be."

"Thank you sir, I'll make sure he knows you feel that way. Take care; I will talk to you later."

"Thank you sweetheart; you take care of yourself and my son. He's a lucky man to have you."

"I'm the blessed one to have him; he is my rock and my soulmate."

"I stand corrected, and with that I say be blessed Zephora." Jackson hangs up and Zephora is left hoping the phone doesn't ring or vibrate again for a while. She walks over to Marcus' bed and presses the button for the pain pump again.

Right after she presses the button, Marcus' dinner tray arrives and she has to wake him up so he can eat it.

Marcus is so drugged he can hardly sit up without falling over. Zephora helps him but under her breath she laughs at him even though she knows she did it to him. Ultimately, she has to feed him because he is too high to hold his own fork and can barely focus enough to eat. After he eats, Marcus falls back asleep and Zephora positions herself back in the recliner in the corner. One of the nurses brings her a pillow and a warm blanket to which Zephora responds "thank you so very much." The nurse nods, turns out the light and closes the door behind her.

As quickly as the doors closes, it reopens again; and the figure that breaks through the darkness and emerges from the light is Charlie. She is well rested and refreshed ready to relieve Zephora for a while. She gives Zephora the items she requested and attempts to get her to go home for the night and sleep in her own bed. Reluctantly, Zephora accedes to Charlie's constant begging and relinquishes her post.

"Charlie, I will be back first thing in the morning. Call me if his condition changes at all."

"Yeah, yeah, yeah, I got this. Before there was you, I took care of my little brother just fine sister."

"I know, but it's my job now and he is my world."

"Yeah but it's not really your job until I can get you two to exchange I do's."

"Point taken Charlie; I hope to change that as soon as I possibly can my dear."

"I hope so because this man needs to settle down quick."

The two share a short laugh and a hug before Zephora walks over to Marcus' bed and gently and passionately places her soft lips on his forehead for a delicate, but meaningful kiss. Then she reaches over to press his pain pump again when Charlie shouts, "What are you doing?"

"I'm pressing the button so he can continue resting."

"Have you been doing that this whole time?"

"Of course; what's the problem Charlie?"

"He is supposed to be able to press it for himself when he needs it for pain. How is he supposed to know how he feels if you keep him comatose?"

"Oops! I just didn't want him to feel any pain for a while. Look, doesn't he seem comfortable and at peace to you?"

"Zephora girl, you have lost your mind; I understand but really, you are funny. Go home for a while; I'll take over and maybe you can actually talk to him when you get back."

"Like I said, oops; I'll see you in the morning. I have some things to take care of anyway. Bye."

"Yeah, bye girl;" With that, Charlie throws Zephora her keys and Zephora leaves the room, leaves the wing, and leaves the hospital for the first time since they arrived. She can't wait to get into her shower and just stand under the hot water and let it rinse away the stress and weight she has been feeling.

Charlie pulls her chair next to Marcus' bed, grabs his hand with both her hands and presses them against her forehead and whispers, "I have so much to tell you little brother, I hope you understand why it took me so long to tell you; I hope you can forgive me." She places his hand on his chest, slides the chair back to its original position and takes up the post in the recliner in the back corner of the room. That chair is becoming familiar with all of Marcus' loved ones, and is probably looking to start a relationship with one or two of them while Marcus sleeps through it all.

It has been a couple of hours since Charlie arrived and replaced Zephora as the one sitting with Marcus. The supervising nurse comes in Marcus' room to check on her patient. She checks his IV bag, sees that it is nearly empty and replaces it with a new one. She then checks his pain pump and notices it is low, and chooses to disconnect it. She approaches

Marcus, and decides it is time for him to wake up and go for a walk around the east wing of the floor.

"Mr. Howard, it's time for you to get up and take a walk. C'mon wake up now."

Marcus is groggy and slowly opens his eyes and responds to his nurse. "I'm awake, I'm awake."

"It's time for you to get up and go walking. We have to get your respiratory system back to full swing."

"Okay, give me a few minutes and I'll be ready."

"Mr. Howard, I will be back in five minutes to get you. Get up and wash your face and we will get you on the move." The nurse leaves the room and Marcus sits up and lets his legs dangle over the side of the bed. He looks towards the corner of the room and sees a body stretched out in the recliner and thinks its Zephora and calls out to her.

"Zephora, can you come help me please?"

"Now Marcus, you should know your sister by now."

My bad sis; but, can you come over here and help me please?"

"Of course I can, but will I; that is the question."

"Girl, get your butt over here and help me now!"

"So pushy little brother, so pushy." Charlie walks over to help Marcus to the bathroom. When she reaches him, he immediately gives her a hug, and the two siblings slowly walk to the bathroom with the IV rolling with them. Once there, Marcus grabs the sink with one hand, reaches for a face cloth with the other, and pushes the door closed with his right foot. His big sister waits patiently leaning against the wall on the other side of the door. Marcus lets the water get hot, and then makes sure the cloth is soaked by the water before wringing it out and pressing the hot cloth against his face. The heat instantly awakens and rejuvenated him. He rinses the cloth in hot water again and then lets it rest on top of his head before pulling it over his face again. Now refreshed and feeling alive, Marcus takes the time to brush his teeth and tongue and rinse his mouth before soaking the cloth again and just letting it rest on his face to complete his revitalizing process. After relieving himself and washing his hands, Marcus lets the top down on the toilet, takes a seat, bows his head and presses his hands together in preparation of prayer.

Dear Lord, thank you so much for taking such good care of me and allowing me to wake once more giving me new life and the opportunity to be better now than I ever have been before. Thank you for taking care of my family and friends and for looking after my beloved Zephora. Father, I send a special prayer out to Angelo's grandmother. Comfort her and give her peace as she battles for her life. Father God give Angelo strength and courage to deal with whatever happens; give him peace Lord and comfort him through it all. Bring them all home safely Lord, and if it is Your will, allow Angelo's grandmother to come with them on their return trip here. Lord bless my doctors and nurses and their families; they give so much of themselves to others Lord and I pray and request you give back to them 100 times what they give. Lastly Father God, I pray You forgive us all of our many sins and open our eyes to the sins so that we may repent and work harder to please You. It is in Jesus Christ's holy name I pray; Amen.

Tears stream down Marcus' face as he feels the presence of the Holy Spirit in that small bathroom and stretches his head toward the ceiling and praises God with earnestness and conviction. And on the other side of the wall, Charlie, who has been tuned in to her little brother's prayer the whole time, is on her knees thanking God and beckoning the Holy Spirit to anoint her and her brother with a fresh and new anointing with tears flowing down the creases in her face. Marcus opens the door to the bathroom and embraces his sister.

"I love you Charlie and I'm so glad you chose to stay here with me."

I love you too Marcus and I'm so proud of you." Charlie is crying so hard, Marcus can barely make out the words she is speaking. The two siblings praise and worship God together for a few more minutes and because they are so

51

engrossed in their own personal church service, they do not notice their newest member, the supervising nurse, standing by the door having a praise party as well.

The three worshipers wind down their praise and the nurse interlocks her left arm with Marcus' right arm and the two slowly walk out the door and turn right to start their east wing walk.

"Mr. Howard," the nurse begins, "I did not know you were such an incredible praise warrior. Are you a pastor somewhere?"

"Thank you nurse… what's your name ma'am?"

"My name is Samantha sir."

"Well thank you nurse Samantha; and no I am not a pastor anywhere. I'm just a man who loves God and love praising Him."

"That's good to know; too few men proudly stand for God wherever they go. Now don't walk too fast, this is our first outing and we don't want to overdo it."

"I understand Samantha, but I only have two gears, go and stop. I've been at stop too long and now, I'm ready to go.

"You may think you're ready to go, but today, we will be taking it slow until I think you are ready mister."

"Well thank you nurse Samantha for your candid approach; I so look forward to taking this long walk under the florescent lights with you as my guide again."

The two share a good laugh while taking one short step after another until Marcus begins to hit a nice stride; and just as he does, the two are back at his door.

"Well Mr. Howard, you did a good job; you're a little crazy but well on your way to helping yourself recover faster.

"Thank you nurse Samantha….."

"Please, it's just Sam, Mr. Howard"

"And it's just Marcus, Sam; but like I was saying, thank you for all your help and support. I look forward to seeing you later for another of our long walks."

Samantha leaves Marcus' room waving and Marcus waves back from the chair next to his bed. Sam closes the door behind her; five seconds later, the door reopens and Marcus looks up wondering what Sam may have forgotten. As his eyes reach the door, the silhouette is that of his own personal angel, his beloved Zephora. Marcus rises from his chair and Zephora ducks under his left arm and places it around her neck and escorts Marcus to his bed. Before he sits on the bed, he gently grabs her face with both his hands, pulls her close and engages her with a long passionate kiss that seems to last for at least an hour. Marcus slowly pulls away from their kiss, but Zephora pulls him close again and they engage in another long passionate kiss.

"Get a room!" Charlie shouts from the recliner in the corner.

Marcus breaks their kiss to reply to his sister, "This is my room." The three laugh and Marcus leans down and sits on the edge of his bed with Zephora's help, and then he turns to lie down. He adjusts his bed so that his head is raised halfway up and his feet are just slightly elevated. Zephora finally speaks after she catches her breath still reeling from their enchanting kisses.

"Hi baby, I guess it's fair to say that you missed me," she states.

"I guess I could say the same thing about you my love."

"Fair enough Marcus. I missed you baby, and I'm glad to see you're feeling better."

"I am feeling better Ms. Sherman and it seems like that walk I took has helped me breathe a little bit better too.

"Yes it has Marcus; it doesn't seem like there's a problem with your lungs after those passionate kisses."

Charlie puts her recliner in the upright position and interrupts the two love birds to interject.

"Listen you two love birds, I hate to interrupt what I know is a happy reunion, but I have something important I need to tell you Marcus and I'm not really sure how you're going to take it, but I can't keep this secret any longer." The tone in Charlie's voice causes everyone and everything in the room to stop moving. Even the ticks of the clock seemed to slow down. One second took five before it clicked again. In the amount of time it took for four seconds to click off the clock, Marcus and Zephora stopped paying attention to one another, and turned their heads toward Charlie instantaneously, both with bewildered looks on their faces.

Marcus' bottom lip quivers as he searches for the right words to say. He can tell by the tone and sound of his sister's voice that something terrible has happened to her. His eyes are darting back and forth as he tries unraveling Charlie's secret in his mind so he won't have to ask what happened. In the several seconds that clicked off the clock, that were taking what seemed like minutes, Marcus went from being scared to know what happened, to being sad that his big sister has been keeping what he imagines is an awful secret, and then to angry that someone has hurt his sister. Marcus has always prided himself as the protector of the women in his family, and even the women that have become his close friends, part of his superhero complex. He failed to save his baby sister, she's dead, and now he believes he has failed to protect his big sister too. Based on her tone, he knows something is terribly wrong and he can't help but think it's his fault. The more he thinks about it the madder he gets and now he's not even sure he wants to know what Charlie has to say, but he has no choice except to hear how he has failed someone he loves again.

"Charlie, what's wrong; what happened, who hurt you? When I find who ever hurt you I'll…"

"Marcus, calm down, let her speak and stop assuming. She doesn't need you to be angry right now, just understanding."

Marcus knows Zephora is right and takes a deep breath to calm himself. "You're right Ze; I'm sorry Charlie. Go ahead precious, I'm listening, we're listening with an understanding ear, not an angry one. Okay?"

"Thank you Marcus." Charlie's tone is different now, calmer but with a hint of fear in it. She is about to have a conversation that she has thought about having for a longtime. And now that she's started it, she wishes she could take it back, but it's too late to turn back now; forward is the only direction she can go. She can feel fear trying to hold her back, whispering in her ear, "Stop don't do this, you know what he told you." Yet, her heart is screaming, "Be brave, it's time Marcus knows the truth." Charlie swallows deep and clears her throat. She gets up from her seated position in the corner recliner that she's been cheating on the waiting room couch with and walks behind it to push it closer to her captivated audience and plops back down in it. She clasps her hands together in front of her mouth and nose, takes a deep breath and says, "Where do I begin. It all started such a very long time ago, where do I begin."

Compassionately, Marcus responds to what he hears as a cry for support. "Start from where ever you want to call the beginning. We're here to listen to you, so you'll get no pressure from us as to what you say or where you start babygirl. Just let your heart lead you and go from there."

"Thanks Marcus; I needed to hear that and just hope you still love me when I'm done."

"Charlie, there is nothing you could ever say that can change how I feel about you, or how much I love you dear sister, nothing."

With that being said, Charlie settles back in her chair, crosses her right leg over her left and places her hands comfortably on her knee. She takes a deep breath and begins to speak.

CHAPTER V

Angelo has gotten tired of waiting for Zuri to come back from his grandmother's room and takes the initiative to walk down to her room on his own. This gives Veronica the opportunity to return a text she received from Zephora. While reading the text, Veronica smirks and shakes her head in disappointment at the choices her best friend made and carefully texts her reply.

> *Hey Ze how you holding up sista? Things here are super crazy, exciting and yet fragile. Granny is stable but we are unsure how long she can hold on but she has every reason to. All things considered, I'm great. I'm so glad I got to meet my sweetie's grandmother. Hope Marcus is feeling better and stop pushing that button so your man can wake up. Listen girl you know how I feel about that call you made but if you don't, I hate that choice but now you gotta hope it doesn't bite you in the butt. No matter what, don't call or text him again. And for Goodness sake tell Marcus before he finds out without you telling him. That would be a serious problem. Anyway, check out the picture I'm sending & tell me what you think. See ya Love ya*

Veronica carefully takes a picture of her engagement ring to insure Zephora can see it sparkling and then sends it to her BFF. While doing so, Saphera catches a glimpse of the ring and her eyes grow two sizes.

"Oh my God Veronica; did Angelo ask you to marry him in there! That ring is stunning baby. I am so happy for you."

"Thank you Mrs. Sherman. With everything that's going on I forgot to come in here and tell you. But yes, Angelo got on one knee in front of his grandmother and asked me to marry him. He was so cute. I love him so much."

"Congratulations baby Congratulations! I cannot tell you how happy I am for you. Did you tell Ze yet?"

"I just sent her a picture of my ring and I'm waiting for her to call me."

"I know she is going to be as happy for you as I am."

Veronica and Saphera share a joyous hug and engagement giggles. The two sit down to talk about all things wedding and marriage.

Meanwhile, down the hall, Zuri and Angelo are sharing themselves with Angelo's grandmother. The three are connecting in ways neither ever thought possible. Teleza is soaking up all the air shared by her two favorite men and she finds herself silently praying for more time on this earth. But before she can finish her prayer, Zuri asks her, "Teleza, are you doing okay?"

She responds, "Yes, I'm just tired baby; but you boys keep talking, it's making me feel better." Having her two men surrounding her, the one she lost and the one she saved is the joy overshadowing the reality that the pace of her heartbeat is beginning to slow. She manages to hold on to the smile on her face as she listens to her boys' voices. They are so excited to be in her presence together that they fail to notice the change in her. Teleza, however, can feel her heartbeat slowing and it sounds loud in her ears like the beat of an old African drum calling her home; boom boom, boom boom, boom boom. Her eyes are heavy and she blinks them ever so slowly; "I'm ready now Lord," she thinks to herself.

Zuri and Angelo are paying more attention to each other, talking and laughing together, not noticing the eventual end that is happening right in front of them. Teleza finds the strength to place Zuri's hand on top of Angelo's with her hands on top of both. They instantly turn their heads in her direction. Everything seems to be happening in slow motion now. Teleza's eyes blink slowly, she looks at Angelo then Zuri, her lips turn a lazy smile and her heart is now beating once every five seconds, now eight seconds, now only once more. Her eyes slowly close and she exhales one final time. Zuri jumps up and yells, "WE NEED A DOCTOR IN HERE!" Angelo grabs his grandmother's hand and yells! "GRANNY, GRANNY; GRANNY WAKE UP!"

Both men are in shock at this uninvited turn of events. The doctor and nurses push them back as they attempt to revive Teleza. But it's too late, she's gone, gone home and there is nothing anyone can do to change it. The elation embraced by Zuri and Angelo has changed to sorrow for the two warriors and the change is neither welcomed nor accepted. The tears begin to stream down their faces, both their lives are changing for the better because of this old lady with two names and they embrace each other, visibly overcome with pain and sadness. Saphera and Veronica hear the commotion and come running down the hall. The two men stop leaning on each other's shoulders and reach for their respective lady and cling to them instead, neither having a word to say, only tears being shed. The matriarch of their family is dead. The skies in Tampa darken and rain begins to fall as if the pain and sadness Zuri and Angelo feel over the death of their beloved Teleza is also felt in the heavens.

Charlie's heart is burdened, for years she has carried this secret with her; a secret that has prevented her from having any close relationships and held her captive. But now, she is ready to free herself of her lifelong burden by revealing her surreptitious past to her brother and his fiancé. As she begins to unravel the past, she notices Zephora's breathing has changed.

"Zephora, what's wrong with you; are you okay?"

"I don't know, but something is wrong; I can feel it."

Marcus chimes in, "Baby what's wrong, what's going on?"

"Something is not right Marcus, I can feel it, something is not right. I think something is wrong with my father."

"Call him Ze," Marcus demands. "It will put your mind at rest. Charlie, can you hold on one minute for Ze to call her father?"

"Sure, I can wait," Charlie responds.

Zephora walks to the corner to make her call and gets Zuri's voice mail and tries again with the same result. "It keeps going to voice mail Marcus."

"Don't panic baby, just call Veronica," Marcus shouts back. His attention is split; he is aware of his sister's solemn demeanor as well as the panic in Zephora's voice all while dealing with his increasing pain level.

Zephora had not even looked at the texts she received earlier from Veronica because of Charlie's need to talk to her and Marcus. However, she must call her best friend now to alleviate the feeling in the pit of her stomach. Veronica's phone rings four times before she answers it.

"Hey Ze," Veronica answers the phone whispering. She had to walk away from Angelo to answer it.

"Roni, is everything alright?"

"No, Angelo's grandmother just passed and everyone here is pretty broken up about it. I will have to call you later girl."

"Oh no, give him our condolences and our love; you go and we will talk to you guys later okay."

"For sure Ze, because we have a lot to talk about, and check the texts I sent you. Bye."

Zephora ends the call and slowly walks over to Marcus and Charlie to tell them the bad news. Marcus looks in her eyes and instantly knows what she has to say. He reaches his hand out for hers and she comes over and they share an embrace. Marcus is smart enough to know that his sister cannot wait any longer or she'll bolt, while they are hugging, he whispers in Zephora's ear, "we will deal with this later," she nods and takes her seat next to his bed as close as she can get. Marcus looks over to his sister and says, "Okay sis, you have our undivided attention."

Charlie takes a deep breath and prepares herself to tell the story of her shame to the one person she knows will not hold it against her, her beloved little brother.

"Marcus, you know how difficult things were for me when we were kids before I left our mother's house."

Marcus rubs the top of his bald head and responds. "Yeah it really was leave or die in my opinion. I honestly thought she wanted to kill you."

"Well, going to live with Jackson was the worst thing I could have ever done."

"Charlie, what happened; what did he do to you sis?"

"Marcus, I need you to just listen and not interrupt me please, or I will never get this out. You gotta promise Marcus."

"Okay, okay, I'm listening. I promise I won't say a word until you say I can speak." Marcus' pain level has increased from a three to a five but he is refusing to push the pain button so hc can listen attentively to his sister.

"Thank you Marcus, this is tough enough as it is. I warn you, it will be hard for you to keep your promise, but I expect you to just the same." Marcus looks at his sister and nods his head. He adjusts the head of his bed up a little more and folds his arms across his chest. Zephora takes the opportunity to calm him down by unfolding his arms and insisting they hold hands; Marcus doesn't fight her and she begins to gently and slowly rub the top of his hand with her thumb and softly smiles at him. Charlie takes another deep breath, sits back in her chair so her eyes won't meet her brother's and begins to tell her life's secret shame.

"When I got off the plane in Jersey, there was no one there to meet me. I called and called but no one answered the phone, so I sat on a bench in the airport for hours. I was thirteen, in a new city, and no one cared where I was. I continued calling and still got no answer. I only had five dollars when I got there and the snack machines ate them up. It was ten o'clock when Jackson arrived to pick me up. He didn't speak or help me carry my bags; he made hand gestures to direct me to the car. I said, "Hi Daddy," he said nothing. I said, "Daddy I'm hungry," he still said nothing but this time he at least turned his head in my direction. Before we reached his house, he stopped at Mickey D's, ordered me a quarter pounder with cheese meal with an orange soda. Even though I didn't tell him that's what I wanted, I enjoyed it. I was so hungry; it took me less than ten minutes to devour it. I said, "thank you Daddy," but he still didn't speak to me. So I asked him if he was mad at me, and he just stared at me with deep wrinkles in his forehead between his eyes while we just sat in the car in the driveway. Finally he turned to me and said, "Things are going to be different for you here. The world is a rough place, and it is my job to make sure you are tough enough to handle it. Do you understand?" I said, "Yes sir." He said, "Yes sir what?" I said "yes sir I understand;" and with that we got out of the car and went into his house. It was dark in the house and he directed me to the only room that had a light on. He told me to put my bags in the corner and sit on the bed and wait there until he came back. The room was painted a drab beige color. The bed had no headboard and was pushed into a corner of the room with a nightstand that had one drawer and an open space at the bottom next to it. In the opposite corner was a matching four drawer chest. There was a short round pink lamp on the nightstand with a lamp shade that was gray and extremely dusty as well as everything else in the room. As I looked around the room, I was overcome with sadness.

When Jackson came back, he had a leather belt wrapped around his right hand leaving about a twelve inch loop hanging down from his hand. He locked the door when he came in and in the same motion turned towards me and began beating me. He didn't stop until I had cried so much that no more tears came from my eyes and he knew I thought he would kill me. After which, he said to me, and I quote, "I gotta make you tough cause life is hard."

Marcus' eyes begin to swell up and he shouts, "That bastard!"

"Marcus you promised," Charlie reminds.

"You're right, I'm sorry; please continue."

"Thank you. Well, after he left the room, I lay there sniffling wanting to hold myself but I couldn't because I was in pain from head to toe; I didn't even want the covers to touch me. So I got in the bed and just laid there very still, to minimize the pain. And just as I got comfortable and was falling off to sleep, he came back in the room and locked the door. He put his hand over my mouth and raped me; and because it was my first time, there was blood everywhere. He made me get up and clean everything up including him. Again he said to me, "I gotta make you tough." He told me if I said anything, he would cut my wrists and make it look like I killed myself. When I finally went to sleep that first night, I was a different person than the one who left you Marcus. I was a daddy's girl; I loved my father. I thought he loved me and I couldn't wait to be living there with him. But when I went to sleep, I was forever changed, damaged, but I had to survive; so I suppose he did make me tough."

Marcus drops his head and tears drip onto his sheets. He whispers, "My God." Zephora reaches up and rubs the back of his neck; she too has tears flowing down her face. As difficult as it is, Marcus keeps his promise and doesn't interrupt. He is in pain, filled with pain and anger and presses his pain pump button, but it isn't designed to take away most of the pain he's feeling now. Zephora hands Charlie a box of tissues from the nightstand beside Marcus' bed; Charlie blows her nose, wipes her eyes and continues her story.

"The next morning I got up early, packed my bags in an attempt to run away; however, when I opened the door to my room, he was standing there waiting for me with a belt in his hand. He pushed me back into the room and told me if I ran he would find me and if I told he, would kill me. He demanded I change my clothes and get ready for breakfast and then school. When I went into the kitchen for breakfast. I got the surprise of my life."

Marcus lifts his head up and looks at his sister and asks, "What else could he surprise you with than finding out he was an abuser and a rapist?"

Charlie chuckles and continues. "I found out that your father had a new wife and two more children."

"What!" Marcus shouts. "Why didn't you ever tell me this; better yet, why didn't he ever say anything?"

"Because Marcus, he doesn't want you to know and he threatened me and told me not to ever tell. But you are interrupting and stopping my story."

Marcus responds, "I digress, please continue."

"Thank you." I walked in the kitchen and politely said, "good morning." I was greeted by this sweet lady who became my step mother. She said, "good morning Charlie, how are you today? My name is Jan and this is Christine and James, and we have been expecting you. I hope you slept good last night." To which I responded, "Yes ma'am," after catching your father's eye. Christine was four and James was two and they were both beautiful and pleasant children which almost caused me to go into shock. So the start of that first day was good. Jan took me to school and gave me a beautiful mother-daughter talk. She told me I could depend on her for anything, I need only ask. She was a nurse and she worked nights; finding this out left me hopeless since she wouldn't be there to stop Jackson from having his way with me. Your father picked me up from school and the trip home was quiet. Every night Jan would make dinner, put the little ones to bed and then go to work. Once she left, your father would come into my room and rape me, every night. This went on until I graduated high school. When I graduated, I wanted to get as far away as I could; so I joined the military and the rest is history that you already know."

"Charlie," Marcus hoarsely said, "I'm doing my best not to cry because I'm so outraged by it all, but what I don't understand is why; wait, I'm sorry, I know the answer to that question."

"What question?" asks Zephora.

"You know, why she never told me this before now," Marcus responds.

Marcus then turns to Charlie, "But Charlie, that's not important now; what is important, is that you feel safe enough to tell me now. And now that you chose to tell me, are you okay and what do you want me to do with this knowledge? Because you know what I want to do, but I don't like the thought of prison being in my immediate future; and hey, where are our young siblings now?"

Charlie looks at Marcus with tears rolling down her face and responds, "The year before I graduated high school, there was an accident. A drunk driver came up an exit the wrong way one night, and Jan and the kids were killed instantly when he hit them head on. Jan and James had picked up Christine from ballet and they were on the way home when it happened."

Charlie lowers her head and begins to cry almost uncontrollably. Marcus is stunned and dismayed. Zephora gets out of her chair and goes over to Charlie and just holds her in an attempt to get her to stop crying. Marcus' heart is broken for his sister. He cannot believe the tragedy and pain she has had to endure alone.

"Oh my God Charlie, you gotta be kidding me. I'm sure you had developed an incredible relationship with them all."

"Yeah, I did. Jan and I were pretty cool; and, me and the dynamic duo, that's what I called them, we were best buds and I truly miss them all dearly. After they died, your father got worse; he drank a lot more, beat me more and raped me repeatedly, daily. And he loved to brag to me about how he did worse to our Mother. And, oh yea, how he stole her birthright, you know, that ring he gave you."

"What!" yells Marcus?

"That's right; it's not his heritage that got you your crown, but your Mother's. But the way he bragged about beating her down, I doubt she remembers or even cares."

"That explains a lot!" Marcus exclaims.

Zephora, who has been in tears along with Charlie for the last fifteen to twenty minutes, reaches for Marcus' trash can and throws up. Marcus sits up on the side of his bed with a look of utter disgust on his face and rubs the back of her neck while she leans over the trash can gasping for a breath. Charlie hands her back the box of tissues and kneels down beside her to comfort Zephora and rubs her back. Charlie had just dropped a mega bomb in the room and caused the equivalent amount of emotional fallout. While Zephora catches her breath and attempts to recover from the emotional shock waves caused by the explosion, Marcus feels it necessary to ask Charlie one more loaded question.

"Okay big sister, you certainly caught us off guard and I must ask; is that it, because if there's more, you may as well get it all off your chest. I promise, you will certainly feel better when you do."

"Well," Charlie starts; and when she does Marcus' eyes open a little wider and he raises his head. "I was going to keep this one; but since you asked, during those years I had three abortions: one at the age of thirteen, one at age fifteen, and another at age seventeen. By the way, all three were your father's"

Zephora starts to vomit again and can't seem to stop crying. Marcus is now speechless and climbs out of his bed to tend to his beloved fiancé. The two of them are in total shock from another totally unexpected bomb Charlie just dropped. And just when they thought she was finished, she continues.

"For all three abortions, Charlie begins again; he took me to one of his friends who is a doctor and he wouldn't leave the room while the doctor performed the abortions. The two of them talked about fishing and told jokes to each other while he would remove life from my body."

"No wonder you ran to the military instead of taking that full scholarship to Brown University. Babygirl, have you ever talked to a professional about all of this?"

"I did Marcus, I had a military shrink. It's the only other time I spoke about all of this. She told me I needed to tell you; it has just taken this long for me to be ready to say it all to you. And I really needed you to know. I'm fine now and there's no need for you to defend my honor, he will get his; if not in this life, for sure in the next. Most people who are abused only have one abusive parent, we just happened to have two. But I will say this, if I had not talked to the Good Doctor, I wouldn't be here today. She literally saved my life because I was self-destructing from the inside out."

"She didn't save your life Marcus retorts, she repaired it. You saved your life by being brave enough to get help and by being strong enough to survive it all; and not because of anything Jackson did or the both of them did to you, but because of everything God created in you. He created you strong enough to overcome anything you encounter. I'm so very proud of you and glad you're my sister. Just know that from now on, I got or should I say, we got your back always."

"I second that," exclaims Zephora.

"Thanks you two; I feel better now that you know about it. I just hope you're okay Marcus. I know you, and I know you want to hurt your Father."

"You're right, it would be so easy to crush him right now; but instead, I'm going to let go and let God. It is not an easy thing to do and I would much rather handle it myself my way; however, this is not my fight, it's the Lord's. But what we can do right now is pray about it."

"Yes, let's," says Charlie with tears of joy in her eyes because all she ever wanted was her brother's love and respect, and now she knows she has it despite her past which had always caused her a great deal of shame. Now she is free to live without ignominy and humiliation, and with an unburdened heart and the love of her beloved brother. She is definitely ready for prayer.

Marcus reaches for his sister's hand and the hand of his darling Zephora. The two ladies in turn hold hands forming a circle across Marcus' bed and bow their heads in preparation of his prayer, when in walks Pastor Chappell who just happens to be coming to check in on Marcus at that moment. "Can I join this prayer circle?"

"Absolutely Pastor," says Marcus as he raises his head. "Would you like to take over and lead us in prayer?"

"No sir Marcus, you continue and I will just be a part of your circle, if you don't mind please."

"Of course Pastor," Marcus embarrassingly replies and then takes a deep breath, bows his head, closes his eyes and readies himself to pray. As he does, Zephora and Charlie raise their heads and look around at each other, and then at the two men who both have their heads bowed and eyes close. They quickly bow their heads and close their eyes in anticipation of Marcus' prayer.

Marcus, now extremely nervous because of the surprise visit by Pastor Chappell begins. *"Father God, I thank You for my sister. I thank You for creating such a woman of strength and courage. I pray for her continued strength and courage. I pray that you will continually bless her life with a refreshed understanding of love, real love. The kind of love that is You so she will not be plagued by the poor example of our earthly parents. I pray healing for Charlie, mental, physical, emotional and spiritual healing; Father, I pray that Charlie be able to forgive those who mistreated her and that she will no longer be bombarded by the nightmares of her past, but dream only of the promise that is her present and her future. Father bless her with a heart to please You always. We all ask that you forgive us of our sins, both in thought and in deed. We pray for our parents Father that they may be forgiven. Father God we love*

You; we thank you for the presence of Pastor Chappell and pray you will continue to bless him and fill him with Your Holy Spirit. You are awesome God and forever providing us with what we need. We worship You always with our every action and praise You continually. In Jesus Holy name we pray. Amen." Everyone else follows with a resounding *"In Jesus name, Amen!"*

After the prayer, Marcus shakes Pastor Chappell's hand and thanks him for visiting. Pastor Chappell asks Marcus how he is doing and when he expects to getting out of the hospital. Before he can get an answer out of Marcus, Dr. Lott enters the room with his nurse to get some vitals and to let Marcus know that he is healing nicely and quicker than expected. While he is talking to Marcus with Zephora attentively listening in, Charlie and Pastor Chappell are in the other corner of the room chatting it up.

While listening to Dr. Lott, Marcus has an incredible idea and before Dr. Lott leaves, Marcus asks him and his nurse to hold on for a moment.

CHAPTER VI

It's been two days since the death of Angelo's grandmother. Her orders were explicit as given by her attorney; she is to be cremated within three days of her death and her last will and testament to be read the day after her memorial service. Angelo hasn't had much to say since his grandmother's death and it has taken all Veronica can do just to get him to even acknowledge her in conversation. Saphera has been having the same problem with Zuri who is equally devastated by the loss. The two couples are staying at Angelo's for the duration of their visit and with the two men barely speaking; the ladies go out for lunch together.

"So Saphera," Veronica questions, "I bet this is the last thing you expected when you guys agreed to fly down with here with us?"

"For sure baby, I thought I knew Zuri's past, but I guess no matter how much you love someone or how much that person loves you, there's always the possibility he could be keeping some part of his past hidden from you. And, it could be because he's buried it so deep he doesn't remember it himself until some tragic event occurs."

"I get that," Veronica responds, "but I hope that Angelo will give me a chance and share his hurts and pains with me, as well as his love."

"Child, let me tell you something," Saphera retorts, "a lot of that will depend on you and how you choose to love him and how you teach him to love you."

"What do you mean, how I teach him to love me?"

Saphera puts down her fork and places her hand lovingly on top of Veronica's, takes the time to chew her food well and swallow it; and then with the voice of an adoring mother expresses her heart. "Sweetheart let me tell you something, no person is born knowing how to love another, you have to teach him how you want to be loved and learn how he needs to be loved. If you don't, he will love you the way he was loved and how he knows love to be, and you will do the same. Zuri and I have had so many years apart and I actually thought he was dead. Now that we are back together, we have to learn how to love each other again and if we ignore this fact, we will be setting ourselves up for failure."

"That's a good word Mrs. Sherman, I will remember that; but what are we going to do about our grieving men right now?"

"Let them grieve, they just lost the most influential person of their lives even though it was at different times. Angelo deserves some time to adjust to life without her. My husband lost her, got over it, found her again only to lose her once more; so I think this is extremely traumatic for him. But your future husband had her all his life and hasn't had to live without her. It takes time to get use to the change that loss causes; so, he needs time to deal with that. We are their support group; it is our job to handle things for them until they recover. Do you think you can do that?"

Veronica looks up at Saphera and without hesitation gives a resounding, "Yes," and the two ladies smile and finish enjoying their lunch. While they are relishing their dessert, Saphera takes the time to order two meals to go for their ailing men and then continues enjoying conversation with Veronica and enjoying their desserts.

Back at Angelo's, Zuri is coughing as he comes out of his room and sits in the living room with Angelo who is going through a box of pictures of him and his grandmother. For the longest time the two men say nothing to one another; they just pass pictures back and forth with the occasional smiles and laughs between the tears streaming down their faces. Angelo notices that Zuri is coughing again.

"It looks like the two of you shared a wonderful life together," Zuri utters.

"She was my mother, grandmother and my father all rolled into one. I could always count on her to know the right thing to say or do in every situation I got myself into. She was so wise, and she shared that wisdom with me; sometimes I got it and sometimes I didn't understand it at all. I hope that one day it will all make sense to me. By the way, are you alright, I keep hearing you coughing."

"I'm sure I'm fine; it's just a little cough. Anyway, when I was a boy, she was the one who tucked me in at night and told me stories. There was one story that was my favorite and the way she told it, made me want to hear it over and over again. What was the name of that story?"

As Zuri searches his mind for the name of the story, he begins to cough again. Angelo is thinking about his favorite bedtime story his grandmother read to him. Then, the two look at each other and concurrently shout, "JOSHUA AND THE LION!" They laugh and begin talking about all the sounds she would make as she read the story to them. They both remember how at the end she would emphasize the character traits Joshua displayed in the story and that a warrior should make a part of his life's code; then, like a chorus, they began to recite them. "INTEGRITY, HONOR, RESPECT, PERSEVERANCE, EXCELLENCE, COMMITMENT and SELF-CONTROL, these are the traits of a warrior that make him accountable, responsible, successful and whole."

"She drilled that rhyme into my head until I could recite it on cue," states Angelo.

"Me too son, me too," Zuri says with a bit of reverence in his voice.

The two share a quiet moment together both looking down at the floor. They look up at one another, smile and continue going through the box of pictures.

Because they were on the run when he was a boy, Zuri had no pictures from his youth to share. Then Zuri remembered, he had one photo to share with Angelo.

"Angelo I have one picture to share with you. I have had it in my wallet for so long, I almost forgot it was there; I had it laminated so it wouldn't get damaged."

Zuri reaches into his pocket and pulls out a worn brown leather wallet that had obviously been around for a while; but, you could still tell it was an exquisitely made alligator skin single fold wallet. In a pocket within the wallet behind his driver's license, social security card, government identification and a tri-folded hundred dollar bill, Zuri pulls out the picture. It is in black and white and although it's laminated, the edges of the picture itself were worn and the picture looked as if it had been taken with an extremely old camera; if not for the lamination, it would surely fall apart.

"This was the first and the only wallet my father ever gave me," Zuri says, "and this hundred dollar bill was in there when he gave it to me. He told me it was for emergencies only and that I should try not to ever spend it, and as you can see, I haven't. Anyway, here's the picture; it was taken the last time we were all together. Two days later, we split up and I never saw Teleza or my brother again. Okay so, in this picture are my father, Teleza, me and do you know who this is?"

"Is that who I think it is?" Angelo asks.

"It most certainly is," Zuri replies.

Angelo lets out a big "WOW," smiles and sighs. Before the two men can get into the particulars of the picture, their ladies walk in and the guys choose to postpone the conversation until later. Saphera and Veronica arrive with lunch for the guys who are definitely in the mood for eating now and are in much better spirits, to the ladies surprise. They all head to the kitchen for the guys to eat and the ladies proceed to put on some coffee and get their men something else to drink when Veronica whispers to Saphera.

"Wow, they are in a much better mood than before we left."

"I told you, they just needed some time and from the looks of it, some time to reminisce about their respective time spent with that wonderful old lady; I noticed the picture box on the table."

"I totally missed that; but either way, I'm just glad to see them smiling and laughing again," Veronica responds.

Saphera and Veronica find four wine glasses in Angelo's cabinets and bring them to table and take a seat with their men. Veronica retrieves a bottle of merlot and joins in the conversation that has the two men laughing. It's Friday afternoon and tomorrow is Teleza's home going memorial service. The arrangements have all been made for an 11a.m. service at the funeral home's chapel. Per the instructions of her will, Teleza requested that Angelo be the only one to speak at her memorial service, as well as it being short and joyous.

A couple of hours have passed and the two couples have been engaged in conversation on a variety of subjects before Zuri takes the opportunity to quiz Angelo on his preparedness for tomorrow's proceedings.

"So son, do you know what you're going to say tomorrow; have you thought it over; you need some help?"

Angelo hesitates; he glances out of his back window and then turns and stares into the beautiful brown eyes of his fiancée, he reaches up with his left hand and gently moves her silky black hair from in front of her right eye, and turns to respond to Zuri's questions. "I think I have it under control sir. She left me with enough memories, advice and love for me to know what to say. I just hope I can get through it without being overcome with emotions."

"We understand baby," Veronica ripostes and she takes her hand and rubs it across his cheek while her thumb softly grazes his bottom lip; "I know it was difficult for me when I lost my grandfather six years ago."

"However, Angelo declares, I would rather not think about all of that right now; how about we all go to a movie tonight. It will give us a chance to get out and share a few more smiles together before tomorrow."

The group rises from the table and prepares for their outing. The ladies clean off the table as the guys make their way to the living room and take a seat until the ladies finish in the kitchen. Angelo grabs his keys and prepares to drive but when they get outside, Zuri has already called for a limo to pick them up. Shocked, Angelo runs his hand over his head from front to back, locks the front door and reaches for Veronica's hand and shouts, "ALL ABOARD," as he opens the door for everyone to get in and the family of four rides off into the night for a movie, dinner and drinks.

Meanwhile, back in Atlanta, Marcus receives news from Dr. Lott that he can go home tomorrow. His hospital bed is surrounded by Zephora on one side and his big sister Charlie on the other. Dr. Lott is standing at the foot of the bed with Marcus' chart in his hands as he reads off the list of Marcus' dos and don'ts, as well as the medication he will be sending home with Marcus and the prescriptions he must get filled.

Marcus is looking at Dr. Lott as he rattles off this information he wants him to know. However, Marcus' mind is somewhere else. He can't help but think about what his best friend is going through and trying to figure out how he can help him. Then he turns his attention to Zephora; she is attentively listening to Dr. Lott; asking questions. Marcus is no longer focusing on what the doctor is saying, his mind is on Zephora and he's thinking to himself: *God thank you for blessing me with such an incredible and complete woman. I know she is going to take good care of me. She's beautiful and oh so fine; thank you Jesus for blessing me with a woman who is so perfect for me. I can't wait to get her home with me feeling better; boy oh boy, the fun we will have. Down boy, we have a room full of people here; let me get my mind back on the good doctor and what he's saying.* With that Marcus can hear the doctor again.

"Marcus do you understand everything I just read to you or do you need me to go over anything again?" Marcus turns and looks at Zephora, smiles and asks her.

"Babylove did you get all of that?"

"Of course I did Sweetheart; you know I always got your back and you know I'm going to take such good care of you baby," Zephora says with a sexy tone to her voice.

"You two are a mess," Charlie chimes in.

Dr. Lott and his nurse do their final check of Marcus' vital signs. They check his heart, his lungs, and his blood pressure, and check his wounds to insure they are no longer bleeding and give them a fresh dressing. As he is preparing to leave, Dr. Lott feels compelled to say one final word to Marcus.

"Marcus, I hope you realize as I do, that you are a very blessed man. I don't say this to all my patients, but every time I come into this room; I can feel the presence of God in here. I feel compelled to tell you that God has a calling on your life. Your recovery has been nothing less than miraculous. With an injury as severe as yours was, I shouldn't be sending you home yet; however, you are doing so well, I cannot find a single reason to keep you here any longer. And if you don't mind, I would like to say a prayer for you."

"Dr. Lott, I would be honored sir," Marcus replies humbly, "and may God bless you for even offering to share your prayers to me."

Charlie, Dr. Lott and Zephora are again surrounding Marcus' bed, this time the four of them are holding hands, their heads are bowed and their eyes are closed as Dr. Lott begins to pray.

"*Father God and Gracious Master, we thank you for blessings us with another day on your earth. We thank for our health. We thank you for food, clothing and shelter, and pray that those who are without today receive all that they need tomorrow and the days that follow. I come here today Lord to thank you for Brother Marcus. I thank you for the healing power you have placed inside him Father God. I thank you for the miraculous healing you did inside of Marcus that spread to every other patient on this wing of the hospital. Gracious Master make it known to Marcus the plan, purpose and destiny You have for his life. Lord bless his family and I pray that Your favor rest upon them. I pray that You anoint them with Your Holy Spirit now and every day going forward from here. Touch Brother Marcus Father God and continue to open his heart and his mind; place the words in his mouth to say as You put him in situations to bless the lives of others. Give strength to this incredible woman You have blessed him with; may she always remain by his side. Father God prepare them for the good and the bad, for the trials and tribulations they may encounter in the future and grant them the strength, the knowledge, the understanding and the wisdom to lean on You in times of trouble and need, and Father God teach them how to forgive one another for they are stronger together than apart. Father God, we love you, we give you the praise, the honor and the glory for whatever success we have and may achieve in our lives and we worship only You Lord for all the days of our lives. And Lord show Sister Charlie that she is important to You, that You love her and show her where You want her to be. And Father we end this prayer with: Our Father in heaven, hallowed be Your name, Your Kingdom come, Your will be done, on earth as it is in heaven. Give us today our daily bread, and forgive us our sins, as we also forgive those who have sinned against us. And lead us not into temptation, but deliver us from the evil one; for thine is the Kingdom, the Power and the Glory; forever and ever, Amen."*

Marcus gets out of his bed, gives Dr. Lott a strong manly hug while at the same time thanking him in truth and sincerity. After the hug Marcus shakes Dr. Lott's hand, places his left hand on top of Dr. Lott's hand; then changes it to a brother shake, pulls him in so that are shoulder to shoulder, and whispers in his in ear.

"Doc I love you man. Thank you for taking such good care of me and my family and thank you for such a beautiful prayer. I am humbled and strengthened by it. God bless you and your family brother, and I'll see you in the morning at check out."

"Rest well tonight Marcus and you too Mrs. Marcus."

"You too Dr. Lott," Zephora replies, "And were you serious when you said everybody on this wing is miraculously healed starting with Marcus?"

"Yes ma'am, I am very serious; the whole thing has renewed my faith and trust in God as well as our Lord and Savior Jesus Christ," replies Dr. Lott.

"Praise God," shouts Zephora, "and good night."

Marcus, Zephora and Charlie begin to talk amongst themselves about Dr. Lott's claim and are all empowered by it. Zephora gives Charlie the keys to her car and home and tells her to go get a good night's sleep at her house. Charlie has no problem agreeing, grabs her purse, gives Zephora a hug, kisses Marcus on the forehead and says goodnight as she gladly leaves the hospital headed to Zephora's for the night.

Marcus and Zephora are finally alone for the night. Marcus adjusts his bed and Zephora comes over and climbs in the bed curling up beside Marcus who scoots over to give her room. She gets under the covers with him and gently lays her head on his chest. With his left hand, he interlocks his fingers with her fingers on her right hand and the two simultaneously take deep breaths, close their eyes and drift off to sleep without saying a word to each other but both having smiles on their faces until Marcus opens his eyes, turns his face towards

Zephora's, kisses her soft lips three times and whispers. "Good night my love; rest well, tomorrow we finally get to go home."

Zephora opens her eyes, smiles at Marcus and kisses his full lips three times back and then kisses the tip of his nose before closing her eyes again as his are already and the two love birds drift off to sleep. Right before they enter into their restful state, Zephora's cell phone beeps and vibrates alerting her that she is receiving a text message.

"Go ahead and get that baby it could be important," Marcus says in a half sleep state.

"I'll just check it in the morning Marcus." Zephora groggily responds.

"It could be your mother or Veronica with some news at this late hour; I can't imagine who else it could be; so, it is probably in your best interest to get now rather than later," Marcus reiterates.

Rather than go back and forth with Marcus, Zephora reaches over and picks her phone up off the nightstand and opens her text message without reluctance for she and Marcus to read. Without looking to see who the message is from, only searching for the starred box, Zephora presses the box and they read the late night message:

> *You know we should be together baby I can't*
> *understand why you are ignoring my texts and*

not returning my calls. I NEED TO HEAR
FROM YOU NOW BEFORE I COME & GET
MY GIRL (LOL).

Zephora's eyes stretch three sizes over normal and begin to well up with tears as she glances up to see the name attached to the message and knows Marcus is doing the same. Her heart is pounding fast and hard and everything seems to be moving in slow motion as she blinks her extra-large eyes praying it's a prank from Veronica. As her eyes reach the top of the page, out of the corner of her eye she can see that Marcus' eyes are there as well. They simultaneously read the name on the phone. Zephora's heart drops into her stomach, her head drops and tears begin to trickle from her eyes as well. Marcus' heart begins to race, his pulse quickens and his eyes grow to the size of a golf ball as he turns to Zephora with consternation.

The name on the phone read: Chris Caldon.

CHAPTER VII

Consternation turns to anger as the realization of the situation smacks Marcus in the face. Without a word to Zephora, Marcus slowly gets out of his bed, places his IV bag on the mobile stand and roles it with him as he holds his tongue and takes a seat in the recliner in the far corner of the room. His blood is boiling and his blood pressure rising as he holds his temper in check despite the pain he is feeling. It feels as if someone has stuck a dagger in the middle of his chest and though there is no blood and no actual dagger, he can't stop the pain.

Zephora thought she would be able to avoid this; she thought she could keep Marcus from finding out and now that he has, she dreads dealing with it all. How does she tell the man that she loves and that loves her more than and better than anyone ever has, that while he was away fighting the would be kings and pawns to defend their love for one another and for their ability to marry one another that she called on another man, a friend, a man whom she was once engaged to, to comfort her? How does she tell him that she was weak and in her weakness this other man who unbeknown to her never got over her and took her advances of friendship as advances of renewal of love. How does she defend her choice even though if she could, in a heartbeat, she would take it back? How does she get him to understand, to see that she knows it was a mistake, one she would give anything to take back? One thing Zephora does know is that if she doesn't go to him right now, she could lose his trust. And what is friendship and love without trust?

Marcus can only see betrayal, can only feel betrayed and can only think why. He is hurting more than any physical pain can touch. He waited so long to find the one woman whom he could give himself over to completely, the one woman with whom he wouldn't have to change for, with whom he could be himself with; he waited for Zephora. And now she has broken his heart into bite sized pieces. Marcus is known for not being able to forgive easily. As hard as he loves, it is that hard for him to forgive. He knows he's not perfect; but, in love he expects perfection, it has been his life's goal to find perfect love and with Zephora, he thought, he knew he had found it. But what now, what about his perfect love notions now?

Zuri and Saphera allow Angelo and Veronica to have the limo all to themselves for the ride back home. As they walk along the beach hand in hand, the elder couple cannot believe how their lives have come full circle. That which was once lost has been found and is now stronger than before. Real love will overcome every obstacle placed before it because love, real, genuine love is the strongest force there is and Zuri and Saphera know this all too well. Their walk is interrupted abruptly by a deep bronchial cough from Zuri that ended with a hurling spit riddled with blood polluting the white sands of the beach.

"Zuri is this new or have you been hiding this from me," Saphera questions Zuri with love and concern but issues it with a firm hand.

"I really hadn't given it much thought until now; the cough has never been this bad and it's definitely the first I've seen any blood. You know I don't have room for secrets from you my love." Zuri replies honestly and nearly out of breath.

"Well that's it, we're going back to Angelo's; our walk is over, and when we get home…"

"Yes, I know, straight to the doctor. It's probably nothing, we have just been in this Florida heat too long," Zuri interrupts. He tries to make light of the situation as to not worry his beloved wife; but, he is extremely concerned by this knew development. He is used to seeing his own blood but not like this; not to mention, the burning pain in his chest. He takes the hand of his wife and starts the walk off the beach with a slower pace than when they started and with more questions, more fear and pretentious smiles.

Saphera releases the hand of her husband and wraps her arm around his arm instead and smiles. She's putting on a brave face for him as to not alert him of her apprehension. She has seen this kind of thing before and is hoping and praying as they walk for the lessor of two evils.

Zuri reaches in his pocket and presses a button on the car remote sized object in his pocket. As they reach the parking lot, a car pulls up, a new Cadillac XTS, equipped with a polite driver who hops out of the car and opens the back door for his passengers to enter. Once in the car, Saphera glances at her husband, smiles and shakes her head in disbelief at Zuri's perfect timing and thinks to herself, "How does he do it? How does he still manage to make her feel like he did when they first met after all this time and separation?"

Meanwhile, on the other side of the city, Veronica is enjoying an impromptu tour of Angelo's home city from the back of a limo. Angelo is an informed host as he is able to seemingly tell her the history of the city, as if he was a tour guide. She hangs on his every word, watching the changes in the contours of his lips as they form words and utter sounds; and, it's turning her on. Finally, she can take it no longer; she reaches over, grabs his face with both her hands, and with Angelo in mid-sentence, passionately locks his lips in an affair with her own and he welcomes her advances and simultaneously pushes the button to close the privacy glass between them and the driver. Their kiss lasts for several minutes, until it is interrupted by intense eye contact between them; after which, the intimate contact begins again. Suddenly but slowly Angelo pulls back and pulls out his phone. Veronica is puzzled by his action as she is sure he is enjoying himself. As she starts to question him, he places his finger across her sexy lips and proceeds to make his call.

"Jerome, I need to ask a favor of you." The voice on the other end of the phone intently listens to the request of Angelo as does Veronica. After the call, Angelo lets down the privacy window and gives the driver new instructions as to their destination. Angelo and Veronica relax back into their seats, her hand clutched in his resting on the arm rest that separates them. Angelo raises her hand to his lips and gently presses his lips against it while staring pleasurably into her eyes. Then he whispers to her, "sit back darling and enjoy the ride." Veronica sits back, crosses her legs and does as instructed without anxiety or trepidation. She only wishes they could get back to their pre-phone call activities, but hopes they can continue them later, much later and hopefully longer; her heart quickens at the thought.

Change happens, and on a consistent and continual basis. Few people ever stop to think about how unfailing change is. Life offers up new orders every second. Those instructions create new wonders that undoubtedly have an effect on all those who journey through life. Some of those orders stop life, and some take life on an unanticipated path that renders what seems like no choice; however, there is always a choice in life no matter how it seems.

Change is offering up new paths for Zuri and Saphera who leave the beach with unanswered questions about Zuri's medical woes, for Angelo and Veronica who are taking a trip with a new and unexpected destination, for Charlie the truth has presented her with a new outlook and a fresh approach to life unshackled and for Marcus and Zephora, change has brought a dark cloud over their always sunny skies challenging the survival of their love. However, change is a constant Marcus and Zephora are used to, but usually it is them against the world, not them against each other. The thing about change is that it offers a lifetime of firsts.

PART 2

The Seeds of Change

CHAPTER VIII

As he sits in the recliner in the corner of his hospital room with his head in his hands, Marcus is reminded of a Bible passage almost as if it was being read to him by someone standing just behind his left shoulder. *"Love is patient and kind, love does not envy or doubt, it is not arrogant or rude. It does not insist on its own way; it is not irritable or resentful, it does not rejoice at wrongdoing, but rejoices with the truth. Love bears all things, believes all things, hopes all things, and endures all things."* He looks back to see who is behind him, but no one is there; however, sitting in front of him is Zephora with her eyes red and full of tears. It's time to break the silence; it's time to actually listen to her explanation. Things can't change or move forward if there is no communication. Just as he opens his mouth to form words to speak, his phone rings. Marcus gets up, walks around Zephora without even looking at her, and picks up his phone from the nightstand and sits on his bed to answer it.

"Sire, this is Bengono from the council; do you remember me?"

Marcus replies with a befuddled look on his face, "Yes I remember you. Why are you calling me so early in morning?"

"I apologize to you Sire, it is afternoon here and the difference did not occur to me." But it did occur to him; he wanted to catch Marcus off guard and hopefully delirious from being awakened in the middle of the night. "I hope I did not wake you; however, I have urgent information to share with you concerning our ancient Tribal Laws."

"You didn't wake me and I'm sure you know exactly what time it is here. I don't have time for games Bengono, so how about you get to the point of this call so early in the morning." Having dealt with his people before, Marcus knows all too well that strength is what they respect.

"I meant no disrespect Sire," his voice now flustered by the directness and clarity he receives from Marcus. "There is a matter in the laws that cannot be overlooked. You have less than thirty days to stand before this council and the families of the council with your wife or the council has the right to choose a wife for you from those who are next in line for you to marry."

Marcus hesitates before speaking in order to choose his words wisely. "First, I want a complete copy of all the Tribal Laws, including the ancient ones overnighted to me immediately. Second, I don't know if you realize it or not, but I am still recovering from the gunshot wounds I suffered at the hands of Kwazan while saving the life of my betrothed. And third, because of that, we should be given extra time to appear before the council, which by the way, I look forward to doing."

"Sire, I will have the copy overnighted to you today. I apologize for the actions of Kwazan, and I am sure he received his just reward for his betrayal; however, it does not matter when it comes to the Tribal Laws. Our ancestors had to deal with difficulties as well when it came to the fulfillment of the laws, yet here we are. I suggest you quickly marry Ms. Sherman and look to appear before us three weeks from today to satisfy our Tribal Laws because there is much work to be done if we are to change the course of our country and our people as you spoke of when we met last."

"Bengono, be so kind as to provide me with pictures of the council members and their families as well as their financials, including yours, along with a copy of all the Tribal Laws. I look forward to seeing you in three weeks with my new bride. But let me be very clear Bengono, if anything should happen to me, my family, my bride or her family before we get there, I am holding you personally responsible. I hope I have made myself clear." Marcus knows he must always deal from a position of strength when dealing with his countrymen.

"Your instructions and warnings are crystal clear Sire. I will prepare for your arrival; however, I must warn you of the bad blood some of the council families have expressed because you and your bride know so little of our culture and way of life and would rather see you with a bride who is familiar with our customs to help you in your transition from the United States to Malawi. I am and will be loyal to you, my King, and wish you would not hold me responsible for the actions of others."

"While I appreciate your loyalty, I would be remiss to believe you have no idea of who has a serious problem with me and is willing to do anything about it. So, I stand by my previous assertion. Good day Bengono."

"Good day Sire." Bengono hangs up the phone feeling less empowered than he thought he would be before making the phone call. He placed this call while sitting in a room with the other ruling council members and they are taken back by his demeanor. One of the members looks at Bengono and says to him, "Well, do we move forward or not?" Bengono glares back at him and calmly states, "I would not suggest it, but do what you like; however know that I am out of it."

Zephora makes her way over to the bed and sits down beside Marcus hoping to be able to deflect from their situation by asking him about the intense phone call. "Marcus what happened, what's wrong?"

The expression on Marcus' face changes from one of deep thought, to one of intense anger as he turns to look at Zephora. "You should be less concerned about my phone call and more concerned with explaining that text you received from Chris Caldon."

Zephora takes a deep breath, lets it out and begins to explain her transgression. "When you were away in Africa, I felt all alone and reached out to what I thought was an old friend. I had no idea he was still hung up on me; I was going crazy, I didn't want to bother Angelo because he was busy with running your company and Veronica was there for me to a degree, but I wanted to hear the voice of a friend other than the two of them. There are times when the voice of a friend is what a woman needs to hear to comfort her, and that's where I was at that time; and my man, you, were halfway around the world. Once I realized I had made a mistake by calling him, it was too late, he was fixated on me and nothing I said could get rid of him. I will gladly show you all the text messages between him and me so you can see it really was innocent on my behalf. My mistake was being weak enough to think that another man's voice could bring comfort to me when what I really wanted was to hear your voice. Marcus, please forgive me, I didn't mean to hurt you in any way."

"Yeah okay," Marcus replies, "I'm not one who takes betrayal easily. In fact, your actions have cut me deep, but what can I do about it now? I have to make a choice on whether I can truly trust you or not."

"Marcus you know you can trust me. I just made a bad judgment call. I'm asking you, begging you, please forgive me. I will never betray your trust or confidence again."

"Now that you have lied to me, why should I believe anything you have to say? Why should I trust you? What really is the word of a liar worth?" Marcus wants Zephora to feel as much pain as he is feeling; he wants his words to cut her with the same depth as the one she cut him with. As he watches the expression of her face turn to pain and the tears stream down her beautiful face, he feels both vindicated and sad. As Marcus walks to the chair in the corner, he realizes by hurting her he has caused himself even more pain.

She says nothing back to him, she just sits in front of him and cries profusely. He has done the one thing he never ever wanted to do, he made his beloved Zephora cry and broke an impossible promise for anyone to keep. He has hurt the one which he holds to be most precious to him. No matter what she did, he knows he has no right to lash out at her out of his pain, to seek revenge. He ponders it all and decides to give himself a break, noting that he is 'only human' and realizes that he should give her a break too. Marcus sits back in his chair, rests his left elbow on the arm and places his chin between his thumb and forefinger as he watches the love of his life weep because of what he said to her. The smugness he felt earlier is all but a distant memory; he watches her cry and is filled with immense sadness. Everything in him tells him to reach out, pick her up and hold her in his arms begging her forgiveness. But how can he, she hurt him too; what's a man to do; too many emotions to decipher, he's so conflicted, he sits there a moment longer. Unable to take watching his beloved cry any longer, Marcus reaches for Zephora and without hesitation she embraces him tightly, enough so that he cringes in pain as her breasts are pressed into the wound across his chest; but she doesn't let up. Instead, Zephora, still heavily bleeding tears, she pulls Marcus even tighter and whispers in his ear while dripping warm tears on his hospital gown that soak through to his shoulder and stream down his chest and into his wound burning as they penetrate Marcus' stitches; yet, he doesn't pull away.

"Marcus baby, I'm so sorry for hurting you, for betraying you and for lying to you. I promise you, I will never lie to you again," she whispers, her voice trembling as she speaks.

"Zephora, you hurt me; you have no idea the hell I experienced over there. You think you had it rough here, you think you went through hell? You have no idea what hell is; but I didn't break, I didn't have a moment of weakness and flaunt with the idea of another. My first and every thought was you, I got through by focusing on you, on us, on our love. But, I understand and I forgive you; but baby, I will be holding you to your promise, just as I hold myself to sharing the best of who I am with you."

The two sit down and talk about how to insure that communication, trust and compromise wrapped in integrity has to be the rule of thumb for their life together. Marcus is exhausted and in pain; he needs to and must lie down if he is going to be ready to leave the hospital in a few hours. The emotional rollercoaster has taken its toll on Zephora as well. The two lie closely together, Zephora curled up on her side and Marcus's body synchronized with hers, in the small hospital bed and he allows their reconciliation to clothe them like a warm blanket, as they both are eager for some much needed rest. Just as they are nearly asleep, Marcus' phone vibrates in the pattern for a text. The two simultaneously respond "What now!"

Although Zuri and Saphera and Angelo and Veronica went in separate directions after going to the movies, somehow they manage to arrive back at Angelo's home about the same time. As they enter the home, the four are all smiles and engage in some small talk before retiring to their rooms. Zuri notices that Veronica does not go into her room but follows Angelo into his room, quietly closing the door not to draw attention to the change in her venue.

The next morning before anyone else is awakened, Veronica sneaks out of Angelo's room into her own as to go unnoticed. Zuri, an early riser, looks up from reading, and watches her from the living room. Shortly thereafter, Angelo emerges from his room and goes into the kitchen to put on a pot of coffee only to be startled by Zuri sitting in the living room.

"Where are you going my boy?" Zuri whispers.

Angelo jumps and lands in his martial arts on guard position, ready to strike whoever is speaking when he notices it is Zuri. "Man you startled me, I wasn't expecting anyone to be up so early; what are you doing up so early?" Angelo replies

"O just sitting here getting some reading done; and you, why are you up so early?"

"Well," Angelo begins, "I figured I would get coffee ready and begin preparing breakfast."

"Really, and why did I see Veronica coming out of your room, or should I say sneaking out of your room this morning and seeing you two sneak into your room last night or earlier this morning should I say? Didn't you tell me the two of you were keeping your relationship sacred until marriage? What happened man, what happened?"

Angelo hesitates before speaking, pondering what to say and how to respond to the various questions. "Well sir, let me tell you exactly what you saw. She was, I mean I was, no we were; what I mean to say is that yes she accompanied me to my room and yes she left my room early in an attempt to keep it a secret. As for the rest, I would like to respond to it all later over breakfast with Veronica sitting next to me."

Zuri laughs and shakes his head. "Angelo, everybody slips up now and again, don't," he is interrupted by Angelo.

"It's not like that at all, I promise you. Just wait until breakfast please," Angelo chimes in.

Zuri sighs and goes back to reading but not before he is overwhelmed by a coughing spell that ends with small chunks of gelatinized blood spattered in his hand which he hides from Angelo by wiping it off in the handkerchief he keeps with him.

"Are you okay Sir?" Angelo asks with great concern and at the same time approaching Zuri and placing his hand on his shoulder.

"I'll be alright Angelo, but could you please get me a glass of water?"

"No problem, I'll be right back." Angelo rushes into the kitchen, retrieves a glass from the upper cabinets to the right of the sink and gets water from the water dispenser on the refrigerator door and rushes back to Zuri spilling it a little along the way and not being concerned about it. Once he is sure Zuri is okay, Angelo proceeds to begin to prepare breakfast. Today is a big day for him that will no doubt drudge up unresolved emotions and hopefully answer his many questions about his beloved grandmother.

Just as Angelo finishes preparing all but the scrambled eggs, the ladies emerge from their bedrooms with stomachs growling, ready to eat. Angelo steps out of the kitchen and sounds the breakfast alarm, "ladies and gent breakfast is ready. Please join me in the kitchen for an enchanting meal and conversation; and oh yeah, good morning ladies." Angelo has prepared a genuine family breakfast which includes bacon, turkey sausage, grits, pancakes, extra strong coffee, orange juice and now that everyone is seated around the table he is topping the meal off with his special cheese eggs with mushrooms, onions and tomatoes.

You can always tell when a meal is truly delicious by the lack of conversation and the abundance of chewing, lip smacking and mm's you hear; and Angelo has just created that kind of meal. Everyone has gorged themselves on the meal that Angelo has placed before them and now they are sipping on coffee and patting their stomachs. Finally Zuri breaks the silence. "Angelo, where did you learn to cook like that; never mind, I know where. I'm sorry I mentioned it."

Angelo drops his head for a second, then raises it again and responds to Zuri, "Its okay, I'm cool now, not over it, but cool."

"Baby, this was a truly delicious meal. I had no idea you could burn like this," Veronica chimes in.

"Yes Angelo, an absolutely enjoyable breakfast, the best I have had in a while," Saphera retorts.

Angelo is pleased that everyone has enjoyed the meal and thanks everyone for their kind words. Now that everyone is done praising him, Angelo thinks it's about time he starts today's first dialogue. He raises his juice glass and taps it three times with his fork. "Last night while Veronica and I were riding home in the limo, we both agreed that we had never experienced love like this before. We also agreed that we've never experienced this kind of friendship in a relationship like we have with each other. It reminded us of the kind of friendship and love we have watched and admired between Marcus and Zephora. We also watched as fate or whatever you want to call it pull them apart again and again, and we decided that we didn't want that to happen to us. I have an announcement to make; or should I say, Veronica and I have an announcement to make."

Before Angelo can finish, Zuri and Saphera are holding hands with their mouths and eyes open wide in anticipation of what they believe Angelo is about to say. Just as Angelo is about to break he and Veronica's announcement, Veronica jumps up from the table and shouts, "We're Married," as she sticks out her hand to show off her beautiful ring that houses a two carat marquise cut diamond solitaire flanked on both sides by five horizontal baguettes per side that get smaller as the ring narrows and is set in twenty-four carat white gold. Angelo looks at his new bride, smiles and calmly says, "That's right, last night we got married."

Saphera heard the words but is caught in the glare of Veronica's ring. She grabs Veronica's hand to get a closer look. "This is a magnificent ring. This cut is my favorite; the color is fantastic and the clarity, what else can I say, except Oh My God it's beautiful! Congratulations girl!"

Zuri grabs Angelo, hugs him and pats him on the back exclaiming, "I'm proud of you son, you did well; you had me going but you did good, congratulations son congratulations! Have you told Marcus yet?"

"We texted right afterwards, but chances are he was asleep. He'll get it when he gets up this morning."

"Oh my God, Zephora, come here!" Zephora is in the bathroom of Marcus' room preparing for his release later and upon hearing Marcus' shouts she runs out.

"What Marcus, what happened, what's going on!"

"Remember that text we got last night right before we went to sleep? Well, it turns out it was Angelo."

"Okay, is everything alright? Did something else happen down there, are my parents okay; what's going on Marcus, what happened?"

"Calm down Ze, everyone is fine as far as I can tell, he texted me to tell us that he and Veronica got married!"

"Are you kidding me; that's fantastic; I knew those two were right for each other! This is so awesome! I need to call Veronica and you need to call Angelo so we can tell them we got married too!"

CHAPTER IX

"No Ze. No one can know yet that we are married, until we get back from Africa. Those royal families over there take the Tribal Law extremely serious; and for whatever reason, they don't want us together. But it doesn't mean we can't celebrate with Angelo and Veronica when they get back in town."

Zephora doesn't respond immediately; she disagrees with Marcus, and believes that the best thing is that everyone knows they are married. However, she doesn't want to get into another argument with him so she feels it best to go along with his way of thinking. "Whatever you say baby," she responds, trying not to sound sarcastic and failing miserably.

Marcus senses Zephora's tone but chooses not to respond to it because he doesn't want to get into another argument. Marcus smiles at her and continues to prepare for his release from the hospital and texts Angelo:

> *That is excellent news brother. We love you both and can't wait for you to get back and we'll celebrate. I'm going home today.*

Both Marcus and Zephora have chosen to be dishonest in their conversation with one another as opposed to stating how they really think and feel about the other's plan on how to deal with their present dilemmas; a recipe for marital disaster.

Its 11a.m. and Marcus' nurse comes in to administer the papers for his release from the hospital. Marcus and Zephora are more than ready to get out of there; he has seen the inside of this hospital far too often in the last few months because of his heritage and the Tribal Law that comes with it. First it was the threat on Zephora's mother's life, and then, the bullets he took to save Zephora's life; they are truly ready to get out of there, for good this time.

When the nurse returns, she brings a wheel chair and Dr. Lott's post-surgery instructions which include minimal physical exertion. "I called Charlie to come pick us up and take us home." Zephora asserts. It will be the first time Marcus and Zephora enter his house as one. It will officially mark the beginning of their new life together. They look into each other's eyes and smile the way you smile when you're both excited and afraid at the same time. Zephora takes out her phone and texts her mother to let her know they are leaving the hospital, finally. And with that, they start their trek downstairs and receive well wishes from the hospital staff, as Marcus has been a popular and lively patient.

Downstairs, Charlie waits for them with excitement and apprehension. Now that she has told her shame to Marcus and

Zephora, she feels free, free enough to build a new life for herself. However, she now has to tell her brother of her plan and hopes he gives her his blessings. It seems like she has been waiting for him for hours to come through those doors. Finally, she sees Zephora emerge from behind the darkness of the doors followed closely by the nurse pushing Marcus in the wheel chair. She jumps out of the car trying to contain her excitement. Charlie hugs Zephora as she greets her and then helps Marcus out of his wheelchair, hugging him the whole way and kisses him on his cheek. "Littler brother, I'm so glad to see you leaving this place."

"Hello big sis, it's good to see you too. You look good, you look different good; it brings a smile to my face to see you like this. What has you looking so happy?" Charlie smiles at her brother and helps him in the car. As she's insuring he's in his seat, she responds to his question. "I'm just glad to see you getting out of here little brother."

They thank the nurse for her assistance, Zephora jumps in the driver's seat and Charlie hops in the back. Before pulling off, Zephora turns to Marcus and says, "are you ready to go home Mr. Howard, to our home? Marcus turns to his beloved Zephora, realizing that for the first time he really is finally and officially married to the love of his life. So much has happened; he has endured so much pain, and passed all the trials to get to this place. Nothing had previously gone the way they had planned; but on this day, he can look at her beautiful face and answer her in the way he has wanted to since he first realized she was born to be his wife, in the way that makes it all worth it. The gravity of the realization of the tremendous debt they both have had to pay has tears forming in his eyes as he reaches up and gently brushes his fingers across Zephora's cheek and proudly says, "Yes Mrs. Howard, let's go home."

Meanwhile, in Tampa, Angelo, his new bride Veronica, Zuri and Saphera are at Angelo's grandmother's attorney's office for the reading of her will, per her instructions. This is the final part of Angelo's and Zuri's terrible ordeal; however, it is through the tragic loss of his grandmother that has brought him the realization of family and the importance of having someone who loves you as much as you love them.

"Ladies and gentlemen, I'm ready for you now," says Matthew Hillberg, the attorney. They enter the conference room of Matthew's office and they all take a seat around the oval shaped conference table with Angelo taking a seat at the head of the table closest to the door. Matthew closes the door and sits at the head of the table on the opposite end ready to begin.

"First let me tell you, it is a pleasure to see you all again even under these tragic circumstances. Mrs. Henson entrusted her will to me a little over a year ago when she had her first heart attack scare. Angelo, she knew this time was coming but she didn't want to worry you. She felt that if you knew about her heart condition, it would prevent you from realizing your dreams; that is why she concealed it from you." Angelo drops his head in sadness, because even though she didn't want him to know, he knew because he always kept tabs on her by keeping in contact with her doctor. So he knew what Matthew is saying is true.

"Second, this Will comes to you via a video, as well as a written copy. It was Mrs. Henson's wishes that you watch the video; after which, I will come back into the room with your copy Mr. Henson, and we can finalize it by signing all the necessary documents. Let me assure you that I have not watched the video, nor have I read Mrs. Henson's Will as she instructed. You will be the first to know what she has to say. I will turn on the DVD player and leave the room. You can knock on my office door when it's over. Thank you." Matthew turns on the player and leaves the room.

The two couples intensely and intently watch the flat screen television awaiting Angelo's grandmother to speak to them from beyond the grave; and then, it begins.

"My darling Angelo, if you are watching this, it means that I have passed on to be with my Heavenly Father. I don't want you to be sad, because truly I am in a much better place. After hearing what I have to say, mourn me and then go live your life; and remember I will always be watching over you.

Son you come from a proud and noble family. Your ancestors were really Kings and Queens. Your real family name is Netumba; my given name is Teleza Nushumba. I had the pleasure of being the nanny of your father, Zakwani, and his older brother, Zuri. Your family has been estranged from your people for a very long time, too long because of an act of bravery to help another noble family who was falsely accused of treason and exiled. This also made your family an enemy of the governing families and exiled as well. Both exiled families were to be hunted down and killed by tribal assassins in order to keep the truth hidden. With the wealth your family possessed, they were able to avoid these assassins for many, many years. All of that son is ancient history; so here is the part that is important to you. As I previously stated, I was your family's nanny and besides your real grandparents, no one loved your father and his brother more. One day an assassin came calling and your grandmother, Shera Netumba gave her life to insure me, your father and his brother's escape. We later met up with your grandfather and I had to tell him his wife was dead. I had never seen a man so devastated as he was; he truly loved your grandmother.

Together, your grandfather, Zikomo Netumba and I decided that the best way to protect his boys was for us both to take one and run. Once we were safe, we were going to keep in touch only twice a year, on their birthdays, but we were unable to keep that promise because it was just too risky and I only talked to them once more. Your grandfather trusted me with half his wealth and I'm not talking about his money, I'm talking about what he treasured most, his sons. I raised your father the way his mother would have wanted and your grandfather raised your uncle. One day it was reported that Zikomo and Zuri's car went over a cliff and they were both killed and I felt the pain I know your grandfather felt when his beloved wife was killed. Your father and I mourned them for weeks before I convinced him we had to move forward. And that we did. I watched your father grow into a handsome man and meet an incredible young lady, Angel, your mother. I had never seen your father happier than when he met your mother. It wasn't too long after they married that you were born and they loved you more than anything in this world. Your parents were what you young people call jet setters; their jobs took them all over the country and more. One day when you were two, they were going on vacation to Africa and were involved in a plane crash and were both killed. Per their will, I was to raise you as your grandmother. Now you know the truth about your family which is my family too. I never married and never had any children of my own except Zuri, Zakwani and you Angelo Zakwani Henson Netumba; you three were my babies. I hate you never got to know your parents, especially your father and your uncle Zuri; they were all such wonderful people full of hope and promise and now that hope and promise lives in you. I have done the job your grandfather Zikomo trusted me to do. I took care of one of his treasures and saved the future of his family. I lived long enough to see you become such an awesome young man, terrific grandson and enduring friend. Always value the friendship between you and Marcus, you two are destined to do great things together. The wealth your grandfather gave me, I doubled it and Matthew Hillberg, my attorney is instructed to give it to you at the right time; you can discuss that with him when I'm finished. For now remember that I love you and remember everything I have taught you; remember the code I taught you and if you have forgotten it, let me recite it to you one more time for good measure: MY GOD IS FIRST IN MY LIFE, HIS WILL IS MY WILL. I TAKE CARE

OF MY FAMILY AND MY HOME. I RESPECT MYSELF AND OTHERS, I AM RESPONSIBLE FOR ALL MY ACTIONS, I LEAD BY EXAMPLE, QUITTING IS NOT AN OPTION; I GIVE MY BEST IN ALL THAT I DO THUS ENSURING VICTORY NO MATTER THE OUTCOME; I TAKE CARE OF MY MIND, BODY AND SPIRIT; I HAVE A HEART OF GOLD AND I LIVE A LIFE OF INTEGRITY. Be the man God created you to be, live the hope and promise your family desired of you and endeavor to be a righteous man, a man like your father and his father before him. I know it sounds like a lot to be, but if you just be yourself, it will come easy because it is who you are already. And if don't, I WILL come back and haunt you; ha ha ha. I love you Angelo and I know you love me too and miss me just as much as I miss you; but you keep the faith, stay strong and trust God with all that you have and all that you are. Remember baby; rejoice because I have my victory! I love you forever. Bye now and night night.

The video ends and there isn't a dry eye in the room. Angelo and Zuri get up and embrace like a father and son would. Veronica and Saphera join in and the four have a group hug. After a few minutes, Zuri breaks away to get Matthew from his office to finish the proceedings. Angelo is able to just sit there, smile and allow his heart to rejoice and be happy just as Teleza instructed him to while simultaneously wiping away his tears of sadness and replacing them with tears of joy. He knows who he truly is now and where he comes from; from bravery, nobility and honor. Oh, my God he thinks to himself, Zephora is my first cousin. The thought brings a smile to his face; he and Marcus will be family when they get married.

Zuri and Matthew return to the conference room and everyone is anxious to get started. Matthew lays the paperwork on the table and chimes in. "Okay Mr. Henson, your grandmother has left you a substantial amount of wealth; enough to last for three to four generations just as it is now. The portfolio is diverse and a large portion is in stocks, bonds and mutual funds both domestic and foreign. There is an account in Switzerland and one in the Grand Cayman; both accounts were established legally so there is no governmental retribution. There is a checking and a savings account here as well; account numbers and passcode information are in the sealed envelope in this folder. You have immediate access to the accounts here; however, per your grandmother's instructions, the rest is to be turned over to you when you get married, a wedding present to you."

"Well," Angelo chimes in, "as it so happens, Veronica and I were married last night and we just happen to have the certificate with us."

"In that case," states Matthew, "congratulations are in order and I will go and retrieve the other folders."

"Thank you Matthew, I appreciate it," Angelo humbly replies.

Matthew leaves the room to retrieve the rest of the information and the four begin to talk amongst themselves. "Did I just marry royalty, did I just marry a prince," Veronica asks.

"I'm really not sure honey," replies Angelo. "What's the real deal Uncle Zuri?"

"Well nephew, as a matter of fact, we are part of an ancient nobility where leadership is determined by Tribal Laws and yes, son, you are a prince in the royal court of this generation and for the next 100 years; and then, it will be another royal family's time to rule. However, our King and Queen are Marcus and Zephora and we serve them just as they should first serve us."

Angelo leans back in his chair, takes a deep breath, looks at Veronica and slowly lets it out; he takes Veronica's hand and shakes his head. Matthew returns to the conference room with the rest of the information for Angelo to sign. "Okay Mr. Henson, we are ready to get this completed." Page after page is explained to Angelo and presented to him to sign until they reach the final page. "Mr. Henson, this page releases my firm from any more obligations and turns it over to you; or, if you choose, we can do for you what we have done for Mrs. Henson for years. With our guidance and her instructions we have almost tripled what she brought to us which was already a substantial amount; the choice is yours."

Angelo takes little time to respond with his choice. "Well Mr. Hillberg, my grandmother trusted you and I will do the same for now. You can continue to manage all stocks, bonds and mutual funds, as well as the Cayman account; and I will take total control over the accounts here and the one in Switzerland."

"Very well Mr. Henson, we will do as you have instructed. I will email you monthly reports on all of your affairs. We appreciate your business and look forward to a fruitful relationship just as we had with your grandmother. It was a pleasure meeting you all; I have another meeting to attend; however, feel free to utilize the conference room for the next thirty minutes, if necessary. Again, it has been a pleasure." Matthew shakes everyone's hand before leaving the room.

Angelo picks up his folders of information, stands up, looks at the faces in the room and makes a statement; "Let's go home family, let's go home. No words are spoken as they file out of the room one at a time. Suddenly, as Zuri is leaving the room, he is overcome with a coughing spell that seems to go on for several minutes and causes Zuri to stop in his tracks and double over from the viciousness of the coughs and the pain it is causing him. Angelo drops his folder and turns to help Saphera with Zuri. As he does, he can see blood dripping from Zuri's nose. He immediately reaches for the tissues which are conveniently located on the end table in Matthew's waiting area. Angelo gets Zuri to sit down in the chair next to the end table. Veronica picks up the paperwork from the folder that is now all over the floor and then joins Angelo and Saphera in surrounding the now seated Zuri.

Angelo's eyes are the size of quarters and his heart is beating three times the normal pace out of concern for his uncle.

"Uncle Zuri what is wrong with you; and don't tell me you're okay because all this blood says you're not. I just found out you are my uncle and I need you around; we need you around. So tell us what's going on so we can help you; I can't lose you too, I just can't."

CHAPTER X

It seems like a lifetime since Marcus has slept in his own bed and as he slowly makes his way around the sidewalk to his front door, the comfort of it is on his mind. With his new bride at his side, Marcus is happy to finally be home; and to be home with Zephora as his wife means the dream has come true. What God told him has come to fruition and he is excited about it from head to toe.

"Come here Mrs. Howard, it's time I carry you over the threshold."

"Now Marcus, you know Dr. Lott said no physical exertion for the first two weeks of being home."

"My love, there is nothing exertive about picking you up and walking through OUR front door; unless you have gained some weight that I can't see."

"No silly; I actually have lost a few pounds. However, I just don't want you to get hurt; plus, I have a much better way for you to exert yourself."

"Yeah, now you're talking; however, nothing is happening until I first carry you over this threshold." And with that being said, Zephora drops the bags she is carrying, unlocks and opens the front door, turns, faces her new husband, places her arms around his neck, places her lips on his and begins to kiss Marcus slowly and passionately until her tongue is occupying space in his mouth on top of and around his tongue. Simultaneously Marcus places his left arm around her back, bends his knees into a half squat, reaches his right arm under her thighs and lifts his bride with ease, opens his right eye to line up his entrance and slowly steps across the threshold of the door all while ignoring the pain in his chest that feels like his stitches are ripping open. Now that they are through the door, Marcus unlocks his lips from Zephora's, kicks the door shut with his left foot and says the words it has taken him what seems like an eternity to get out. "Welcome home Mrs. Howard; welcome to the start of our new life together. I love you."

Zephora is overcome with emotion. She was beginning to think that they would never get to this point, the beginning of their life together. Tears of joy are streaming down her face as Marcus gently places her feet on the floor. She remembers the last time she was in Marcus' living room and they came close to crossing a line she is eager and legally able to cross right now.

"Husband, why don't you make your way upstairs while I get everything out of the car."

"Absolutely; but you know what we forgot?"

"Whatever it is I will take care of it; you just get up those stairs."

"Okay."

As she makes her way to the car, it hits her like a ton of bricks: Charlie is still in the car. Charlie has moved from the back seat to the front seat and is shaking her head and laughing.

"Okay, now that you two have had your intimate moment, can you give me the keys so I can leave this little love nest please."

Zephora cannot believe she forgot all about Charlie being in the car. "Girl, I forgot all about you even being here. Here are the keys and I will see you later because I have got to go."

"Thank you sister; I know the drill, your house has become my second home which incidentally I need to get back to real soon. I will give you guys a call sometime late tomorrow."

"Don't bother Charlie; we'll call you if you get my meaning girl."

"Zephora, you are a mess. Bye girl." Zephora waves to Charlie as she hurriedly makes her way back into the house to her husband whom she hopes is ready, willing and able to consummate their marriage. She locks the door behind her and decides to give Marcus a little more time by putting away the bags she brought in the house.

Her work is done and now it's time to play. She makes her way up the stairs calling out to Marcus with every step. "Oh Marcus, Marcus baby, here I come ready or not. I hope more ready than not because your queen is hot!" Halfway up the stairs, there is a knock at the door. At first Zephora ignores the door because she has business to take care of; but then, it dawns on her that Charlie may have forgotten something or may need something. She bounces back downstairs and opens the door, saying Charlie's name simultaneously as she turns the nob. "Charlie, what did…" Her words are interrupted by a white handkerchief being thrust over her mouth, as she is pushed back into the house, gently laid to rest on the floor and the door quickly and quietly closed.

The assailant looks out the window insuring that no one saw what happened and that no one is out there now. Picking Zephora's limp body up, the attacker takes another look outside and carries her fireman style out the front door, closing it quietly and places Zephora in the trunk of a burgundy, late model Lexus 430; license plate number KZR 598. Marcus wakes up after nodding off waiting for his bride. He makes his way down stairs, noticing the rug at the front door is crinkled and he makes it to the door just in time to see the car peeling out of the driveway and down the street. Taped to the door is a note that simply reads: FINDERS KEEPERS.

Meanwhile, back in Matthew's office Zuri is surrounded by his family and Matthew's staff when Matthew brings him a glass of water which Zuri pushes away. "I'm alright now thank you." Zuri attempts to get up but is pushed back down gently by a hand firmly placed on his shoulder.

"Uncle Zuri, please take your time and catch your breath."

"Angelo is right Sweetheart," Saphera chimes in, "that was the worse one yet. I've got to get you back to Atlanta; you're scaring me."

With deep concern, Angelo begins to probe Saphera for answers. "How long has this been going on; what exactly is wrong with my uncle Aunt Saphera?"

"I have only just noticed it since we have been down here and with each episode, the cough gets worse and now there's blood coming up with the cough. We need to get back home so we can see our doctor about this." Saphera retorts.

"As soon as we get out of here and back to my house to pack, we can leave. I'm ready to get back to the ATL anyway."

Zuri, being an astute individual, catches that Angelo has begun calling him Uncle Zuri, like he has been missing not having one all his life, and is calmly overjoyed about it but hiding his emotion from the group. He watches Angelo's every move and mannerisms and for the first time he sees the resemblance of his little brother in Angelo's eyes. He has gained a lost part of himself back in Angelo, and he can't wait to build a meaningful relationship with him; he has so much knowledge he needs to share and to pass on.

Saphera and Angelo help Zuri to the limo and Veronica is following behind them with Angelo's folder of papers gripped tightly in her hands. Once in the limo, Zuri instructs the driver to call the pilots to get them back to the jet and have it fueled and ready to go in four hours. The ride back to Angelo's is a quiet one; everyone is seemingly in deep thought.

Zuri is concerned about his health. He has seen this type of thing enough to know that it isn't good; it's just a matter of how bad it is and if it's too late to reverse the damage. Saphera is frantic about the condition of her beloved husband. She just got him back and she doesn't want to lose him now; they are just getting to know one another again and he is really trying to build a relationship with his daughter whom incidentally she hasn't heard from in a couple of days. Zephora usually texts her mother once a day just to say hi. Angelo's mind is racing. He has a new bride, a new uncle and a need to spend time with both. Veronica is ready to spend time with her new husband; she is ready to whisk him away from all the family drama and go on their honeymoon. Then it hits her, *"oh my God, we're rich; I unwittingly did what my mother always advised me to do and married a man who is well off, and to top it off, I married him because we are madly in love. Hooray me."* Her next thought is, *"I really miss my parents, one day I'll have to tell Angelo the truth."* She looks around the limo and realizes no one is smiling. She catches Angelo's eye and he smiles and winks at her. The two are holding hands; but Veronica releases her hold, leans her head on Angelo's shoulder and wraps her arm around his, and with her other hand pulls his arm close to her, places his hand on her thigh which gets an immediate reaction, just what she was hoping for. Zuri and Saphera are watching the young lovebirds; they glance at one another and Saphera thinks Veronica has the right idea, cuddling with her man, and follows suit.

Just as they arrive at Angelo's, Zuri's phone rings, vibrates, rings; it only does that when the person on the other end knows to put a U in after his number for urgent. He looks down to check who's calling him; it's Marcus.

Marcus' heart is beating a mile a minute and it's causing extreme pain to his chest, but he can't think about that now. First thing is to write down the license plate number before he forgets: KZR 5, "Damn it!" he exclaims, "What's the rest of the number!" Next, he must call Zuri and then he can call the police. He reaches for his phone but he doesn't have it; it's on his night stand charging. He looks up the stairs dreading the trip back up in his weakened condition; but his beloved is in trouble, nothing else matters not even his own health. Without hesitation he runs up the stairs grimacing with every step. He makes it to the top of the stairs and doesn't stop until he gets to his phone. As he dials Zuri's number followed by a U for urgent, he realizes the room is spinning. He hears the phone ring once, twice, a third time before he hears Zuri's voice. "Marcus, what's wrong; where's Zephora! Marcus!"

Marcus is able to only get out a couple words, "Zuri, in trouble.." before he falls to the floor and passes out opening his wound as his body bounces off the floor like a half flat basketball. On the other end of the phone Zuri is shouting into the phone that is laying on the floor under the bed, "Marcus, Marcus, Marcus;" however Marcus is unable to respond.

"Driver, call the pilots and tell them to be ready to leave in twenty minutes," Zuri shouts. Everyone in the car is now sitting on the edge of their seats and instantaneously shouting, "WHAT HAPPENED!" Zuri explains that he believes Marcus is in trouble; he used the urgent dialing method and was only able to get out a few words before the line went dead. Zuri barks another order at the driver, "Take us to the airport now!" Without hesitation, the driver complies with his orders. Zuri makes an attempt to call Marcus back and the phone rings until it goes to voice mail and Zuri hangs up. He immediately tries to call Zephora and her phone rings several times before it clicks, as if someone is answering it but no one says anything. Zuri presses the record button on his phone in an attempt to record all the sounds he hears and then he speaks.

"Hello, hello; who is this, let me speak to my daughter right now!"

A Mickey Mouse sounding voice on the other end of phone answers; "You're not the one I want to talk to. Where is Marcus; he is the one I want to talk to."

Zuri responds, "You got me and if you know anything, you should know that if you have my daughter, it would be in your best interest to let her go now."

"You speak to me as if you are in control." In the background Zuri can hear Zephora screaming. The Mickey Mouse sounding voice continues, "Now listen to me, if Marcus doesn't call me in the next six hours, I will send you a piece of your daughter to the address where I took her from."

"Okay buddy, take it easy; I'll have Marcus call you as soon as I get to him. Is my daughter hurt; let me talk to her for just a minute so I can hear for myself that she is okay please."

The voice on the other end of the phone puts the phone up to Zephora's ear so she can talk into the phone. "Daddy is that you?"

"Yes baby I'm here."

"Where's Marcus? I'm fine Daddy, please find Marcus. I'll be okay."

"I'm coming baby, I'll be there soon; I'm coming." Before he can say another word, the voice snatches the phone away from Zephora's ear and at the same time Zuri has another coughing spell and hands his phone to Angelo. Angelo doesn't hesitate to speak to the voice.

"Listen whoever you are, we will have Marcus call you back on Zephora's phone and at that time, it would be in your best interest to let her go."

The voice doesn't respond to Angelo, only hangs the phone up. Zuri recovers and calls his number one team and tells them to get to Marcus' house and check on him now. He instructs them to report back in the next thirty minutes. Saphera has been patiently waiting for Zuri to tell her what has happened to her baby, but Zuri seems to be ignoring her as he sends the recorded message to his number two team for analysis with the same thirty minute time frame for some answers. No sooner than he finishes with the message and looks up, Saphera grabs his face with both her hands, looks directly into his eyes and speaks calmly but firmly to Zuri.

"What has happened to our baby; tell me what is going on right now Zuri."

Zuri stares right back at her, takes her hands in his and quietly responds to her. "Someone has kidnapped her and seemingly only wants to speak with Marcus, who I cannot reach on the phone. I have sent a team to his house to check on him and I have a team analyzing the recorded phone call so we might find out where she is being held. Right now, she's okay but we have got to get to Marcus quickly or…"

"Or what Zuri, or what!!"

"I don't know; we just need to get to Marcus as fast as possible so we don't have to find out."

"Zuri, don't let anything happen to my baby or…"

"Or what sweetheart;" Saphera pulls her hands away from his, gives him a blank look as if she was looking right through him and then begins to cry, and Zuri buries her face in his chest.

Finally, they have reached the plane and it's ready for takeoff. Veronica comforts Saphera and helps her to the plane as Zuri and Angelo begin to talk about how to proceed.

CHAPTER XI

Zuri's first team reaches Marcus and Zephora's home to find the front door closed but unlocked. They breach the door cautiously with their guns drawn, calling out for Marcus as they clear the first floor of the home. The team leader has Zuri on the phone with him, who is now on the plane tapping his knee nervously with anticipation of what they might find. As they make their way up the stairs, Zuri is constantly asking for a report; his team leader has never heard him like this before. Zuri is usually so calm under pressure. Reaching the master bedroom, they find Marcus passed out on the floor next to the bed with blood visibly spreading throughout his shirt.

"Mr. Howard, Mr. Howard, can you hear me; Mr. Howard," shouts the team leader. Marcus is groggy but conscious, trying to get his bearings.

"Who are you; what are you doing here?"

"Mr. Netumba sent us to check on you after your phone went dead during communications; I have him on the phone now. Are you ready to talk to him?"

Marcus shakes his head and slowly responds, "give me a minute please." Marcus slowly gets off the floor, walks over to the recliner in the corner and takes a seat. The number two man of the team tears opens Marcus' shirt and takes a look at

Marcus' wound which has a slow but steady stream of blood coming from it. He looks over at the team leader and orchestrates a nod which informs him that Marcus is okay.

"Mr. Netumba, Mr. Howard is groggy but fine. We are tending to his wound and he will be ready to talk to you momentarily," the team leader reports.

Zuri takes a deep breath and manages to calm himself before he responds. "Thanks J.R., that's good news. Please go downstairs and see if you can ascertain what happened. Get your kit and see if you can pull some fingerprints while I see what information I can get out of Mr. Howard. Time is of the essence J.R. We will be landing in about twenty minutes; be ready to brief me when I arrive."

"Yes Sir Mr. Netumba; I'm on it. I found Mr. Howard's phone under the bed; he has it now so you can call him directly and I look forward to speaking with you when you land sir." And with that, J.R. hangs up and gets busy following his orders. Just as C.J. finishes changing the dressing on Marcus' wound the phone rings for Marcus; it's Zuri.

Marcus is not ready to talk to Zuri yet, not ready to tell him how he got careless and lost his daughter; however, he knows Zuri won't hold him any more responsible for it than he holds himself. Marcus knows what's most important, it's that they find out who took Zephora and getting her back. "Zuri, I'm sorry I lost Zephora, I don't know what happened."

"It's okay Marcus, the main thing is that we get her back. Tell me what you know about what happened; start from the time you guys arrived at your home."

Marcus chooses to omit some minor details as he starts his recollection of the events. "Well, when we arrived, I went upstairs, changed clothes and sat on the side of the bed. Zephora went back downstairs to get our belongings out of the car and see Charlie off. I heard her come back inside, she said she would be up after she put some things away downstairs and at that point, I lay back on the bed and closed my eyes. The last thing I remember before nodding off is Zephora saying she was on her way up, hearing the doorbell and then hearing Zephora say Charlie must have forgotten something. I woke up a few moments later wondering where she was, I went downstairs, saw the rug crinkled, the door cracked open and heard a car backing out of the driveway and peeling off."

"Marcus, were you able to see the license plate number of the car?"

"Truthfully Zuri, I did; however, I was only able to remember the first four numbers. The car was a late model Lexus sedan. I apologize Zuri, you know me; I'm not usually like this."

"Marcus, stop apologizing; aren't you on medication and recovering from getting shot to save my daughter's life?"

"Yes sir, but…"

"But nothing Marcus, it's okay; you've done your job, now let me do what I do, better than most. When it counted, you didn't let me down and I promise you, I won't let you down now or my daughter. We will be there in ten minutes and I will have her back to you and the rest of us in less than twenty-four hours. We are coming directly to you from the airport and my guys will be setting up headquarters there because when I get there, we have to call this clown back."

"Wait Zuri, what do you mean call him back; you've talked to him, what did he say, what does he want?"

"I called Zephora and this clown answered her phone. I was able to talk to her to get proof of life; however, this clown, and I say "this clown," because I cannot tell if it is a male or female, the voice was distorted. But what is important, is that this clown only wants to talk with you and we have to be able to use this to our advantage. You have to keep this clown talking long enough to get a trace. Most people believe you have to keep someone talking for sixty seconds to get a trace; however, we don't need nearly that long."

"I'll be ready when you guys get here; I hate that I'll be seeing my family and friends again under these circumstances

141

but I really need you all now. I want my wife back in one piece and alive Zuri; so, I'll be glad to follow your lead." Marcus realizes at that moment that he mistakenly said wife; he wasn't ready to let the cat out of the bag just yet. He finds himself hoping Zuri didn't catch on to what he said.

Zuri believes he heard Marcus call Zephora his wife; however, he knows Marcus does that all the time and thinks nothing of it. Besides, he is focused only on getting his daughter back for Marcus, Saphera and for himself; not to mention, introducing her to her first cousin for the first time. "Marcus I will see you shortly; hold on son, we will get her back." Zuri hangs up the phone, turns to Saphera and embraces her with all that he has in him, and she returns the embrace with just as much compassion.

Marcus finds himself overcome with emotion and steps into his walk in closet and closes the door. *"Father God, I am not sure why we are being tested so much; I am truly at my wits end. Please bring her back to me; You said she is my wife and I'm ready to embark on our new life together. I'm ready to let the whole world know she is my wife and forgive me for holding back. If this is my fault, please forgive me Lord. Keep her safe, keep her spirit high and protect her from any harm. And Father, whoever this person is that has taken my Zephora, change his heart, temper his spirit and help him to see the error of his ways in order to make the right choice and give me back my bride. Father, I know You are in control, I trust You and I love You. In Jesus Holy name I pray. And Lord, You know I'm ready to be whoever I need to be to bring her home."*

Now that Marcus' prayer is over, he is now ready to fight. He is ready to fight whoever has taken his beloved wife and his movements will be nothing short of hostile; for this person has kidnapped the queen of Malawi and the person or persons will feel the full weight of her king. Marcus has the look in his eye that he had back in the dungeon of Malawi and even though he's not one hundred percent fully recovered, he is still a force to be reckoned with. He first makes a call to Bengono, the council leader. "Did you or any other of the council members attack and kidnap my wife?"

Bengono hesitates before he responds, "Your wife, you are married, since when?"

Marcus is exasperated by this. "Answer my question you old fool and don't question me!"

"My apologies Sire; I know of no one who has ordered such a travesty. After our last conversation, the council agreed that no actions are to be taken against you unless you and your wife are not here within the allotted time, of which there are only three weeks left Sire."

"And you are positive there is no rogue member who would defy the council?"

"Absolutely Sire."

Marcus hesitantly believes the assurances of Bengono; however, he is still angered by Bengono's arrogant tone. "Fortunately Bengono I believe you; however, when we arrive in Malawi, I am going to personally deal with your arrogance and insubordinate tone myself in the ways of our ancestors and in front of the entire council so no one will ever try me again. I suggest you get your affairs in order and prepare for our arrival because like it or not we are coming to rule."

"Oh my God, Sire, please forgive me, I meant no disrespect."

Marcus rebuts quickly, "Then you should not have disrespected me. I have shown you nothing but respect and at every turn you have chosen to insult and disrespect me. Well enough is enough, and you will learn, I am not to be toyed with."

"Sire please, please, forgive me. I am here to serve you and believe me, I meant no disrespect. It is my job to insure that our new King is not weak; and to that end, is the only reason I have ever challenged you. I am your servant always. I will send one of our best men to assist you in your search for our Queen."

"There is no need for that; I will have it handled before he arrives. And as for being my servant, you will serve me well as a message to the rest of the council once I fulfill the rest of the Tribal Laws. Good day Bengono." Marcus hangs up the phone and begins to pace back and forth trying to remember the name of the guy who sent Zephora the text two days prior. He sits on his bed tapping his foot, racking his brain trying to remember the name but cannot.

Meanwhile, downstairs he hears J.R. greet Zuri at the door. "Finally," Marcus remarks and he runs the twenty feet from his bedroom to the top of the stairs and because of his condition he is out of breath. He looks down, sees the older and younger couples enter his home and while trying to catch his breath, he calls out to only one of them. "Veronica," he shouts, "What is his name, what is his name; I know you know; you have to know!" He is panting at the top of the stairs holding on to the railing and weaving back and forth barely able to stand.

Angelo darts upstairs and grabs his best friend who falls into his chest wrapping his arms around Angelo as he does. "Gotcha Marcus, I gotcha," Angelo helps Marcus back to his bed, lays him down propping pillows behind his head trying to make him comfortable. Marcus' eyes are tightly closed and a tear squeezes its way from between his eyelids and rolls down the side of his face resting in his ear. Angelo leans down and whispers to his friend, "I'm here now Marcus; rest, I will get her back." Marcus opens his eyes and the tears that were trapped under his tightly closed eyelids poured out like dew pouring down a leaf that can no longer hold it. When the tears have cleared from his eyes, he looks up and his bed is surrounded by Zuri, Saphera and Veronica with Angelo sitting on the side of the bed. "She knows Angelo, Veronica knows who it is," Marcus whispers.

All eyes turn towards Veronica and she tries to figure out what Marcus is rambling about. What is it she is supposed to know? Marcus pushes himself up into a seating position on the bed and begins to rant again. "It's got to be her ex and Veronica knows his name."

Finally Veronica realizes what he is saying; her eyes open wide, she snaps her fingers and questions Marcus. "Do you mean Chris, Chris Caldon; I told her she should have never called him, that guy is unstable. But no, she swore she needed some moral support."

Marcus nods his head yes and then slides back down into a laying position and closes his eyes when Saphera notices blood making its way through his shirt again. "Zuri, you and Angelo have a name, go find this guy and bring me back my baby; Veronica and I will take care of Marcus."

Zuri and Angelo head back downstairs to put the wheels in motion. They have the partial license plate number Marcus provided and within minutes, Zuri's two teams have found three possible locations where Chris Caldon could be keeping Zephora. One location is Chris' home, the second is his mother's home and the third is his grandparent's home, which they left to Chris. The job now is to locate the burgundy Lexus with a license plate number beginning with KZR 5. Zuri inputs the particulars into his search program, all except the name just in case they are wrong: burgundy Lexus sedan and the four known digits. The program searches through a list of possible numbers and returns a hit in less than two minutes. Zuri checks the registration for the car and it is a match for Chris Caldon's burgundy Lexus and Zuri exclaims, "We got him, we got the sucker!"

Zuri knows he has only three hours left before Marcus has to call this guy back, he plans to catch him before that. "Okay gentlemen, we have three possible locations; team one will check out the perpetrator's house, team two will go to his mother's house and Angelo and I will go to the grandparent's house."

Marcus, who is now patched up, has been listening from his room and slowly makes his way downstairs and interrupts Zuri, "Don't you mean you, Angelo and me because there is no possible way I'm staying here?"

Zuri knows better than to argue with Marcus on this point because he would do the same. "Okay Marcus it's your call. Gentlemen, be precise, be concise and don't make any mistakes; my daughter's life is at stake. Now let's go get the job down."

The three teams head out leaving Saphera and Veronica at Marcus' home. Saphera has never been good at waiting so she coaxes Veronica downstairs and into the kitchen to prepare a meal. She believes her baby will be hungry when she gets back and lucky for them Marcus keeps a stocked kitchen. "Veronica darling help me make my baby's favorite meal and tell me why she called that awful Chris Caldon; I could not stand that boy when she was dating him."

"To be honest Mrs. Sherman, I think the pressure of not being able to talk to Marcus and preparing to marry that devil Kwazan, I think she just wanted to hear a familiar male voice and Angelo was so busy running Marcus' company to call that often. I told her it was a bad idea and after their first conversation, she realized I was right and didn't call him anymore, as far as I know. What's Ze's favorite meal anyway?"

"Well Veronica, she just loves homemade macaroni and cheese, baked chicken and rice, candied yams, collard greens, and corn bread; and Marcus, he just happens to have everything we need right here."

Meanwhile, under Zuri's direction, the three dispatched teams have nearly reached their various locations. Zuri, Angelo and Marcus' location is the farthest away therefore, they will know if the other teams have found Zephora before they get there. Team one calls in and reports all clear at their location and just as Angelo pulls up to their location, team two calls in and reports the same. Zuri commands teams one and two to reconvene at his location and tells Marcus and Angelo that they will hold position until the other two teams arrive.

CHAPTER XII

It's dark and all three teams are at the third location, Chris Caldon's grandparent's house. The house is a colonial style red brick home with four large white columns in front, side entry garage with a daylight basement. Zuri is ready to give instructions to his men, when he falls prey to another coughing spell coupled again with spitting up blood and extreme sweating. This is Marcus' first time witnessing Zuri's fit and he's mortified. Angelo taps him on the shoulder and assures him that Zuri will be alright.

Angelo has been privy to Zuri's plan of attack and decides to take over for Zuri until he is able to speak again. "Team one, check to see if the car in question is in the garage; clear and secure the rear of the house. Team two; once we are sure the car is here, clear and secure the right side of the house so we can gain entrance through the front door. Once you guys have cleared and secured those locations, team leaders one and two, Marcus and I will penetrate the home will clear the house starting with the first floor and then the basement; team one will follow us in and clear the second floor. Everyone clear on their instructions?" The team gives Angelo the same respect as Zuri and respond with a resounding, "Yes sir!"

Zuri finally catches his breath and is able to speak to Marcus and Angelo. "Angelo you did a good job instructing the team, I'm proud of you. Now, this is the first time you two boys have been involved in a mission like this and when your heart starts pounding in your chests, stop moving, take a few deep breaths, clear your mind of all fear, and remember only the mission; to rescue Zephora. Now, I'm going to give both of you something and I wouldn't do it unless I thought both of you could handle it." Zuri reaches in his jacket and pulls out a black 9mm automatic pistol and then reaches in the small of his back and pulls out a nickel plated 380 automatic pistol. He hands the 9mm to Marcus and the 380 to Angelo and gives them instructions. "Do not put your finger on the trigger unless you intend to pull it; and, you only pull it if you have no other alternative. Do you understand?" Both Marcus and Angelo look down at their weapons, then look at each other and nod their heads up and down signaling that they understand.

Each team member is supplied with an ear bud from Zuri's briefcase of gadgets to insure they stay in contact with one another. As darkness falls over the city, the teams, all outfitted in black camouflage gear, is ready to move into their various positions. Zuri gives the order; "Engage," and team one moves to check the garage and secure the back. Team one reports in and confirms that the burgundy Lexus is in the garage, then moves to clear and secure the rear of the home. Simultaneously, team two is moving to clear and secure the front and right side of the home. Now that teams one and two have accomplished the first phase of the plan, Marcus and Angelo move in to enter the home. The two best friends are both proficient in martial arts and have often trained together; however, this is only the second time the two have entered into a real life or death situation together; the first time, they were successful and they hope they can do it again. Focused on what is at stake, they breach the front door slowly, split up and clear the main floor of the house. Angelo reports in; "main floor clear" and team two enters through the front door and head upstairs as team one remains out back to keep it secured.

Marcus and Angelo meet up at the basement door and notices light coming from under the door. The two look at each other, pull out their weapons, take off the safeties and prepare to open the door. Marcus reaches for the nob, it's unlocked and he gently and slowly pulls the door open. As he does, Angelo moves to the side so that he is in view of the basement stairs as the door opens. They are able to completely open the door without an event and are now headed downstairs. Halfway down the stairs, Angelo, who is in front of Marcus, is slowly taking his next step and when he does the stair creeks. Both he and Marcus instantly stop moving.

The stairs are carpeted with a wall on both sides all the way down to the bottom where you can go either left or right. The two friends hear movement in the basement and noises that sound like someone has their mouth covered and is trying to speak. Marcus, hearing the sounds, rushes pass Angelo down the stairs and to the right. Angelo follows him down but goes to the left. When Marcus looks up, what he sees makes him stop in his tracks and hold his weapon in firing position.

There in front of him is his beloved Zephora seated in a chair with her legs duck taped to the front legs of a captain's chair of a dining set, her arms are taped to the arms of the chair, tape is over her mouth and a medium brown skinned man of slender build, glasses and curly hair wearing a navy blue Dickey's workman suit holding an eight inch knife with a partially serrated blade and an ivory handle against Zephora's neck. The florescent lights of the basement flicker as Marcus takes a quick glance around the basement before he makes a move or says a word.

The carpet stops at the bottom of the stairs. The rest of the floor is gray painted concrete. The walls are also concrete and painted the same gray color. The ceiling has exposed beams and pipes decorated with a plethora of spider webs, some with the dried shells of cockroaches. Out of the corner of his eye, Marcus spies Angelo who is in position and hidden from the perpetrator; now he is ready to speak to the man holding his woman.

"Okay man, take that knife away from her neck; I know you don't want to hurt her," Marcus begins.

"What's it to you and why are you in my house? This is none of your business. I want you to leave; get out!"

Marcus pauses and takes a deep breath before responding. "I can't do that. Why don't you tell me your name and why you have this beautiful young lady tied up?"

"I'm Chris, Chris Caldon, and this is my grandparent's house; you have no right to be there. And this beautiful young lady is my girlfriend and we're playing sex games; so please leave."

"So you're Chris Caldon. Well Chris, I'm sure this isn't your girlfriend because she's my wife and you kidnapped her from our home. And now I want her back; and you are going to give her to me. I hope we can do this the easy way; but, I'm prepared to do it the hard way, and I would prefer if you didn't test me." Everything Marcus is saying is heard by all the team members and the other two teams have just made it to the basement. The four men fan out; take positions that give them a perfect view of Chris and turn on the red laser lights on their sights and point them directly at his head.

Chris looks up and sees all the red lights pointed in his direction and starts to get nervous and presses the blade against Zephora's neck just enough to break the skin. Zephora's eyes are as big as saucers and her pupils are the size of marbles. She stares at Marcus and tears begin to stream down her face. Marcus stretches his hand out to Chris. "Now Chris, you don't want to do that; take the knife away from her neck. I know you don't want to hurt her, I know you care about her. Remove the knife and these fine gentlemen will put their guns down."

Marcus' voice is calm but his heart is beating so fast its ready to jump out of his chest. He has been in dangerous situations before and even jumped in front of a bullet for Zephora; but this is different, he can see the blood trickling down her neck and it's making him crazy. He still has an ace in the hole; Angelo is still hidden with his weapon trained on Chris and he's ready to put his finger on the trigger. The four other men holster their weapons and step back behind Marcus. No one notices Zuri coming down the stairs; his movements are slow and deliberate. He turns left at the bottom of the stairs and quietly takes a kneeling position behind and to the right of Angelo, with his automatic pistol already cocked and ready to go.

"Okay Chris, their guns are down and now I need you to MOVE the knife AWAY from her neck and tell me what's going on so we can all go home alive and well." Chris takes the blade off of Zephora's neck, but keeps it close to her; and then, with tears running down his face, he starts to speak.

"I've been alone my whole life; I only got this house because there was nobody else to leave it to. My mother gave me up as a baby and doesn't want anything to do with me, never has. The only person that ever showed me an ounce of attention is sitting right here in this chair; and when she left me, I was all alone again. Then one day out of the blue, my angel called me and I was saved again from my loneliness. So now she is mine forever. So I would appreciate it if...." Before he can finish his sentence, Angelo turns on the red light on the sight, aims it at Chris' left temple, slowly places his finger on the trigger of his 380, breathes in and before he squeezes the trigger, a bullet zings passed his ear. The bullet was shot out of the barrel of Zuri's weapon and it leaves Angelo temporarily stunned and a little off balance.

Chris is dead before his top teeth leaves his bottom lip while pronouncing the f in if. As his body is falling, Marcus dives for Zephora's chair and pushes it back just in the nick of time as the serrated blade of the knife passes in front of her face grazing the tip of her nose as Chris' lifeless body glides slowly to the floor.

Zephora is hysterically screaming behind her taped mouth with her blood staining the gray duct tape, slithering down her chin and dripping onto her blouse. Marcus is stretched out across the floor seized in pain from the acrobatic move he performed to yet again rip his beloved's life from the claws of death. Angelo drops his weapon to the ground almost as fast as he was about to pull the trigger and races towards Marcus and Zephora to check their condition. Teams one and two run over to check Chris; one of them kicks him to see if he's alive. As his cold limp body flips over on the floor, they are all astonished to see the accuracy of the shot. The bullet penetrated the left temple through a mole the size of a sharpie tip and exited the right side of his head leaving a gaping hole upon which the insides of Chris' skull oozed out onto the floor and splattered the wall causing the four team members to turn their heads in disgust. They find a blanket to cover what's left of Chris' head.

Angelo approaches Marcus, who is lying on the floor at Zephora's feet. Marcus hasn't moved, so Angelo turns him over. With tears streaming down his face, Marcus grabs Angelo's face with both hands, peers into his eyes and whispers, "What did you do, Angelo, what did you do?"

Angelo removes Marcus' hands from his face and sits him up against a table; then, still without speaking, cuts the tape that binds Zephora's legs and arms and carefully pulls the tape off her mouth and wipes the blood off her face and neck. He then turns to Marcus and whispers, "I didn't do it." Zephora hugs Angelo tightly and whispers, "Thank you," then turns to help Marcus to his feet slowly so she can fade into his arms overjoyed to be alive. They grab Angelo; pull him in and the three of them engage in a group hug that finds both Marcus and Angelo apologetic and thankful. As they release from their hugfest, Zephora turns around and standing at the bottom of the stairs is her father, patiently waiting his turn to embrace his daughter. She slowly walks over to her father with Marcus in tow, as she refuses to let go of his hand until she has reached Zuri's out stretched arms.

The other four men know their job and go about the business of handling cleanup. They place Chris' body in a black body bag and scoop up any brain matter they find and dump it in the bag with him. They clean the floor and the walls and drop all the dirty and bloody cleaning rags in the bag with Chris' body as well. They carry him out to the van to team two, who immediately pull off. Team one goes back into the house and down into the basement to report to Zuri. J.R. approaches Zuri who is still clinging to his daughter and addresses him.

"Sir, cleanup is complete and disposal will be done through the usual channels."

Zuri turns and standing next to his daughter with his arm around her neck, smiles and replies. "J.R., I appreciate you and let the rest of the men know how grateful I am as well for their service."

"Thank you sir, it is an honor as always."

Just as he turns to leave, Zephora stops him. "J.R. is it; I need you to please do me a favor. Bury Chris in a casket and give him a nice head stone please with his name on it with the words, 'Good Man, Great Son, and Trusted Friend.' Okay, thank you."

J.R. turns his gaze towards Zuri who nods giving his approval for his daughter's request. He then turns and makes his way back upstairs, out the front door and into the van with his partners and they head out to complete their tasks.

Back in the basement, Zuri gathers his three loved ones on the other side of the basement to converse with them before they leave. "I need the three of you to listen to me. First, my sweet daughter, I am so glad you are alright. I hate I was compelled to have to kill that man; however, I would do it again in a heartbeat to save any one of you. And Marcus, again you've risked your life to prevent harm from coming to my daughter. I am so proud to call you my son. The three of you are my children and I love you all dearly. Now listen to me carefully, what happened here tonight could haunt you all for a long time to come; however, I want you to try to put this out of your minds; forget about it please. What I was forced to do was a necessary evil to save Zephora's life and to keep Angelo from doing something that would haunt him forever. We will not speak of it again; and when we get to Marcus' home, let me explain the situation and the surrounding circumstances okay, if necessary? Now let's go home."

Zuri turns and goes up the stairs, followed by Angelo then Zephora with Marcus, whose injury has gone unnoticed by everyone, bringing up the rear. Because he is behind everyone else, no one notices his racing heartbeat or that he has only taken three steps before he collapses and falls back down the stairs.

"Marcus," Zephora screams in terror as she runs back down the stairs to his aid; and then, she shouts, "Daddy help, Marcus collapsed!" Instantly Angelo and Zuri dash back down the stairs to help Zephora get Marcus up to his feet; but as Zuri reaches the bottom, he is overcome with another violent coughing spell until he passes out on the stairs right next to the ailing Marcus.

Zephora screams again, "My God Daddy; Angelo what's wrong with him?"

Angelo doesn't respond, he instinctively steps over Zuri to get to Marcus. "Marcus, Marcus," Angelo shouts and slaps

Marcus to generate alertness in his fallen friend. Marcus' body jumps and he opens his eyes with a look of shock and awe on his face. Angelo shouts at him, "Marcus Focus," and once he has his attention, he checks his readiness. "Marcus can you walk," Angelo barks, and Marcus nods yes. "Good; now Ze put his arm around your neck and help him up the stairs while I carry your father out of here."

Zephora follows Angelo's instructions and she and Marcus slowly make their way up, making eye contact after every step. Once they make it to the top, Zephora notices that her blouse feels damp and looks down to see blood on it coming from Marcus that had not been previously recognized because of his black clothing. The blood scares her but she contains her fear so that she doesn't pass it on to her ailing husband who unbeknown to her already knows he is bleeding. She keeps him walking towards the front door.

Meanwhile at the bottom of the stairs, Angelo fireman carries Zuri up the stairs and hurries right behind Marcus and Zephora. "Get a move on it you two, Uncle Zuri isn't exactly light you know."

Zephora quickly responds, "Marcus is injured too Angelo, we're moving as fast as we can." They finally reach the car and Zephora straps Marcus into the front passenger's seat and Angelo fastens the unconscious Zuri into the back seat behind the driver's seat and Zephora gets in next to her father. Angelo slips his left hand into his back pocket, pulls out the keys, and hops into the car while seemingly simultaneously pushing the key into the ignition, sliding it into gear and peeling off with the tires screeching, as they speed away from the scene.

"We need to get them to the hospital," Angelo looks back and says to Zephora. Before she can respond, the barely conscious and listening Marcus touches Angelo's arm to get his attention to insert his response.

"No hospital; take us home," Marcus rants.

"You guys need to go to the hospital Marcus, not your house."

Zephora interjects emphatically, "Angelo, please do what he says, I know my father and he wouldn't want to go to the hospital. Take us home, my mother will know what to do. She is there, right?"

"Yes she's there. Just remember, if something goes wrong, I'm saying it's your fault," Angelo retorts and he chuckles and makes a left on Pryor Street to head towards Marcus' house. Zephora smiles, finding Angelo humorous; then her mind drifts back to what Angelo said back at her kidnapper's lair and she says to herself, *Uncle Zuri.*

"Say Angelo, what did you mean when you said, Uncle Zuri isn't exactly light?"

Angelo laughs and says, "I meant he was heavy."

Marcus, who is hanging on to consciousness, turns his head towards Angelo waiting to hear why he said it as well; but before he can answer, Zuri regains consciousness and finds Zephora holding his hand, Marcus half conscious and Angelo driving like a bat out of hell.

"Angelo, where are we?" Zuri manages to slur.

"We're almost at Marcus' house sir," Angelo quickly retorts.

Zephora, annoyed that her father didn't take the time to address her first, calmly turns her entire body towards Zuri to insure he knows she is addressing him. "Daddy you scared me half to death. You mind telling me what's wrong with you?"

"Well, baby," Zuri slowly begins, still trying to get his bearings, "we are not sure yet, your mother and I will be going to my doctor in the next couple of days; but I'm okay now."

"Well father, since you can't tell me what's wrong with you, can YOU tell me why Angelo called you Uncle Zuri?"

Zuri hesitates for a minute and responds with, "Well, I'll tell you after we get Marcus taken care of."

Before the conversation gets volleyed back, Angelo pulls into Marcus' driveway. He and Zuri lift Marcus from his

163

seat to carry him into the house. Zephora pushes open the front door, moves to the side so Zuri and Angelo have room to bring Marcus in. Saphera rushes to the door, expecting to see her daughter; however she is met by the horror of seeing Marcus barely conscious, which sends her over the top and she faints before Zephora can make it through the door.

"Mother," Zephora screams rushing to Saphera's aid. Veronica runs from the kitchen and together with Zephora they get Saphera to the couch. There is no time to celebrate Zephora's safe return, Marcus is injured and bleeding and Saphera lays unconscious on Marcus' couch being fanned by Zephora and Veronica.

It seems this family is forever tormented with pain and strife; however, through it all they stick together and help one another. Marcus receives more trouble than most, but never complains about it. Maybe it's his faith or maybe it's the deep abiding love he has for Zephora; mostly likely, it's a combination of the two. Whatever the case, it will take the love of them all to endure the trouble of the day.

Angelo sits Marcus on his bed, takes off his shirt, and notices that Marcus' stitches have opened in a few places. Angelo lays him down so Zuri can clean his wound and butterfly the exposed areas of Marcus' stitches. Meanwhile, Zephora has applied a cold, wet compress to Saphera's forehead and she begins to come around. Veronica rushes to the kitchen to keep dinner from burning and makes it just in time to turn off the oven and save the day in her own way. Back upstairs, Zuri has patched up Marcus and medicated him with antibiotics and Vicodin prescribed to Marcus by Dr. Lott, plus a sleeping pill he found in Marcus' medicine cabinet for good measure. For the moment, all is calm in Marcus Howard's home and the family can breathe a sigh of relief. Once again, the family has banded together and avoided the worst case scenario.

CHAPTER XIII

Marcus has been sleeping for twenty-four hours straight and Zephora is doing an incredible job of watching over him. Lest bathroom breaks and eating, she has stayed by the side of her husband waiting for him to wake up. The time has given her the opportunity to think about how her lapse in judgment caused the death of a man, someone she once cared deeply for. She kneels on the opposite side of the bed from Marcus, bows her head, brings her hands together and prays. *"Father God forgive me for my betrayal of what it means to love. Forgive me for betraying the man You sent to me who loves me so fiercely; and, forgive me for betraying You. In my time of need, I chose not to count on You but to be weak and call Chris to play a role that was not his to play. My weakness caused his death and for that I am truly sorry; and I hope and pray Father that You can please forgive me. Thank you for sending Marcus back to me, for keeping him safe and for saving his life. I repent for betraying you, Marcus and myself. Father I love and worship You above everything. I thank you for Marcus; I know he truly loves me and I thank you for the second chance to love him too. Thank You for bringing my father back to my mother and allowing them to share their love again. Thank You for hearing my prayers, thank You for forgiving me and thank You for Your love. In Jesus Holy name I pray.* With tears streaming down her face, Zephora crawls into bed next to Marcus, gradually slides close to him, gently lays her head on his chest and closes her eyes to take a well needed and deserved rest.

Zuri and Saphera have finally made it to his doctor's office. Zuri doesn't usually sit and wait in a waiting room and this time will be no different. Even though Dr. Phillips' waiting room is completely full, Zuri and Saphera bypass the registration window, walk through the 'Doctors Only' door, and take a seat in Dr. Phillips' office. Dr. Phillips' P.A. saunters into patient room three, whispers in Dr. Phillips' ear, takes over the examination of his patient and Dr. Phillips removes his gloves and tosses them in the garbage, as he walks out the door asking his patient's forgiveness while doing so.

Because of Zuri's governmental clearance, a visit to his doctor gets him V.I.P. priority service which means absolutely no waiting. "Zuri, long time no see; why don't you come this way," Dr. Phillips pleasantly addresses Zuri as he ushers him and Saphera to patient room seven. "Who is this lovely young lady you have brought with you today?"

"This is my beloved wife Saphera. How have you been Doc," Zuri replies taking a hold of Saphera's hand as they walk down the long hall.

"I have been well Zuri; and, business has been great fortunately, but unfortunately, if you know what I mean. So tell me, what brings you here today?" As Zuri starts to open his mouth to respond, he is overcome by another one of his coughing spells, this one as violent as the others. Saphera helps Zuri into the room and lays him on the doctor's table.

Dr. Phillips has known Zuri for more than ten years and never heard him cough like that before; however, he hasn't seen him in at least three years. As he starts his examination of Zuri by listening to his chest, he has an idea of what is causing Zuri's violent episodes which include coughing up blood, but keeps it to himself until he can complete his observation and get some x-rays. He does his best not to show any change in emotion to his friend and his wife by making small talk. However, he knows it is probably serious because of Zuri's symptoms. "Zuri, we need to get you down to x-ray. I know you probably have a lot questions but if you don't mind, can you save them until after I have had a chance to review your x-rays? My nurse will be here shortly to take you to x-ray so sit tight for a few moments." Zuri nods his head and Saphera whispers thank you and finds the strength to muster up a smile for Zuri, as Dr. Phillips walks out the door.

Angelo and Veronica are camped out at Veronica's apartment doing what newlyweds do and doing everything they can do to escape the last few days. They go from the bedroom to the kitchen and then back to bedroom. For now they are content to drink champagne and feed each other chocolate covered strawberries while watching movies. Veronica breaks from the kissing and eating to actually say something.

"Sweetheart, do you think Marcus and Zephora are alright?"

"Well my love," Angelo starts and then goes back to kissing Veronica from her lips to her neck and then back to her lips before finishing his sentence; "if they are not, Zephora would surely call."

"But she won't Angelo, her pride, her pain or both will make her think she can handle it on her own; you don't know her like I do."

"I'm just as concerned as you are baby; so, let's go by there in the morning. But for the rest of this day, it's going to be all about you." With that Angelo pushes Veronica's hair to the side and kisses the back of her neck, pulls her blouse over her head and begins to gently massage her shoulders and back and his lips softly follow his hands down to the small of her back. Once there, he kisses from the middle of her back to the left side and then turns her over and begins kissing her stomach up to between her breast as his hands touch everywhere his lips missed and more. Angelo has successfully taken her mind off Marcus and Zephora. She is only thinking about Angelo now and returning the pleasures he is gracing her with. Their bodies meld together, filled with expressions of love drenched in perspiration, champagne and the juices of love; their mouths no longer saying words, only creating the sounds of laughter and lover's chatter. Right now, their world consists of only each other, their love and sheer contentment and absolute gratification.

Charlie has just arrived at Marcus and Zephora's home; she has been making choices about her life and is ready to share them with Marcus to hopefully get his blessings. It is important to her to know what he thinks; he has been the only person in her life who has never turned his back on her and his opinion and encouragement is all she needs to move forward. She rings the doorbell four times before she hears a voice from behind the door screaming, "Give me a minute, I'm coming." Anxiety sweeps over her like a tidal wave as she awaits the opening of the door. She hopes Marcus approves of her plan, she thinks it's a good one but it wouldn't be the first time; however, the tidal wave of anxiety is starting to recede and a buildup of courage flows through; and with it, Charlie decides that no matter what Marcus thinks, she's taking the opportunity.

"Who is it; Charlie is that you," Zephora yells from midway down the staircase. After her traumatic experience with not checking first, there is no way she is getting any closer to that door until she is sure who is on the other side.

"Yes Zephora Howard, it's me Charlie; now can you let me in please?"

Now that identification is established, Zephora makes her way down the stairs and lets her new sister-in-law in. The two exchange hugs, Charlie drops Zephora's keys in her hand and they head up to see Marcus. When Zephora left him, he was still asleep; however, between the excessive doorbell rings, women squawking and the door slamming, Marcus has made his way back to the land of the living. He has propped himself up into a sitting position with a couple of pillows behind his neck and back. His eyes are fixed on the bedroom door awaiting the return of his bride. Zephora opens the door and because she is looking back swapping witty banter with Charlie, Marcus sees her first and the sight of her brings a massive smile to his face.

"Hello Mrs. Howard," Marcus says in a deep sexy voice. Zephora is caught completely off guard. She did not expect to hear his voice and surely didn't expect to see him sitting up in bed with that smile she loves so much staring back at her. The newlyweds are so focused on one another that neither acknowledges the presence of Charlie in the room.

"Marcus baby how do feel?" Zephora lovingly inquires, as she sits on the edge of the bed with both her hands on his face stroking his cheeks with her thumbs.

"Better now my love, better now," Marcus replies and follows it up by gently pulling her face close to his and resting his lips on her lips that are rose petal soft.

"Excuse me," Charlie retorts, "I hate to break this love fest up, but I am standing here."

Marcus hears his sister but takes his time disconnecting his lips from his bride's before choosing to address Charlie. "Hello my sister, I'm glad to see you too."

"Well I can't tell Marcus, with you leaving me hanging and all," Charlie sarcastically replies while contorting her lips to one side.

Zephora is checking Marcus' bandages while the brother and sister duo exchange witty comments before she interrupts them. "Excuse me you two, but Marcus baby, are you hungry; can I fix you something to eat?"

"I can eat a little something; but, I would like to brush my teeth and take a shower first please."

"Well husband, that sounds good and all, but there is no way I'm letting you get in that shower by yourself quite yet; so Charlie, why don't you go downstairs and watch TV while I help Marcus get cleaned up."

"Yeah, I hear you Zephora, but please just help him shower only and don't try to be rabbits just yet; he is still in recovery mode. Besides, I have something very important to talk with him about." And with that, Charlie makes her way downstairs without even waiting on a reply.

Zephora gets up and closes and locks the door before helping Marcus to the bathroom. Once there, while Marcus is brushing his teeth, Zephora turns on the water in the shower and then with the closet door half open, making sure Marcus can see her in the mirror, she slowly begins to undress. Marcus places his right hand on the granite counter top to support himself while he brushes his teeth. He stares into his eyes in the mirror and then stares at the mostly healed wound on his chest.

As he finishes brushing his teeth and comes up from rinsing his mouth in the sink, Marcus spots the caramel toned and curvaceous legs of Zephora out of the corner of his eye. Without letting on that he sees her, Marcus finishes undressing by stepping out of his shorts and steps into the shower which is equipped with full body sprayers on both ends and a rain shower head that drops down from the middle of the five foot wide six foot long doorless shower. Seemingly not giving a second thought to the sight of his bride, Marcus soaps his wash cloth and begins to wash his muscular body all while being watched silently from the closet by Zephora.

Zephora allows Marcus to completely cleanse his body, while admiring how the water glistens over every inch of her husband's six foot one, well developed frame, as it drips off of him in all the right places. She waits until Marcus turns off the body sprayers, turns on the rain shower and begins to wash his face with his eyes closed before she makes her move. Zephora quickly walks over to the shower, steps around the wall of the doorless shower and walks in behind Marcus allowing her wet body to touch his, pressing her breast gently against his back while she slowly moves her hands gradually up and down his stomach and chest being careful to run her fingers tenderly across his scars as to caress them. She deliberately and lovingly moves her hands up and down his body, each one moving in the opposite direction, down and up his thighs and across the six-pack that is his mid-section. His body stiffens and he turns to face her.

"My turn," Marcus whispers in Zephora's ear nibbling gently on the lobe as the words complete their cycle from his lips. As his lips move slowly down her neck, his hands caress the contours of her toned, but soft back and do not stop until they tenderly encircle her butt, his fingers cupping her apple bottom, as his thumbs caress her ample curves. The two speak no words. As from memory, his lips rest upon hers until they are creased by the smoothness of his tongue which strokes the underside of her top lip; after which, Marcus lovingly bites her chin. Water from the rain shower above encroaching his mouth flows down his chin and onto her breasts. Marcus squats down to kiss her soft and toned abs before rising again to gently kiss her lips splitting them with his tongue slowly causing her to gasp for air.

It is the wettest shower either of them have had in a really long time with water or without. In an attempt to change gears, Marcus grabs the soap and begins to rub it over Zephora's caramel skin, suds maneuvering their way down and around her many curves until they circle the drain. Marcus uses his hands to wash her body; his method causes her to gasp even more and Zephora believes he isn't clean enough either so she engages in the dirty job of washing him clean. More suds circle the drain. Her body is soft and wet and his body is hard and damp; they grab a towel and head for the bed. This is essentially their wedding night, the first time the two of them have been naked together and so far they are both pleased. The foreplay is over and now they can finally collect their physical reward for being patient and obedient. Marcus' wounds and condition aids in them taking their time; their bodies swirl together like a chocolate and caramel treat ready to be devoured. They give a new understanding to the term making love as they slowly, carefully and joyfully explore every inch of each other and the room.

The lovers are blended and sticky like milk duds left in a hot car in the middle of July. Back to the shower, this time only to get clean except their lips are locked together with the water drizzling down their faces and over their bodies. She washes his back and he washes hers; he washes her breasts and she washes his chest. They enjoy being able to explore each other's body without thought of penalty and are able to thank God as they celebrate their love on every level. They finally make it out of the shower and manage to even get dry this time. Zephora takes the time to lotion Marcus' body from head to toe and his muscles tighten as she massages him and she is bent on loosening them up.

Marcus returns the favor. Zephora lay on her stomach as Marcus massages the lotion into her soft and supple skin, smiling the entire time at how blessed he is to have such a beautiful woman as his wife, lover and friend. Marcus turns his bride over, as he does, she closes her eyes as he has her totally relaxed. He massages the lotion into her shoulders, around and on her breasts, and over her tummy causing her to giggle as it tickles just a little. He turns his attention to her thighs and she opens them to give him access to her inner thigh. As he lotions her left thigh, he can feel the heat emanating from between them; he leans over to gently blow in an effort to cool her down but it has the reverse effect and they begin making love again. For the last three hours the two have not spoken a word but have understood each other completely. Finally, Zephora breaks the silence by posing a question, "Baby, are you hungry?" Marcus responds with a hearty, "for sure."

"Do you mind if I invite mother and father as well as Angelo and Veronica over to join us? Charlie is already here; at least I hope she is still here, so everyone can see you are feeling better."

"Sounds like a plan; I'll text Angelo and you text your mother. We do have food right?"

My mother made enough food to feed several people for a whole week; so if they don't come to eat, it will all go to waste."

"Cool, let's get this party started. Marcus responds, I'll be down to help as soon as I get dressed."

"Okay Baby but take your time please, I need you to remain a healthy and frisky young man," Zephora replies with a smile, as she walks out the door closing it behind her and texting her mother as she walks down the stairs. Marcus texts Angelo before he gets up, and waits on a reply before he moves; Angelo's response is favorable and they are on their way. Marcus doesn't know it yet, but the same is true for his in-laws.

Marcus takes his time and gets dressed. As he reaches the bottom of the stairs, he is met by his sister who pulls him into the family room to finally have their chat before his guests arrive. Charlie wastes no time in letting her brother know she is leaving and not planning on coming back for a while. Marcus perceives there is more and is careful not to interrupt even though Charlie has paused for a minute. Charlie takes a sip of water and explains that their Great Aunt Madam Zigumba has invited her to the Bahamas to learn the business with the intention of taking it over. She explains to Marcus that she sees it as the break she has been praying for and that she didn't need much convincing to want to go; Charlie fell in love with her Great Aunt, her business and the Bahamas when she was there last year. The entire time Charlie is speaking, Marcus is smiling and slightly nodding his head. Charlie finishes her news with, "And, I'm leaving tomorrow." Marcus stands up, pulls his sister up and embraces her with love and affection.

"Charlie, I am so happy for you and I can tell this makes you happy as well. Go and create a life for yourself, as well as a future. I will take care of Granny and your mother, so don't give anything here a second thought. I love you so much and I want to see you truly happy. Now let's go help Ze in the kitchen and tell her the good news."

It has been a long time since this group of friends and family has had anything to smile about; however, tonight they are smiling a lot and with good reason. Marcus pulls a bottle of champagne out that he has been saving for months for his first night home with his new bride, but this feels like the right time to open it. His first toast is to announce to the family that he and Zephora got married while he was in the hospital. He then follows it up with a toast to his bride; "to my beautiful bride, the third time is the charm. It took us three attempts to get married but if that's what it takes for me to be filled with this much love, joy and happiness, I would do it all over again; so, Mrs. Zephora Howard, thank you for making me the happiest man alive." Marcus and Zephora kiss and the seven champagne glasses clink together followed by a resounding, "Here Here," and a simultaneous sip of bubbly.

Marcus doesn't stop there; before anyone else can get a word in edgewise, Marcus continues with another toast. "To my best friend Angelo, and to Ze's best friend Veronica, may the love you two share be like a flower in perpetual blossoming." All seven glasses clink again followed by another sip. By now, everyone realizes that Marcus has a lot to say. They all look at one another, smile and await his next toast.

Marcus does not disappoint; he is prepared to give another toast. "This toast is for Mr. and Mrs. Zuri Netumba; you two are the definition of lasting love against all odds. To a future filled with more of the love that created so much love." Clink, clink goes the glasses one more time; however, this time no sips, everyone takes a gulp and look to Marcus for the next toast and again he is ready. "Finally, I would like to give a toast to my beloved big sister. You have endured more than this world knows, been around the world in the military and have done so much for others; however, today we celebrate you doing something for yourself, for your own happiness.

Here's to you taking the Bahamas by storm and finding all the happiness you deserve and more!" Glasses clink one final time followed by drinking.

The seven take their seats and prepare to eat. Marcus asks Zuri to bless the food and he humbly accepts. Zuri thinks to himself for a moment and realizes a long prayer would be overkill and chooses to keep it simple. They all hold hands, bow their heads and Zuri begins. *"Father God, we thank you for allowing us all to be here together to commune with You and one another. And Father let this food be nourishing to our minds, bodies and spirits in the name of our Lord and Savior, Jesus Christ; Amen."* The group follows with Amen. Marcus kisses Zephora's hand, as he always does after the food is blessed, and shouts, "Let's eat," and the family dives into their meal and conversation with one another enjoying food and laughs. Zephora finally gets her question answered as to why Angelo called her father "Uncle Zuri," as Angelo tells them everything that transpired while they were in Florida to see about his grandmother. As they all finish their meal and sit back in their chairs, Marcus pours everyone another glass of champagne and stands up with his raised.

"I am finally pleased to announce that in accordance with Tribal Law, next week we are all going to Malawi, Africa to face the Tribal Council and become the new reigning Royal

Family of our ancestral homeland. We will have the opportunity to work behind the scenes, together as a family, and transform our homeland from a poor country to one of hope and promise. So, here's to love, family, adventure, hope and triumph!"

"Here, here," springs from the family's voices and fill the room.

The joy, happiness and love they all feel has been a long time coming. Each one may have some sort of sadness, pain or pending issue, but they have chosen to put it all aside for now and relish in their individual and family happiness. Because they are all family now, literally, by blood or by marriage, by bonds built over time and through trials; they have chosen to love one another and to be there for one another, no matter what challenges may be waiting in the wings.

PART 3

NECESSARY PREDICAMENTS

CHAPTER XIV

Marcus wakes up and glances out of the window of the jet just in time to see them breach the continent of Africa. He looks around the plane to the rest of the family who is still asleep including his beloved wife and his source of wisdom, his grandmother, Ruth. With the exception of his mother and father, who refused to be in the same space together no matter the occasion, Charlie is the only other family member not taking the trip. Charlie is off on an adventure of her own to find peace, happiness and possibly love in the Bahamas with her and Marcus' Great Aunt Madam Zigumba.

"Please fasten your seat belts and put your chairs in their upright positions and prepare for our descent, as we are in Malawi air space." The words from the captain startle the sleeping passengers. Marcus, who is sitting next to his grandmother, who is seated next to Zephora, reaches over and assists his granny with her seat belt. She fusses with him, slaps his hand away and lets him know she can handle her own seat belt; she has always been feisty. The jet shakes and rumbles hitting turbulence on the way down causing everyone to tightly grip the arms of their seats. Marcus looks around at his granny and Zephora and whispers, "We're here baby," and she smiles at him and returns his whisper with, "Exciting." This is Ruth's first flight ever and she demands that they be quiet while she prays silently. Finally the jet touches down and Marcus can feel his ears popping from the cabin pressure.

"This is your captain and I would like to welcome you to beautiful Lilongwe, Malawi. The skies are blue with a few scattered cumulous clouds. The time is 11:15am and the temperature is a sunny 85 degrees. I hope you have enjoyed your flight and Mr. Howard, I and my team are at your disposal twenty-four hours a day; you need only give me a call with your departure plans and we will be ready. Your ground transportation will be waiting for you when we pull into the hangar. We are glad you are back here in the home land."

The flight attendants are two beautiful young ladies both with short, jet black hair worn in natural, short afros. Their attire consists of burgundy skirts that stop just above the knee with white blouses and matching burgundy five button vests topped off with a burgundy, gold, black and white scarf tied around their necks. The plane pulls into the hangar fourteen and comes to a stop. The lead flight attendant opens the door and immediately the stairs, covered with a plush red carpet, are docked up to the open door. The carpet extends all the way to the back door of the first of three Bentley limos that are waiting to take the royal family to the palace. Also, a part of the entourage are two police cars and four police motorcycles; a car and set of motorcycles in front and the same trailing the limos.

Before anyone gets out of their seat, Zuri is overcome with one of his coughing spells that nearly renders him unconscious. Saphera, now used to Zuri's seizure like fits, fans him to keep him cool. Marcus motions to one of the attendants and when she arrives, whispers to her to let someone know to have a doctor at the palace when they arrive. She nods and leaves to make it happen. Before she can make it out the door, Bengono enters the plane. The attendant relays the message and the situation to Bengono who immediately gets on the phone and calls the royal family doctor, fills him in and instructs him to get to the palace immediately.

Now that he has the doctor on the way, Bengono turns to address Marcus. "Your Majesty, how are you? Is this our future queen beside you? She is absolutely beautiful."

Marcus pays no attention to Bengono as his attention is on Zuri who is finally coming around. Zephora on the other hand, turns and addresses Bengono with a bit of sting to her tone. "Sir, I don't know who you are, but instead of sucking up to me and my husband, can you please get someone in here to help my father off this plane?"

"I apologize Madame, I will get someone right away." Bengono presses a button on his phone and calls for two of the escorts to come and help Zuri. He then kindly lets Zephora know that help is on the way. When the two men arrive, they begin to gently help Zuri, who is breathing erratically, off the plane. As they pass Bengono, he tries to, but unsuccessfully, whispers to them to put Zuri in the second limo. Marcus hears him speaking to the two men and before they can take another step, he stops them. "Stop, put Mr. Netumba in the first limo along with his wife, my grandmother, and my wife and I. Once we are all in, that car had better be on its way to the palace." The men, followed closely by Saphera, nearly run Bengono over following Marcus' instructions. Marcus turns to Angelo and Veronica and tells them, "We will see you guys when you get there. We were hoping to ride with you guys, but we will have to do it later. We have got to take care of Zuri.

"Marcus," Angelo replies, "if you hurry up and get off this plane, we will be right behind you and we'll all leave together. Now come on, you holding us up." Marcus smiles, bumps fists with Angelo, grabs his briefcase and they all quickly exit the plane without saying another word to Bengono who at this time is so mad that you can see the steam escaping from the top of his partially bald head. Marcus helps Ruth get in the limo and Zephora makes sure her mother and father are comfortably in as well. Once Angelo and Veronica have taken possession of the second limo, Marcus instructs the entourage to get moving. Bengono has to run to get into his limo to be a part of the escorted convoy; once in his seat, Bengono instantaneously makes a call.

With the sirens blaring and the lights flashing, the convoy speeds through the streets of Lilongwe, moving so fast there is barely time to allow their eyes to focus on any object. Looking ahead, Marcus can see the entrance to the palace compound. It is on the northern outskirts of the city. The part that Marcus can see above the trees allows him to ascertain that the palace sits on a hill. He taps Zephora and points out the window so she can catch a glimpse of the palace as well. "I hope you're ready for this," Marcus expresses to his bride.

"You forget Marcus my love, my mother raised me to be a queen, as if she somehow knew I would be one day," Zephora replies.

Saphera averts her eyes away from her husband for a moment to glance up at her daughter and son-in-law and give them a touché type smile and then turns her head sharply back to her husband and rubs his face gently with the back side of her fingers. Marcus and Zephora look at each other and laugh quietly allowing their foreheads to come together, then their noses and ends with their lips softly coming together with their eyes closed for what seems like a few minutes before they gradually separate them and their eyes slowly open and they simultaneously say "I love you."

CHAPTER XV

The convoy turns left down a two-way street, separated by a five foot median with twenty-five foot evergreen trees perfectly trimmed in the shape of Christmas trees. The street winds through the hillside for a half mile gradually inclining before ending in front of huge gates that have lion head crests in the middle of each side. The gates are flanked by a twenty foot brick wall that continues to surround the entire royal compound and looks to be as old as the hill it rests upon.

The convoy stops at the guard shack that sits in front of a bridge that spans twenty feet across to the gigantic gates and over a moat that encircles the royal compound. One of the two guards manning the post comes out to meet the lead motorcycle officer, he turns to the other guard, nods and the gate begins to open. The convoy continues on to the palace by following a circular drive. In the center of the circular drive is a fountain in the shape of a large seated lion with water coming out of his mouth.

The first limo stops directly in front of the doors where the palace doctor, a nurse and an attendant await with a wheel chair for Zuri. The driver of the limo jumps out and runs around to open the door and let his passengers out. The nurse and the attendant help Zuri out and seat him in the wheel chair, and the driver helps Saphera out and the five of them rush into the palace heading for the sanatorium of the palace which is the size of a small medical facility.

As they rush in, the palace butler, a tall distinguished looking white gentleman with salt and pepper hair, a mustache and goatee to match, and he has an English accent fitting all the stereotypes of a butler rushes out. He leans into the car to help Ruth out of the limo and he cordially speaks to her with his impressive English accent, "Good day Madam, allow me to assist you please. My name is Oliver and my staff and I will take care of your every whim."

His suit is gray, his shirt white with black onyx cuff links, his vest is black, his tie is deep burgundy and his gloves are white. Ruth takes his hand and smiles as she slowly gets out of the limo and stands to the side waiting for Marcus and Zephora to get out the car and in her best make shift English accent says, "Marcus, I think I am going to like this."

As Marcus and Zephora emerge from the limo laughing with Ruth, they are met instantaneously by Angelo and Veronica who, just like Marcus and Zephora, are astounded by the enormous spectacle in front of them.

"Marcus," Angelo shouts, "look at this place, I can't wait to see the inside!" both he and Veronica's eyes are wide open just like their mouths.

"Calm down my friend, let's not lose our cool in front of all these people. We are the heirs to all we see and after passing all that poverty to get here, I am frankly disheartened at the waste of resources," Marcus replies with a look of disgust on his face.

"Marcus my man," Angelo replies while placing his hand on Marcus' shoulder, "Before you start citing the imperfections of OUR country, let's at least take in the vision that is our legacy without such a holier than thou eye please."

Marcus glances at Angelo, looks over at Zephora who is standing next to Veronica and then takes a look around at the palace and the incredible grounds, smiles and says, "You know brother, you are absolutely right; let's enjoy it for a day or two before we decide to turn this country around."

The two couples and Ruth are escorted through the front doors of their new home. Bengono, who is still outside watches everything unfold with a scowl on his face. The family has paid little, to no attention to him since he entered the jet. As one of the Tribal council leaders, he is now subject to the rule of these outsiders and just like the rest of the council, he is less than thrilled about it. However, Tribal Law is clear and now that Marcus and Zephora are married and their heritage verified, without killing one or both of them, there is nothing that can be done. Bengono thinks to himself, "Maybe Kwazan had the right idea but the wrong plan." With that thought in mind, he makes a conference call and connects with the other council members before getting back to his duty of making sure the royal couple are comfortable and insuring that the country's wedding of the year goes off without a hitch.

With the wedding happening in just a few days, Bengono has his hands full with the arrangements, even though he has the cooperation of the entire palace staff to help. He has hired a wedding planner, a hair and make-up professional for Zephora, a caterer and a bakery for the elaborate wedding cake. He is a very resourceful and well-organized man, and despite his feelings for the bride and groom, he plans on putting together a world class event.

As the two couples enter the castle, all their coolness goes out the door as they are overwhelmed by the interior of the palace. Standing in the foyer, Marcus and Zephora look up in amazement. "My God Marcus," Zephora gasps as she speaks, "the ceiling goes up forever; and look at the size of that chandelier."

"I know Ze, have you ever seen anything so beautiful," Marcus responds, his eyes full of wonder.

"Your Majesty," the butler interrupts, "let me show you to your room."

"Not just yet," Marcus reasons. And before he can finish his sentence, Zephora exclaims, "Take us to my father please."

"Yes please." Marcus retorts and he turns to Zephora, gazes at her with his eyes wide open and his mouth twisted to the side. She returns his gaze and cutely says, "Oops!" with her hand over her mouth.

"Oliver, can you show my Grandmother to her room and have someone take the four of us to Mr. Netumba please," Marcus kindly asserts.

"As you wish your Majesty, but my orders are not to leave you and the Queen alone," Oliver carefully states.

Marcus calmly turns towards Oliver remembering that he is only attempting to follow the orders he was previously given and respectfully, but with authority states, "Thank you Oliver, I appreciate that; however, as I am here now, the orders I require you to follow are mine and those of my Queen, if I am not around. And to clarify, your orders are to take care of my grandmother exclusively, as I want her to have the best person helping her. Please assign someone to take care of the Henson's, someone to insure Mr. and Mrs. Netumba have everything they need and finally someone to show my wife and me around. If my grandmother does not need you and you are not busy handling other affairs, you should come find me so we can get to know one another."

"I understand Your Majesty, it will be taken care of just as you have ordered," Oliver respectfully responds. He is used to being spoken to with little to no respect, to put it bluntly, rudely. He smiles and nods to acknowledge Marcus' authority and immediately takes care of his requests while simultaneously escorting Ruth to her room. Before leaving with Ruth, he turns to address Marcus. "Your escorts will be here momentarily Your Majesty."

"Thank you," Marcus replies and he, Zephora, Angelo and Veronica take the opportunity to wonder slowly down the long corridor as they await their escorts. Veronica has said very little since they arrived. She has been wondrously taking it all in. Now that the four of them are alone for a moment, she turns to her friend and chimes in. "Zephora," she starts, "do you feel how plush this carpet is; I cannot wait to take my shoes off and feel it between my toes."

Zephora laughs and banters back, "I hear you girl, and I can't wait to get to our room after we check on my father."

Seemingly from nowhere, their escorts pop up ready to obey any and all requests.

CHAPTER XVI

The four friends and their escort make their way to the medical wing only to find Zuri and Saphera staring into each other's eye and smiling, as Zuri gently strokes his wife's face with the back of his hand; first her cheeks and then her chin. Saphera looks up and sees their family standing there, "come in children, come in." Zuri adjusts his bed with buttons on the side to a slightly seated position, slowly blinks his eyes and begins to speak.

"I apologize for giving you four such a scare; however, I think it's time we talk about a few things."

Zephora's heart drops into her stomach setting the butterflies there into flight and she grabs Marcus' arm to steady herself. Zuri pauses and takes a sip of water before attempting to finish his thought. "We have got to get this wedding done by the end of the week to be in compliance with the law."

"Daddy," Zephora shouts, "Why are you scaring me like that? We did not come down here to talk to you about that, we came down here to check on you. Now how are you doing?"

"Babygirl I'm fine, I just need to take it easy for the next few days. The physician here has given me some unbelievable medication and I feel 100% better. If I had gotten to see him sooner, I might have been able to," he pauses, "start feeling better a long time ago."

Marcus chimes in, "what does that mean sir; what are you saying?" Marcus caught the subtle hitch in Zuri's voice and the glance he gave Saphera.

"I only meant that the medicine here is much more potent than the stuff we get in the US of A, that's all. Now, enough of this talk about me. Why don't you two young couples get out of here and go get settled? I have spoken with our gracious host and he assures me that everything is nearly ready for the wedding. He has left all the information in your rooms for schedules pertaining to fittings for dresses and tuxes. So go get comfortable and we will see you at dinner, I'm going to just rest a while."

Marcus knew better than to argue with Zuri. He and their escort usher everyone out as Zuri requested. As they left, Saphera breathed a sigh of relief and laid her head on her husband's chest.

It seems that Marcus and Zephora's suite is on a wing all to itself on the top floor and Angelo and Veronica's room is one floor down and on the opposite side of the palace. The escort offers to take Angelo and Veronica to their room first since it is closer and then come back and take care of Marcus and Zephora. Marcus instructs him to just take care of his friends and that he and his bride will be fine.

Before going up to their suite, Marcus and Zephora take a detour to check on his grandmother. He knocks on her door and begins to open it as he says. 'Hey Granny, you okay, you have everything you need?"

"I'm fine son; this bed is so comfortable, I'm not sure I ever want to get out of it. Plus, that Oliver guy, he is extremely nice, and by the way, he is taking care of me and if I need anything, I just need to press one button on this phone and he will be here in a jiff he says. In a jiff, have you ever heard anything so funny." The three of them share in a laugh about it and Marcus kisses her on her cheek as he and Zephora make ready to leave Ruth to rest. She looks exhausted, it has been a long day already especially for an old lady who has finally made it to Africa, the home of her ancestors that she had heard so many stories about; and, knowing that her grandson will now claim the birthright of his father and his father's father and his father's father before him.

Before Marcus and Zephora reach the door, Ruth calls out to them, "Marcus, come here son, there is something I have got to tell you, something I should have told you a long time ago, but either way, it's time you know.

"Know what Granny, what is it that I need to know?" Marcus is facing the door as he speaks and he slowly turns around, as he does, his eyes meet Zephora's eyes and they both have a look of bewilderment on their faces. What now, what more can be revealed about his life or about the Tribal Law he is subjected to. Marcus and Zephora pull two chairs next to Ruth's bed, sits down and Marcus gently takes his grandmother's hand in his and quietly says, "Granny, what is it that you have to tell me, what is it that I don't know?"

Ruth takes a sip of water from the glass on her night stand, licks her lips and as she looks up at Marcus, tears begin to slowly stream down her face.

"Granny what's wrong, what's the matter?"

"Nothing's wrong baby, I am actually happy that I am able to tell you this, this important revelation about who you are." Marcus and Zephora stare at each other and then look back at Ruth but say nothing; however, Marcus thinks to himself, *"I know who I am; at least, I think I do. What could she possibly tell me?"*

"Listen to me Marcus and do not speak until I finish," Marcus nods and Ruth continues. "My Husband, your grandfather, John Henry, and I had two children. Esther, the woman you call your mother is my second child. My first child was her older brother and his name was Marcus. Esther had

Charlie when she was young and she and Jackson, the man you call your father, were so very proud of Charlie because she was my first grandchild. Well, a few years later my son Marcus and his wife Nicole had a child, my second grandchild, you.

Marcus and Jackson were good friends in those days, they were like brothers and we were all one big happy family in those days. One day your grandfather decided he wanted to come here to Africa and open the doors to his heritage, his beginnings and he wanted to share that with his son. John knew the history, he knew about the exile of his ancestors and he wanted to see if it was time to be able to reconcile their place. Before they left for Africa, we all sat down as a family and he spoke to us. It was me, Esther, Jackson, Marcus, Nicole and of course John; and this is what he said: *"I do not know what to expect when we get there so while there we will not speak of children or any other family members just in case we are not well received."*

"My beautiful son Marcus, then turned to his best friend Jackson and gave him the ring that his father, my husband, had given to him and uttered these prophetic words:" *"This ring has been in my family for generations and was given to me by my father as did his father and his father before him and so on and so on."* He said: *Jackson, if by chance we do not make it back, you are to give this ring to my son when you recognize he is ready to receive it, and I charge you with raising him as your own; however, I truly expect you to give this ring back to me when we get back."* "We all laughed about it and the next morning John, Marcus and Nicole boarded a plane and went to Africa. John called me once during their trip and told me he thought everything was going well. Two days later they were on their way back, your grandfather called me from the plane. He said to me:" *"Ruthie my love, you have always been and will always be the best thing that ever happened to me. I love you more now than I ever have before and because of you I am a king and my kingdom is you."* "I said to him I love you too John and tell Marcus I said I love him too, okay? He never responded to me because the phone went dead and little did I know that it was because the plane had exploded and crashed into the Atlantic Ocean killing everyone on board including my husband, my son and his wife."

The tears are streaming faster down her face, her nose is running and Marcus can only sit in awe with his mouth wide open. Zephora reaches over to the nightstand, grabs the box of tissues and hands some to Ruth and then notices the tears running down her husband's face and hands him some too. Marcus sits in silence with his head down; Zephora grabs his hand and daps the tears before they drop into his lap. Ruth wipes her tears and blows her nose.

Her voice is shaky and her hands are trembling but she finds the strength to continue. "Now you know the truth son. You are the son of my first born child Marcus and his wife Nicole. I know it may seem like your whole life is a lie but it's not; you were raised by your family, for your family, and we did it all to protect you from the people who killed your parents and your grandfather. If they had known that you or Charlie existed they would have tried to kill you too. I hope you understand, I hope you're not angry and I hope you still love me."

Marcus just sits in his chair with his head down, his elbows resting on his knees and his tears are dripping on the thick pile carpet sinking in and disappearing like they were never there. Marcus watches his tears vanish into the carpet and the room is silent, so silent he can hear his tears hit the carpet after they fall from his weary eyes. He wonders to himself, "what next, what more could there possibly be about my life that I don't know." Zephora is rubbing Marcus' back but she doesn't utter a word; she wouldn't know what to say anyway. What do you say to someone who just found out his parents aren't really his parents, they're his aunt and uncle and his real parents died because of the same Tribal Law he is subjected to now.

"Granny, thank you for telling me the truth, thank you for telling me who my parents were and thank you for loving me. I always knew I was different, at least I know why now. It's okay Granny, I'm okay; this doesn't change who I am, it helps me better identify with who I am and I'm grateful for that, I really am. So again, thank you Granny. Now you're going to have to tell me all about my father and mother; and, let's say we start tomorrow?"

Ruth smiles, stretches her hand out and gently touches Marcus' face and looks at him eye to eye before she speaks. "Just look in the mirror baby, you are the spitting image of your father and you have the heart and intuitive nature of your mother. Do you remember what I used to tell you when I was helping you with your lesson?"

"Yes ma'am," Marcus replied, "you used to tell me never quit, never give up and I will change the world."

"That's right Marcus; and now, you have that opportunity. Your parents are extremely proud of you, I just know they are watching over you from heaven, and I know they are so very proud of you. And you know what else, I am tremendously proud of you too."

"Thank you Granny for everything, I wouldn't be the man I am today without your love and guidance. God knows my mother, I mean my aunt, and even my uncle didn't seem too interested in guiding me or giving me all the love they could have. I spent my whole life trying not to be like my father, when the truth of the matter is, I don't know anything about my father. I don't know who he really is, so do I know who I am?"

Ruth grabs Marcus' face with both hands, pulls him close and emphatically says to him, "Oh Marcus, I'm so sorry; but, try not to be so hard on them, on us. What happened tore us apart and turned them into different people. Esther lost her brother and father, and Jackson lost his best friend; and as far as they knew, the same could have happen to them. Fear can change a person little by little until you gradually don't recognize yourself anymore. Now you two get out of here and let an old lady get her rest. In the morning I will tell you all about your father; but baby, if you look in the mirror and inside yourself, you'll know your father because you are just like him."

"Okay Granny," Marcus rebuts, "get your rest and we will just see you in the morning and you can tell me all about him. Remember that I love you very much and that will never ever change."

Zephora blows Ruth a kiss, and then she and Marcus close the door behind them as they leave. Marcus is excited to hear more about his parents from Ruth in the morning over breakfast, but he keeps his excitement to himself or at least he believes he's keeping it to himself; however, Zephora knows him well and can sense his excitement, but chooses to keep what she knows to herself.

Now that Marcus and Zephora are gone, Ruth calls for Oliver to bring her some food. He does, and after eating and talking with Oliver for a while, she lays back in her big comfortable bed knowing that she can finally rest easy without any more secrets hanging over her head. She says goodnight to her late husband as she always does, places her glasses on the nightstand, clasp her hands together with her index fingers touching her chin and says her prayers.

"Father God, thank You for granting me a long and happy life, thank You for looking after my daughter and my granddaughter and for keeping my grandson safe through all he has encountered. Please continue to look after him all the days of his life and protect him from the devourer no matter what. Lord I know he is destined for greatness but in order for him to get through the trials and tribulations that are a part of his path, he is going to need You more. Talk to him Lord so he will know You are always there. I humbly ask for forgiveness for all my sins Father, and when my time comes, please allow me entrance into Your Holy Kingdom. I am a tired old lady Father, I've done my best and You have seen my worst; but,

through it all, I have been faithful to Your Word and will continue to do so for as long as you allow me to live. Your will be done in my life, the lives of my family and Your will be done in the lives of everyone everywhere because You are God and Your Word is final. Thank You for Your grace, mercy, peace and Your everlasting love. In Jesus Holy name I pray, Amen."

With her prayers done, Ruth rest her hands on top of her chest, one on top of the other, looks around admiring the beautiful room that was carefully prepared for her and then closes her eyes and allows herself to peacefully drift off to sleep in the lap of luxury and in the Motherland she had heard so much about, both firsts for her long and illustrious life.

CHAPTER XVII

Marcus and Zephora are unable to contain their overwhelming excitement over their elaborate quarters, the King and Queen's suite of the palace, a room of immense size and indulgences. Though the bed is king size, it seems small in comparison to the room's size, even though the room is filled with oversized furniture. After admiring the room from the doorway for a moment, Marcus and Zephora kick their shoes off to feel the plushness of the carpet and wander aimlessly around the room until they reach the bed. They dive on it and roll and playfully wrestle around like kids on the bed together culminating with Zephora landing on top of Marcus. The two are staring passionately into each other's eyes and Marcus whispers, "I love you Mrs. Howard," and Zephora returns his whisper with one of her own, "I love you more Mr. Howard."

Passions ignites and their lips are locked together, their tongues are intertwined and their hands are probing as much of each other as they can through their clothing for what seems like forever before Zephora rolls off of Marcus and lays beside him overcome with excitement, passion and an overabundance of sensual dynamism.

"Marcus, I want you right now!" In what seems like the same breath that ends her last word, Marcus jumps off the bed and makes it to the door and locks it in one continuous motion. Zephora is now even more turned on by her husband's physical dexterity, and immediately begins to remove her clothes. Marcus is giving her a strip tease show as he slowly glides back to the bed. The two cannot wait to allow their bodies to interweave together, but override their desire and replace it with tenderness and take the time to slowly experience every inch of each other's body. Marcus starts with Zephora's big toe and with the precision of a surgeon and the attention to detail of an artist, he gradually and tenderly makes his way up her body, touching everywhere with either his hands or his mouth and in some places both, only stopping to ask her, "do you like that baby," to which she replies, "yes baby, don't stop baby, yes baby."

After they have become a part of the international lovers club, the two fall asleep from exhaustion with Zephora's head resting on Marcus' chest and his right arm draped over her back gently but firmly gripping her fit, but soft arm and the covers pulled up halfway over her curvaceous butt.

Hours later, the water of the shower is warm and inviting and Marcus allows it to caress him, as it cascades down his body. He gently washes Zephora's back who is embraced by the water of the rainforest shower head on the opposite side of the shower. Zephora then turns to face Marcus, and using both hands, she begins to rub soap all over Marcus' body into a thick lather insuring that she doesn't miss a spot. She squats down to lather up his lower extremities giving more attention to parts that she thinks warrant special care to insure they are clean by any means necessary. Marcus appreciates her thoroughness and rewards her by standing her on the shower seat in order to apply the same attention to detail where he feels she deserves, and she leans forward pressing her hands against the glass walls of the shower to grant him access everywhere without complication and he shows her that he appreciates it. The undistinguishable words that she utters tells Marcus that he is doing a complete, thorough and excellent job. Zephora steps down from standing on the seat and ushers Marcus to her previous location and gently forces him back until his buttocks are pressed against the glass. She adjusts the shower head so that the water is flowing down from his chest rinsing the soap from his well lathered body and she uses her hands and whatever else it takes to insure he is rinsed and clean. His muscular body glistens, as the warm water drips down it. Marcus turns the shower head so that the water is running down Zephora's back and soaring off the edge of her curvy and plump booty like over the edge of a waterfall. Their bodies respond to each other's touch like soldiers jumping to attention upon the entrance of the general into their presence.

As they dry each other off, Marcus notices the tips of his fingers are shriveled up like raisins emphasizing how long their shower was. He smiles to himself and continues to gently pat dry the beautiful and inviting body of his wife and his body again responds like a saluting soldier. Zephora smiles at Marcus, drops her towel, pulls his towel out of his hands, pulls his head down as she reaches up to engage him in a kiss. Marcus lifts Zephora causing his biceps to flex. Zephora, excited by this, begins stroking Marcus' bulging biceps as he carefully places her onto the granite countertop and slowly crosses the threshold of her love once more until she moans with desire incessantly, beseeching him not to stop.

Zephora's dress is an incredible sapphire blue. It slopes halfway off her shoulders and curves into a V that stops just low enough to show off a little of her cleavage. It hugs the curves of her body and stops at her ankles with a split that runs up the middle of one leg and stops six inches above her knee. She accessorizes it with a fresh water pearl choker necklace, pearl teardrop earrings, a pearl and diamond bracelet, and compliments the dress with a pair of black five inch heel open-toed shoes with a crystal strap down the center. Her hair is pinned back with a silver, pearl and diamond broach and she leaves one curly strand out that hangs down the right side of her face. Her beauty is unmatched and when she steps out of the dressing room and into the bedroom, Marcus can only manage to say one word, "Wow!"

Marcus too is dressed to impress. He has on a black tux with a three button, single breasted jacket, complimented by a white, collarless shirt with a sapphire and diamond top button cover and a pair of square cuff links with eight square sapphires around the edge and a diamond in the middle matching the button cover. He also has on a five button sapphire blue vest and to finish off his attire, Marcus has on his favorite pair of classic square toed, eel-skinned shoes, a white gold, Cartier rectangular shaped, watch with a sapphire blue dial, an onyx, diamond and white gold bracelet and, he has taken his father's ring from around his neck and for the first time since his last visit to Africa, he places it on his finger just as Zephora walks around the corner.

Zephora responds in kind to the vision her eyes behold, "You are one exceptionally handsome man, Your Majesty!"

Marcus can finally utter a sentence and replies, "With a Queen as extraordinarily beautiful and breathtaking as you are, I better be. Are you ready to grace this dinner party with your presence and meet your African wedding court and their parents who are the rest of Tribal council heads? Because if you aren't, we can stand them up, grab Angelo and Veronica and get out of here."

"I'm ready my love. I feel as though I am exactly where I am supposed to be, exactly where I was prepared all those years by my mother to be; and somehow, where I dreamed a while back I would be. So yes, I'm ready. What about you?"

"Ze, with you by my side, I am ready for anything. You make me feel like I can conquer the world; however, all I want to do is make sure I love you with the best of me for all of eternity and beyond." Marcus takes the left hand of his beloved wife and they walk out of their suite and are met promptly by their two armor bearers.

They are two of the King's captains of the guard who, as the senior captain explains, are sworn to protect the King and Queen with their lives. Marcus tells them to insure that nothing happens to his beloved Zephora. They shout, "yes sire," and confess their loyalty to Marcus and Zephora. One leads the way and the other follows behind as they escort Marcus and Zephora to the royal dinner party that is in their honor.

CHAPTER XVIII

"Introducing, the Tribal King and Queen of Malawi, his Majesty and her Majesty, Marcus and Zephora Howard Sakara." All eyes in the room turn towards Marcus and Zephora, and every individual stands and stops whatever they are engaged in, including the servers, as they enter the grand dining room hand in hand. Zephora is all smiles and Marcus maintains a stoic look, only smiling when he glances over at his beloved and realizes how happy she appears to be. As they step down into the dining room and are lead to stand next to the rest of the waiting Royal Family, a procession line of Tribal Council members and dignitaries, including the current President of Malawi are all waiting to greet, congratulate and shake their hands.

Zephora leans in to hug her mother and whispers in her ear, "I guess all that training you put me through is finally coming in handy mother." Saphera just smiles and nods her head in acknowledgement. As the two reach Zuri, he stops them and with his eyes welling up, ready to pop out tears at any second, he places one hand on the shoulder of Marcus and the other on the shoulder of his daughter and proudly speaks to them. "You two have brought joy to my heart and an eternal sense of pride to my soul. Because of you two, I am in the land of our forefathers and standing in the halls that they too should have been able to adorn. You two are restoring honor back to both our families who were exiled because of their honor and integrity. I have no doubt that you two will change the landscape of this country, and I am glad that I am here to see the beginning of it all. I love you both with all my heart." And with that, Zuri pulls them both in close and hugs them as if he will never see them again; and, the King and Queen return his adulation, respect and gratitude.

Oliver escorts Marcus and Zephora to their seats before they had an opportunity to speak with Angelo and Veronica. Marcus is seated at the head of the table and as Oliver starts to take Zephora to the other end, Marcus stops him and tells him to seat Zephora to his right.

"Your Majesty," Oliver responds, "Traditionally, the Queen sits at the opposite end of the table as," before he can finish his sentence, Marcus stops him and casually whispers in his ear as not to embarrass him,

"Seat my wife at my right, her mother and father to her right, her cousin and his wife to my left and the President and his wife next to them and oh yeah, seat Bengono at the opposite end of the table; and Oliver, please do not ever question me again. Oliver, also, when you are finished here, please go immediately and check on my grandmother and report back to me please." Marcus smiles as he releases the grip he has on Oliver's elbow that is firm but does not cause a scene or embarrass him.

"Yes Sire, my apologies," are the only words that Oliver is able to articulate as he composes himself, delegates to his staff what must be done and promptly leaves the ballroom to handle the other duties set before him. Everyone takes their seats after the King and Queen have been seated. Bengono is highly upset, as he expected to be seated near the King and the President. With him at the far end of the table, are his wife and his absolutely stunning daughter. Her name is Tamrin Makira Bengono and, except for Zephora and not discounting Veronica, she is undoubtedly the second most beautiful lady in the room. She is the former Malawi beauty queen with her silky smooth dark chocolate skin, her jet black hair worn in a naturally curly afro, her exotic features, full lips, gray eyes and her 5'4" flawless and perfectly curved 128 pound frame. She is well known and beloved in Malawi and the pride of her parents, who had hopes of her one day becoming queen.

Bengono leans over to his daughter and whispers, "If you have any hope of being queen my dear, you must take the current Queen's place."

Tamrin, without hesitating, retorts to her father, "me being queen is your dream father not mine, and I wish no harm to befall the King or the Queen."

And with that, Bengono leans back, straightens his bowtie and frowns at his daughter before taking a drink of water. The palace Chaplin makes his way down to Marcus and asks if he is ready for him to bless the table before the food comes out. Marcus nods yes and the Chaplin retakes his position at the midway point of the table and taps his glass with his knife to get the attention of the rest of the diners and in a deep resounding voice declares, "Let us pray."

Marcus takes the hands of Zephora to his right and Veronica to his left and the remainder of the group follows suit and takes the hand of the person next to them and together they bow their heads. The Chaplin has given an incredible prayer filled with gratefulness, sacrifice, sharing, love, prosperity and thankfulness. It's inspiring and sets the tone for the individual conversations Marcus intends to have; however, his first order of business is enjoying the seven course meal that seems to just keep coming one plate after another. After the fourth course, Oliver enters the rooms and from the door, looks it over making sure his staff is adequately serving the King and Queen and their special guests. Now that he is satisfied with the staff's performance, he approaches Marcus and informs him that Ruth is sleeping comfortably. Marcus leans back to whisper in Oliver's ear after receiving the information about his grandmother.

"Oliver, I really, truly appreciate how well you are taking care of my granny; she means the world to me and she told me how much she appreciates you as well."

"Sire, it is my honor to serve you and your family. You have only been here a day, and the palace already has a freshness about it that it has not had in my twenty-five years of service here," Oliver replies.

Sounding like a man who understands what being a king is all about, Marcus responds, "No Oliver, it is my honor to serve you and prove that I am worthy of your service." Oliver nods with respect and with his head held high, makes his way to the kitchen to help support his staff.

Marcus, Zephora and their guests are finally enjoying the last course. Conversation is flying back and forth across the table as the new king and queen are getting to know the Tribal Council, their children, who are of the same generation as the King and Queen, and also the important dignitaries of the country they are adopting. With the exception of Bengono, everyone is having a grand time; and, now that the wonderful meal is over, the palace family and their visitants are ushered to the grand ballroom for dancing and more conversation.

Marcus now has the opportunity to speak with anyone and everyone without the constraint of the dining table and he wastes no time getting to know a little about every gentleman and every lady at the party. With the effectiveness of a politician and productiveness of a businessman, Marcus, with Zephora by his side, is winning over Malawi's movers and shakers with relative ease by introducing them to new and fresh ideas which included them all. Finally, he and Zephora are able to stop and speak with Angelo and Veronica without a chance of being whisked away.

"Angelo is this not the coolest party we've ever been to?" Marcus asks.

"I don't know man, I mean, your Majesty, the music could be jamming just a bit more," Angelo retorts.

"Man, if you call me that one more time, it's going to be on and popping," Marcus remarks.

And just as quick as Marcus said it, Angelo responds, "Your Majesty," and the friends share a laugh that has been waiting all night to happen. While enjoying his friend, Marcus pulls out his phone to text his sister, whom he just recently found out is really his cousin, and sends her a message:

"Hey sis, wish you here, missing you much. Hope you are having a great time bathing in the sun."

As if she has been waiting by the phone to hear from her brother, Charlie responds back immediately:

"Wow, I was just thinking about you. I'm glad you are having a blast and I'm glad you miss me because I miss you too. I wish I was there too but I'm truly glad I am here for sure. I have never been happier in my life. I have a career and a life now that I love."

Marcus texts back:

"I could not be happier for you, you deserve to be happy more than most. I'm proud of you for taking this chance to be happy and succeeding in it. Will call you tomorrow. Love you."

Marcus responds and slides his phone back in his pocket knowing his sister/cousin would not respond back because she never does after he says I love you. For her, that marks the end of conversation.

Marcus, Zuri and Angelo find time to talk about Tamrin and her friends and how incredibly gorgeous they are; just as Zephora, Saphera and Veronica find time to giggle about how handsome Marcus' groomsmen are as well. Marcus pulls Zuri away, asks him if he and the lovely Saphera will stand in for them for the rest of the party, as he and Zephora are about to slip out. Zuri acknowledges that he will help; however, that honor should be bestowed upon Angelo and Veronica. Marcus adheres to the wisdom of his father-in-law and lets Angelo know his intentions and expectations. As expected, Angelo responds, "yes your Majesty," Marcus shoves Angelo, the two have a big laugh, shake hands and Marcus takes Zephora by the hand and slip out through the kitchen, unnoticed by his guests.

Back in their room, Marcus and Zephora cannot wait to get out of their clothes. Marcus opens the French doors and they step out onto their private balcony. The night is perfect, there are no clouds in the sky and the two lovers are astonished at the multitude of stars available to see. Wrapped in each other's arms and a comforter from the bed, the party is but a distant thought as the soon to be crowned Tribal King and Queen pick up where they left off before the party, making up for lost time.

The last of the guests are leaving the palace. An hour before, Zuri and Saphera left the party in the capable hands of his nephew and niece. Angelo and Veronica are now exhausted but pleased with themselves because of the job they know they did at the party. Angelo grabs the last bottle of champagne, two glasses and his wife's hand and slowly make their way to their palace suite. Veronica closes and locks their door, Angelo begins to run a bath and the two take the opportunity to undress one other and settle in a warm bath with their champagne and love, as a nightcap.

Oliver has overseen the cleaning of the palace after the party and is now the last one to make it too his room. It is 3 a.m.; his head hits the pillow and his duties will resume again in three hours. Sleep well Oliver, for unbeknown to you, the morning will bring its own troubles.

CHAPTER XIX

Its 6 a.m. and Oliver feels as if he just laid down. The usual hours of his job traditionally are long, but when there is any kind of event at the palace, there are five to six hours added to the normal day. He is up two hours earlier than typically and the first order of business is coffee and then a shower. Normally it would be the other way around, but today, no coffee, no shower and the day does not start as planned.

Marcus is up early as well. He has a call to make to his operations manager. Its 6 p.m. in Atlanta, the perfect time to conduct a little business. Today is the day Marcus promotes his Operations Manager to the position he originally trained him for. Marcus and Angelo previously discussed the change and to them both it just makes sense. He just hates he has to do this over the phone. Marcus likes to look a man in the eye when doing business; he finds it to be an easy way to judge intent and integrity. However, this time he will be elevating a man who has been in the trenches with Marcus since the inception of his business; and now, Marcus has him on the phone.

"Zachery, how are you this evening?"

"I'm fine Mr. Howard, how are you this morning, I'm sure it's early over there?"

"We are all well on this end. I have been keeping up with our exports, imports, our warehouse production and customer service since I put you in charge of operations. First, I want to say how proud I am of you and the work you've done and have been doing since the beginning of this corporation. You and I have worked side by side for many years and all you have accomplished is excellence from the start until now. However, I must tell you that I no longer need you as my operations manager."

Shock is on the face of Zachery; this is not what he expected to here and his response and the tone of his response reflect his emotional state. "Mr. Howard, I thought you said you were proud of the work I have done? What is the reason you no longer need me as your operations manager?"

The call is a video call so Marcus can see the utter dismay on Zachery's face. "Listen Zach, I believe you have incorrectly perceived what I am saying. I no longer need you as my operations manager because I want and need you as my Vice President of Operations and Production. This position triples your responsibilities, decreases your physical labor and doubles your direct customer relations time. I am not in the business of placing people in positions to fail and I am not going to start now with you. You are well trained and prepared for this new position and I trust you and I know this is tailor made for you."

"I apologize Mr. Howard, I totally misread that."

"It's okay Zach, but do you accept the position?"

"With pleasure Mr. Howard, and I will not let you down. I have been hoping for this opportunity for a long time; and I know, that I'm ready, willing and able to fulfill the duties of the position of Vice President of Operations and Production."

"Well then, congratulations Mr. Zachery Dwight!" Tomorrow when you get in, your new office will be ready for you; and, on your desk will be paperwork for you to complete, an envelope with your benefits package and an envelope with your new job description. There is no more training required for this position; you will answer to Angelo Henson and myself. We are here to support you in any way possible. You can reach us most anytime by phone, email or video chat. I have an expectation of you Zachery and a greater reward than just this position. I believe in you my friend, and it is my honor to know someone like you. I appreciate all the work you have done to this point, and I look forward to watching you grow in this new position. There will be a company memo going out first thing in the morning, so our team will know about your promotion when you arrive at work. I am not sure when I will be returning to the states, but like I said, I am always at your service day or night."

"Mr. Howard, I appreciate this opportunity and I am excited about the challenge. Thank you so much for trusting me; I will not let you down. I probably won't sleep tonight I'm so excited. Again, thank you very much for the opportunity."

"Zach, you earned it. Now, I must go. Have a wonderful evening and I will have Mr. Henson touch base with you tomorrow sometime. Congratulations and goodnight."

Marcus shuts down the video call and decides to sit on the balcony a little bit longer before jumping back into bed with Zephora. From the balcony, he can see for what seems like miles. The sun coming up over the horizon is an incredible sight to behold and as it rises. Marcus feels the warmth of the morning sun on his face and he closes his eyes, smiles and receives the love the suns is freely offering up this morning. After accepting this first blessing of the day, Marcus returns to the warmth of his bed and his bride. Time to start some trouble.

One cup of coffee drank and shower completed. Oliver is officially ready for duty and his first duty of the day is to check on Marcus' grandmother, whom he has chosen to call Mama Ruth. Though he had a long night, Oliver is in good spirits. He whistles as he walks up the stairs and down the corridor to Ruth's suite. *"It's a beautiful morning to be alive,"* he thinks to himself as he reaches Ruth's door and gently knocks on it so that she won't be startled. Oliver has grown fond of her the short time she has been there. That's no surprise, Ruth is known to have that effect on most souls that are fortunate enough to meet her.

Oliver knocks one more time before pulling out his key allowing him access to her room and still no answer. He cracks the door ever so slightly and peeks through the crack to observe if she is still in the bed or up and possibly in the bathroom. Oliver notices that Ruth is still in the bed, however she is not moving. He calls out to her one more time before entering the room. The joyous feeling he relished while making his way to Ruth's room is gone now and distress is setting in. He enters the room slowly, calling Ruth's name as he makes it to her bedside. He shakes her, no response; he shakes her again and still there is no movement. He checks for a pulse…no pulse.

Oliver falls to his knees in tears all the while attempting to control them. Not only is there no pulse, Ruth's body is stiff and cold; she's been dead for hours. "Oh dear God, oh my

God, this is not happening, this is not happening. Pull yourself together Oliver, pull yourself together man," Oliver is talking to himself trying to keep his cool. He pulls the covers over her head, exits the room and locks the door. The cool strut he had to get there is now an all-out sprint as Oliver runs to his office to call for an ambulance and then to call the palace doctor. "Doctor T, I need you to meet me at the King's grandmother's room; she has no pulse and her body is cold."

"My God Oliver, I'll meet you there. Do not say anything to the King until after I have checked her please," the doctor relays.

Oliver waits outside the room for the doctor to arrive. When he does, Oliver lets him in but stays outside and doesn't let anyone enter. The doctor checks Ruth's pulse, puts his head on her chest to check for a heartbeat just to be sure, checks his watch, 8:30a.m., and records the time. He gestures, tracing a cross symbol across his body: head to chest, left shoulder to right. It's now his job to inform the King of the passing of his grandmother, and it's the job he likes the least as a physician, but it must be done and it must be done by him and right now. For now, Oliver's part of this is over; he didn't know Ruth long, but she made an impression on him; enough so, that he has to go to his room and wash his face to cover the tears before informing the staff and getting back to his duties.

Tap, tap, tap, Marcus is distracted by what he believes is a knock on the door. He listens closely but since Zephora didn't hear it, they continue conversing and cuddling. They have had very little time to do so for what seems like forever. Every time they think they can relax, there is another fire that must be extinguished. Little do they know, this time will be no different.

Knock, knock, knock, there is no mistaking it, someone is knocking on their door. The knock was heard by both Marcus and Zephora this time and neither of them is amused by the interruption.

"Can we not get one morning to sleep in Marcus? Is that too much to ask," Zephora retorts.

"You are the Tribal Queen my love, and until we have this wedding on Saturday, there is much that has to be done and things you have to sign off on. So, I'm sure that knock is for you." Marcus throws Zephora her robe, slides on his black silk pajama pants and his matching full length silk rope, waits for her to get dressed and then opens the door.

"Doctor T, how can I help you this morning? Is there a problem with Zuri, did he have another episode?

"Your Majesty," the doctor replies in obvious distress, "It is your grandmother, she, she has passed away in her sleep." Marcus pauses. His pause turns into silence. His facial expression changes from disbelief to a scowling frown. Zephora, who is standing behind him, turns him around and instantly wraps her arms around him in an attempt to comfort him. No words have been spoken since the news was given by the doctor. Zephora has the wherewithal to raise one finger up to the doctor suggesting to give them a moment before closing the door and guiding her husband back to the bed to take a seat. She kneels down in front of her husband, takes his head in her hands and with her thumbs, gently wipes the slow moving tears from his eyes as they are beginning to slither down his faces.

"Marcus, sweetie, I am so sorry, so, so sorry. You have got to get up and go to her room. Just for a moment and then I will handle everything after that; however, this you must do. Come on baby, I'll go with you, I got you. I know how important she has always been to you; I am so terribly sorry." Zephora pulls her distraught husband up from the bed, takes his hand and he takes the first steps and leads her to the door and opens it. Marcus is composed enough when he opens the door to only say a few words. "Lead the way doctor."

Ruth looks like she's asleep. There is a slight smile on her face as if she was dreaming pleasantly when she passed on. Marcus kneels by her bed and lightly rubs her head and leans in to whisper in her ear. "Welcome home granny; I love you, I miss you already. You were supposed to guide me through this." Upon finishing his sentence, Marcus hears "*I did and you're ready.*" Marcus raises up from the bed, turns towards the doctor and gives him his instructions. The doctor nods and Marcus leaves his grandmother's room with a bewildered look on his face. Zephora stays behind and assists the doctor with the final preparations.

Zephora enters their suite and finds her husband sitting on the balcony with a box of tissues and a bottle of cognac on the table. She doesn't bother him but takes the time to call the kitchen and have them bring some food to their room. After which, she pulls out her mobile phone and goes to work. She texts her parents and Angelo, calls Marcus' mother, then his father and finally, she calls Charlie. Within a couple of hours, Zephora had made flight arrangements for the entire family, made arrangements for the funeral according to Ruth's last wishes, which Ruth just happened to have with her, and found a little time to spend with her best friend and her parents.

Marcus hasn't moved from his spot on the balcony, he barely acknowledges Angelo who is sitting beside his best friend in silence, until Marcus chooses to say something, anything. There's a hole in Marcus' heart where the presence of his granny was, and even though he knows that her essence has merely shifted to a different plane of existence, he misses her from this one. Her presence kept him grounded, her wisdom kept him moving forward; and now with her gone, he cannot find the muscle capacity to move at all. It feels as if his heart is about to implode and it is taking every ounce of his strength to hold back the continual tears and keep his heart from that inner implosion. His options are, harden his heart or let it implode, and neither sounds like a good idea. His eyes are welling up with tears, his breathing is becoming more constricted when he hears the still, quiet voice of God. *"Let it go my son, let it go. My love is enough to sustain you."* And with that word, the tears begin to fall and Marcus' chest is filled with pain that extends from the outside in, imploding his heart.

Angelo grabs his phone and texts Zephora:

I need you now!

He awaits a response from Zephora, but one is not forthcoming on his phone because she comes rushing through the door. Without speaking, she positions herself in the chair with Marcus, straddling him so that she gets as close to him as possible, chest to chest, wrapping her arms around him with her face cheek to cheek with his. Angelo places a hand on both their shoulders, squeezes gently and then stands outside their door not allowing anyone to enter. Marcus deserves to grieve

231

without being interrupted. Angelo knows his pain first hand and the thought of it has him wiping tears from his eyes.

Marcus needs this good cry and Zephora is obliged to allow him to do so without ever thinking or feeling any loss of respect for her King. He has lost an unwavering friend, a trusted advisor and a loving grandmother all in one, who has been there for him for as long as he can remember, being each at the same time. Zephora is all he has now, she has inherited the duties vacated this morning. She had hoped to learn all she could from the only grandmother she has ever known; however, like every part of being a wife to this point, she will learn by on the job training and today is lesson one – comfort without judging.

"Marcus today is your day, no one will bother you. You mourn her today and I will mourn with you. My father will take care of our kingdom today. I have spoken with the council members and their families and everyone sends their love and condolences; and, they know my father is in charge for the day. So baby, you have me all to yourself today without a duty in sight."

"Wow Mrs. Howard, you have been one busy Queen. I cannot express how grateful I am in words. Thank you, I don't know how you did it and I don't know what I ever did to deserve such an incredible lady, but I'm glad I did it. You are perfect for me and to me. Now I know why my granny loved you so much. She told me not to ever let you go; not that I needed her to tell me that, but that was just her way of saying she thought you are the real deal. I told her, why you think I want her as my wife; and we laughed together about it. We did that a lot, laugh and talk. She saved the best talk for last; I wonder if she knew last night when we were talking, that I wouldn't see her anymore? I am going to miss that old lady, and our talks. Without her advice, I would not be the man I am today. Now who's going to tell me about my father and my mother? Good bye granny, tell my father and mother, my little sister and my granddad I said hello. Night, night granny, see you again one day, hopefully not soon, but definitely one day."

As Marcus mourns on the upper east side of the palace, Zuri has been called to duty in support of the Tribal King by an impatient and pretentious Bengono waiting for him in the conference room on the lower west side of the palace. Zuri walks into the room and Bengono is pacing back and forth with an impetuous look on his face.

"Bengono, the King is mourning the death of his grandmother; what could you possibly need today," questions Zuri.

Bengono brashly replies, "It would be wise of you to let your Tribal King Marcus know that the tragic passing of his grandmother will not delay Tribal Law. The wedding must happen as planned or he forfeits his crown." Nothing would please Bengono more than Marcus forfeiting, as it would be his daughter who becomes queen if it were to happen. However, his insensitivity is infuriating to Zuri who slowly walks toward Bengono with rage in his eyes.

Upon approach, Zuri's arm is outstretched and his hand tightens around Bengono's neck; and as the weight of his body surges forward, Bengono is thrust against the wall with his air supply significantly cut off and fear entering his heart.

"You pompous jackass, how insensitive you are to bring this foolishness to the palace and the King today as we are all mourning a great woman. I should crush your windpipe so that no words will ever reach your tongue again. Our Tribal King knows his obligations very well and I assure you, he will comply with every portion of our Tribal Laws despite his heartbreaking loss. When I release you, immediately leave the palace and I expect to see you here only two more times: at the funeral in two days and at the wedding two days after that. And when the King and Queen go on their honeymoon, I will personally deal with you as I have grown tired of your ridiculously, mutinous behaviors," Zuri erupts and spews like a volcano in the face of Bengono and then, throws him across the conference table and over a chair simultaneously with the end of his words.

Bengono, in a state of shock, picks himself up off the floor, straightens his clothes and with his hand rubbing his throat, slowly limps out the door looking back at Zuri as he leaves. Zuri, who has an intimidating presence, has been a peaceful man as of late amidst his condition, is clearly disgusted by Bengono and follows him out the door and continues his onslaught by grabbing Bengono's arm to halt his exit.

"When next you enter this palace, I expect you to treat the King and Queen with the utmost respect. Am I understood?"

Bengono turns towards Zuri ripping his arm from Zuri's grasp, and stares at him with half the brashness and twice the respect, as he entered with still rubbing his neck as a reminder, and meekly says, "Yes I understand."

Zuri slides his hands in his pockets as he watches Bengono peel off in his Mercedes leaving the palace. In the back of his mind Zuri thinks, "*I hope Marcus does not think I overstepped my bounds on this one because I just made that man his enemy.*"

PART 4

Until The End of Time

CHAPTER XX

"Ruth Eurika Henry lived a brobdingnagian life. She was fearless, thoughtful and endearing. Ruth Eurika Henry was my grandmother and one of the most incredible women I have ever known. Next to my beloved wife, I have not known anyone, man or woman, with as much strength of character, determination to inspire, depth of spirit or faith in God, as Ruth Eurika Henry, my grandmother. Not to mention, she was extraordinarily beautiful, too. If you knew her, you know what I say is true.

My Grandmother and I often spoke about the accountability of life, the responsibility to live and the integrity to do so righteously. My Grandmother was known also for being tough, but fair. But if you took the time to get to know her, as she was totally approachable, she was extremely kind and loving. If I needed to know anything, I knew I could count on her. She would say to me, "Don't come to me unless you want to know the truth;" and like I just told you, my grandmother and I spoke often. However today, it is my turn to tell you the truth about her, for her. Hebrews 13:7-9 says: *Remember your leaders, those who spoke to you the Word of God. Consider the outcome of their way of life and imitate their faith. Jesus Christ is the same yesterday and today and forever.*

Do not be led away by diverse and strange teachings, for it is good for the heart to be strengthened by grace, not by foods, which have not benefitted those devoted to them.

My Grandmother, Ruth Eurika Henry, was one such leader, and if you knew her like I knew her, you would have known her to have always been the same; and, it was her words of faith that guided me then, and that guide me now. When I was a child, she would say to me, "Please, thank you & you're welcome, never forget to use these terms in seeking what you want and need and for getting to where you want and need to go in life." And one of my personal favorite maxims of hers is, "Bought sense is better than none." However, the meaning of that one eluded me until I was 21 years old. I'll never forget the day I figured out its meaning; I was so proud of myself, and the only thing I wanted to do was call her. "I said guess what granny, I figured it out, I finally figured it out," and she just laughed that big, deep laugh of hers and we ended up talking for hours.

1 Cor. 13:13 says: *So faith, hope and love abide, these three; but the greatest of these is love.* My Grandmother's faith was always strong and securely placed in God; her hope was that my faith would be strongly placed in God as well, and it truly is, and her love of and for God is now providing her the ultimate reward, as she is there in Heaven with Him now.

My Grandmother, Ruth Eurika Henry's words, her strength, hope, faith and love will continue to be a guiding force for me the rest of my life; and, I will use them to chart my path and to guide others with integrity, as she taught me to do. If I am to become an inspiring leader, it will be because of her; if I am going to be a loving and devoted husband, it will be because of her; and if I am to continue learning and growing as a person and a faithful man of God, it will be because of Ruth Eurika Henry, my grandmother.

I bring this eulogy to a close with a word that I believe her spirit guided me to which exhibits an example of her faith, her strength, her hope and her love. John 14:25-28 says: *These things I have spoken to you while I am still with you, but the Comforter, the Holy Spirit, whom the Father will send in My name, He will teach you all things and bring to your remembrance all that I have said to you. Peace I leave with you, My peace I give to you. Not as the world gives do I give to you. Let not your hearts be troubled neither let them be afraid. You heard Me say to you I am going away and I will come to you. If you loved Me you would have rejoiced, because I am going to the Father for the Father is greater than I.*

My Grandmother, Ruth Eurika Henry, is now with the Father. If you knew her, and if you loved her, please be at peace, because she is now with God, our Heavenly Father. Do not let your hearts be troubled, and do not spend too much time grieving. Allow yourselves to feel glad instead of sad, to feel hope instead of fear, to have faith and not doubt, and to feel love and not despair. You know, Ruth Eurika Henry would tell you herself if she was here; or, if you are like me, and you can feel her spirit, you know she is screaming with her arms outstretched, REJOICE!

I am glad that her home going occurred here in the country, the land of our forefathers. Our ancestors, for the most part, were able to put their differences aside and create a set of rules that would be the system of laws that would govern our people for generations. Those rules, those laws, are called our Tribal Laws, and it is because of these laws that my family is here in the first place. My grandmother was ecstatic to be here in the motherland and more specifically, the land of her people. It gave her a sense of pride to be here in the palace, to be a part of the royal family especially after the sacrifices she has made. You see, her husband, who was my grandfather, and her son, who was my father, lost their lives trying to restore our family's honor many years ago; and my grandmother, was responsible for protecting an unwitting future king, me, and the rest of my family from suffering the same fate as her husband and her son. We are here, I am here, because of her quick thinking, incredible courage, limitless sacrifice and enduring faith. She is my hero.

Please stand, and bow your heads as we pray. *Dear Lord, we thank You for Your limitless love and grace that surrounds us always. As we formally commit Ruth Eurika Henry unto Your hands, we pray that Your Holy Spirit will comfort us as we grieve the loss of a friend, a mother, a wife, a grandmother, a teacher and a mentor; but rejoice in her going home to You from whence she came. Grant Your faithful servant entrance into Your Kingdom; and, Father God we thank You for the time You loaned her to us. We need You here in our presence today Father, as we pray that You carry our burdens, as we cast them to You. Bless our family Father God and grant us peace and prosperity, mercy and forgiveness of sins; and we pray, that You keep a hedge of protection around our family, our noble friends and the Tribal Law that unites us. And Lord Jesus, as I put my faith and trust in You and endeavor to serve my people as I am commissioned to do, I pray You guide my heart, my spirit, and my mind like You did my beloved grandmother, as my steps are ordered by You. Bless this country and our fellow countrymen, and let Your peace reign supreme over us. Father God we need You now and always in our lives; we love You, and thank You for granting Ruth Eurika Henry a peaceful home coming; and it's*

in our Lord and Savior Jesus Christ's Holy name we pray.
Amen. Rest in peace Ruth Eurika Henry, rest in peace my
granny."

CHAPTER XXI

Zephora has been waiting for this day more than she has been letting on to Marcus. The thought of walking down the aisle toward Marcus has her excited. Even though they're already married, she still has always dreamed of a wedding with her father walking her down the aisle and her mother sitting on the front row crying; and now, just hours away, her dream comes true. For the last 24 hours, Zephora has been held up in her and Marcus' room, the King's suite alone and away from Marcus, as Tribal Law demands; it's the first time she hasn't slept next to her husband since they got married in the States.

Zephora is contemplating texting Veronica as she steps out of the shower, when she hears her phone vibrating with a distinctive tone. It's Veronica sending her a text:

> *Ze come down to my room, it's time for me to do your hair and make-up.*

Zephora instantly texts her back:

> *Girl I was just about to text you to see if you are ready. I'm married already but I can't stop my hands from shaking just like the first time. On my way, leave the door cracked. TY.*

Zephora slips on her warm ups, grabs her hair and make-up kit and darts down the stairs, turns left and around the corner to Angelo and Veronica's suite. She knocks once and slowly pushes the door open to find her mother there with Veronica. "Mother, what are you doing here," Zephora asks with elation while instantaneously stretching her arms out to embrace Saphera.

"Ah baby, you think I would let my only child, my precious daughter, prepare to be crowned queen and I not be here to help every step of the way; or more importantly, be able to tell her how exceedingly proud of her I am, and how proud I've always been and how honored I am to be her mother?"

"Ah mom, thank you so much. I love you," Zephora cries as the two continue to hug with tears streaming down both their faces, when Veronica runs over with tears in her eyes as well and yells, "Group hug! That goes double for me Ze. And boy, I'm sure glad you guys got all this crying out of the way before we start on Ze's make-up." The three share in a laugh and finish their hugs when Veronica shouts, "Okay ladies, now let's enjoy these mimosas while they're still cold." She passes around the glasses, clears her throat and raises her glass.

"Zephora, you are the absolute best friend a girl can have, that's why I'm glad you're my best friend; and I need you to know, I'm so happy for you, ecstatic even, and as one of your loyal subjects, you can always count on me for whatever you need 24/7; 365 days a year. I love you girl." "I second that my darling daughter," Saphera affirms."

"And before we clink these glasses," Zephora rebuts, "let me say this; I am blessed to have you both, and it is I who is ready to serve you both, if you two beautiful ladies will give me a chance – except for today, today I really need you two because I am all thumbs. Now let's drink!" The three raise their glasses, bring them together and Veronica and Saphera shout: "Hail to the Queen!" They laugh, sip on their mimosa and get to work on Zephora's hair and make-up.

Marcus stands on the balcony and admires the view of the palace grounds while sipping on his coffee. The thought of meeting Zephora at the altar again brings a smile to his face; he can't wait to see her in what he knows will be a beautiful dress walking down the aisle on Zuri's arm. No matter what she has said previously, Marcus knows how important this moment will be to Zephora; and this time, he doesn't have to worry about anyone even attempting to disrupt their ceremony.

Marcus makes a call to Oliver and asks him if Zephora has left their suite yet; and Oliver, who has had one of his staff watching for her departure as instructed by Marcus, lets Marcus know that she has exited the suite. Marcus responds to Oliver with a resounding, "Make it happen Oliver, make it happen!"

Oliver responds with a seldom seen smile on his face, "Yes Sire, immediately."

While Marcus and Oliver are corresponding on the phone, Zuri and Angelo arrive at Marcus' suite, the King's personal guest suite, knock and simultaneous charge through the door with three glasses and three bottles of champagne raised to the sky with shouts of jubilance. Marcus nods ardently to them as he finishes his enigmatic conversation with Oliver. "Who are you two supposed to be, the welcome wagon or the party train," Marcus excitedly queries.

"As your best man my brother," Angelo begins, "it is my job to keep you from getting nervous by doing my best to make you nervous, guarantee you that you're making the best choice of your life and make sure you know I still have that surprisingly beautiful ring. And by the way, what happens to the first one you gave her?"

Zuri, uncharacteristically chimes in, "And I'm here to warn you," he admonishes with a scowl, "that if you break my little girl's heart, I...; and, then he changes his countenance to a smile, "want to express to you from the bottom of my heart, as a father, there is no other man I would rather see my Zephora with. I couldn't be prouder of you; you've shown courage under duress, patience in the face of abhorrence, you've shown sagacity and an unyielding, undying love for my daughter. I am tremendously honored that you are my son-in-law; and I will faithfully serve you as my King."

Marcus calmly questions, "You two do know that Ze and I are already married right?" He then reaches out and firmly shakes Zuri's hand and while holding it says, "Zuri, sir, it is I who will humbly serve you. You have fervently shared your wisdom with me, as if you were perceptively mentoring me from the moment we met in my house that night; and I promise that I will continue to love and cherish your daughter all of this life and the next one to come. And as for you Angelo," Marcus declares right as Angelo pops the cork and begins to pour, "No man could ask for a better friend and confidant than you. We've been through the trenches together, got educated together and trained together. You are my brother, my best friend and a true warrior; and as my best man, don't you lose that ring."

The three warriors share a robust laugh, clink their glasses, hoist them high into the air and together shout "Salute," and down their bubbly. They shake off the immediate champagne rush to the head and continue drinking until the bottles are empty. Marcus looks around at his fellow warriors who are now champagne lounging and looks beyond their red, alcohol, puffy eyes, appreciates their big hearts, their unparalleled honor, their unflinching loyalty and their enduring friendship and love; and as Marcus watches Angelo and Zuri's eyes blink slowly, he decides they have had enough, and relieves them of their duties. "You guys should go and rest, especially you Zuri, and we'll meet back here an hour before show time." The two men get up and help each other leave the suite without saying a word, and gently close the door and stumble arm over shoulder down the hall. Marcus falls back on the bed, clasps his hands behind his head and stares at the ceiling as if it were the Cysteine Chapel. He smiles and whispers, "Lord, I praise You, and I thank You Father God for blessing me so much," as he closes his eyes and passes out.

Oliver and his staff have their hands full; Marcus, their new King, has given them a mission to complete and Oliver is thrilled to complete it. Oliver has been on staff here at the palace for a long time; and in all that time, he has rarely smiled or had reason to do so. In this week since Marcus and Zephora have taken over the palace, despite the emotional roller coaster everyone has been on over the unexpected death of Ruth,

Oliver has experienced more joy than he has in all his years serving at the palace. He became attached to Ruth and her loving spirit within hours of knowing her; and instead of feeling sorrow for her passing, what he senses is adulation and love. He has been trying to comprehend what he's experiencing; he can only attribute it to the arrival of the new Royal Family and because of this new spiritual awareness, he vows to serve the King and his family well.

The staff stands ready to complete the King's mission and Oliver instructs them on exactly what must be done. His dissemination of the mission brings a smile to their faces and they delightfully get to work. While they are working outside in the halls, Oliver uses his master key, lets himself into the King and Queen's suite and gets to work in there and doing so with immense joy in his heart. It's the first time in a long while that he has joyfully followed the special directives of a Royal in the palace.

The deed is done and now Oliver must insure that everything is in order in preparation for the royal wedding. He checks with kitchen staff, they are ready, he checks with his lead server, he is ready; Oliver checks with security, they are ready and he finally checks with the valets, and they are also ready. It seems, that the only staffer who is not yet prepared, is Oliver. He takes the opportunity now to go to his room and get out of his daily uniform, shower and put on his special occasion royal uniform designated especially for royal galas, presidential visits and, as in this case, a royal wedding. Oliver and his staff are all smiles and ready, willing and able to serve the King and Queen, the Tribal Noble Families, Malawi's elected officials, important foreign dignitaries and, of course, the rest of the Royal Family.

Its two hours before the wedding and Zephora, Saphera and Veronica emerge from Veronica's room. Zephora can only stand in the doorway with a look of overwhelming euphoria because of what her eyes behold. Saphera and Veronica are equally stopped in their tracks with wide eyes and opened mouths. Finally, Zephora is able to speak but only a few words, "Oh my God, what has my wonderful man done." Veronica and Saphera follow suit with a simultaneously elated, "Oh my God."

The three ladies stand in amazement at the unbelievable sight before them. The entire hall is covered with the deepest red rose petals speckled with the whitest white rose petals. Every inch of the grand hall is covered, the plush carpet cannot be seen, only red and white rose petals. As far down the hall as can be seen, there are only rose petals. They cover the stairs going up from right to left, every step, only rose petals.

Zephora has not moved and will not allow Saphera and Veronica to move either. She pulls her phone out of her pocket; still astonished at the sight before her and speed dials Marcus. "Marcus, you are a beautiful man. I love you so very much husband. I have never seen such an expression of love and honor as the one before me now. I am truly at a loss for words; I'm holding back these joyful tears so I won't mess up my make-up but I do not think I can hold them back any longer. I cannot wait to see you in a little while. Thank you for making me feel like a real bride and a Queen."

Marcus speaks with a soft, even toned voice, "Beloved, you are a Queen, you are my Queen and the Tribal Queen of Malawi; and, a Queen should walk on rose petals and a bride should walk on them also. I love and adore you and cannot wait to see you later. Enjoy your present; see you soon my love. Bye."

Zephora hangs up the phone, takes a picture, then starts her video camera and slowly begins her trek to their suite escorted by Saphera and Veronica. Neither one of them has ever walked on rose petals before; they are enjoying it immensely as the petals softly crumple beneath their feet. When Zephora opens the door to their suite, again the whole floor is covered with red and white rose petals. On the dresser are two vases of 24 red roses, on the gentleman's chest two vases of roses, on each nightstand a vase of roses, and on the bathroom counter, a vase of roses on each end. Zephora has never seen this many roses in one places at one time before and she is totally, completely and utterly overjoyed.

Veronica is ecstatic as well, but she knows she has to redo Zephora's make-up now. "Zephora girl, I know this is overwhelming, and when I see Marcus I'm either going to kiss him or kill him, I'm not sure which yet. Either way my darling sister, right now, we have to do your make-up again. Come on mama Saphera, we need to get this done in a hurry and we basically have to start from scratch because of all this crying she's doing. I tell you the truth, after this is over I'm going to kill that Marcus for all this extra work we're doing."

With only an hour left before the wedding is supposed to start, Veronica and Saphera feverishly work make-up magic now that Zephora has stopped streaming tears of joy. Once her make-up is complete, they have 30 minutes to converse with one another. Suddenly, Zephora knows what needs to be done before she puts on her dress. "Mother, will you and Veronica pray with me?"

"Of course we will baby," Saphera replies.

They kneel down on a bed of roses side by side and hold hands, as Zephora begins to pray. *"Heavenly Father, we thank You for this moment in time. Thank You for Your continual blessings that flow through heavens open doors. Father we praise You for Your grace and mercy, for Your love, Your peace and Lord, we thank You for Your forgiveness, as we forgive all those who have crossed us along the way. Thankfulness and praise will always be in our mouths, as You have placed us in positions of influence able to help those who are less fortunate than we are. Lord thank You for my dream of a beautiful wedding, thank You for answering my prayers and sending me an incredible husband who loves me. Thank You for surrounding me with loyal friends and allowing me time with my dad and for bringing him back to us; and Lord, I pray that You will heal the sickness that is in his body. Father God, show us how to help the people of this country, our new home. Bless my husband Lord, grant him the strength of character to bring the families together to heal this country. Continue to bless our business back home in the U.S. Lord so that we may continue to provide income for those families. Lord, You have blessed us more than most and I know that to them who much has been given, much is expected and we Lord, are ready to do all that You ask. For we are Your humble servants and follow You wherever You lead us. Jesus we praise your Holy name and thank You for Your sacrifice and resurrection that frees us from the grip of sin. Thank You Father God again for all You have blessed us with and all that is to come. It is in Jesus Christ Holy name we worship and pray, Amen, Amen."*

Angelo and Zuri arrive at Marcus' door dressed and ready to go. Angelo knocks one time and walks right in to find Marcus almost dressed and ready. "Marcus, why are you dragging your feet here," Angelo questions.

Marcus gazes at Angelo as he formulates his answer and then gives it to him. "Angelo, dear brother, there is no way that I am going to lounge around in my tux and get it wrinkled a whole hour before show time? I got time brother, I got time. Did you gentlemen get some well needed rest, especially you Zuri?"

Zuri responds in kind, "Marcus, my son, I am well rested and ready to go. Whatever this medication is they are giving me here, it has me feeling better than I have in a long while which is perfect for my daughter's wedding day."

Angelo gets in on the fun. "Marcus, my brother, I too was able to rest and now that I am revived, I too am prepared and ready to serve you as your best man, my friend. Now will you please get your butt in gear and at least show me that you are excited about this with all these rose petals everywhere? Boy let's go!"

The three laugh at themselves and have a pre-wedding glass of champagne. Marcus only takes a sip of his champagne, sets it down and then makes a request. "Will you two gentlemen join me in prayer?" Of course they agree and the three kneel down around the bed, bow their heads and fold their hands in preparation for Marcus' prayer.

"Father God, we come to You in thankfulness; thanking You for Your grace and mercy, for Your love and understanding, for Your peace and Your forgiveness as we graciously and humbly forgive those who have crossed us now and in the past. Lord Jesus we thank You for watching over us and keeping us safe. We pray that You continue to protect us from the devourer and protect us from the powers and principalities that wish to steal, kill and destroy. Keep Your Angels encamped around us, as we move forward under Your covering. Father we are thankful for all that You have provided and the provision that has not yet manifested. We are thankful for family and devoted friends. We are thankful for bringing us to a new land and we pray that You will guide us in the right direction to heal this land and these people. Teach me how to turn this land of poverty into a land of wealth and prosperity for the future generations of our people. Show us how to bring peace and harmony between the Tribal Families for the sake of the people. Father God bless my wife, fill her with Your grace

and Your strength and I pray Your blessings over our marriage and I pray for the healing of the Holy Spirit for Zuri; heal him from the inside out. Thank You for bringing me and Zephora together and we will always honor You with our love and all that You have blessed us with. We pray Your blessings over this wedding today, that it will be everything Zephora ever wanted it to be. Father we praise Your Holy name. We worship You and only You. In closing Father God and Lord Jesus, we pray for wholeness and all glory and honor are Yours. It is in my Lord and Savior Jesus Christ's Holy name we pray. Amen and Amen and Amen again. Hallelujah and I praise Your name Lord Jesus, we love You Father God with all our heart, mind, body, soul and strength. Thank You Lord Jesus, thank You Father God. Let Your Holy Spirit rain down on us in Jesus name, Amen."

CHAPTER XXII

Standing next to Pastor Jamal Rekab in the pulpit, Marcus has a perfect view of the entrance of the chapel. Dressed in a black three button tuxedo with a seven button vest, a crisp white shirt with sapphire and diamond cuff links garnished in white gold and a sapphire blue tie, Marcus' right leg shakes back and forth like it always does when he's nervous, he watches the people file into the chapel, most of whom he doesn't know or has only seen once or twice. However, as the Tribal Council and their family members enter, he recognizes them all, especially their adult children, the ones who are in his age bracket, the ones whose time it is to take over their parents' positions on the Tribal Council. As Marcus watches them take their seats, he has transformation on his mind.

It doesn't take long for the chapel to fill up. The pews are filled with Malawi's present leaders and future prospects, dignitaries from neighboring countries and ambassadors from around the world. Since the party a few days back, Marcus has taken the time to brush up on who all these officials are, it could mean the difference between prosperity and poverty for the country of his forefathers. Now that everyone has taken their seats, the doors of the chapel close and is instantly filled with captivating music and Marcus' mind is back on the business at hand, and his leg begins to shake once more.

The music changes to Luther Vandross' 'Here and Now,' the chapel doors open and Angelo and Veronica step in arm and arm sashaying down the aisle. They reach the front and Angelo assists Veronica in stepping up on the stage to the left and then takes his position next to Marcus. He nudges him with his elbow and cracks a smile at his nervous and intense looking friend.

"Marcus," he whispers, "you do remember this is just ceremonial and you're already married right?" Marcus slowly turns his head towards Angelo, gives him a nervous smile and responds.

"Of course, I know that; but I also know that this is everything Zephora has ever wanted in a wedding and with everything that has happened, I think I can understandably be a little nervous."

Angelo places his hand on Marcus' shoulder, gently squeezes and reassures his best friend, "Relax Marcus, this day is preordained and will be the new beginning of your incredible and long standing love affair that gives hope to all. Now stand there and be cool and wait for your bride." Marcus shakes off his nervousness and crosses his hands in front of him, right hand over left displaying his family ring for all to see.

The chapel doors open again and in steps Saphera escorted by Oliver. The two of them strut their way to the front and Oliver seats Saphera in the second seat on the front row and then walks out and closes the doors behind him. Once outside the chapel, Oliver grabs one of the ushers and they get to work on completing the second part of Marcus' secret mission. With Zephora waiting in her room for her cue, Oliver again lines the hall, the stairs and her trek all the way to the chapel entrance with red rose petals. Oliver and his helper open the doors to the chapel where just inside on both sides behind the doors are two containers of rose petals; except these petals aren't red, they are white and blue. Oliver spreads the petals across the entire main aisle from the back of the chapel all the way to the front and up the steps to the stage covering any place the bride may step or stand; the two flower spreaders then turn and exit down the outside aisles; one down to the left and the other down to the right leaving the petals untouched by anyone.

The usher at the entrance of the chapel gets the signal to make the call to the bride. Zuri receives the call and shouts to Zephora, "Its time my daughter." He stands up and awaits the emergence of his beloved daughter from her dressing room. Zuri never thought he would ever be able to get to know his daughter; and now, on a day he also never thought possible in his wildest of dreams, he gets to walk her down the aisle. He is rhapsodic and overjoyed, more than proud, his life is now complete, words cannot express his sentiment and nothing can stop the tears from streaming down his face as Zephora stands before him now.

Father and daughter step out of the suite; both realizing and understanding their dreams are coming true and so is the future neither has ever dared to dream of. Zephora wraps her arm around her father's arm, he in turn places his hand atop hers and together, stepping as one, their feet landing on top of the softest of rose petals, each step moving them closer towards a position her mother prepared her for and a future, with Marcus, she is destined for. For Zuri, this means the reestablishment of two families' honor stolen from them long ago and setting right the wrongs of greed and betrayal through his daughter and one of the most honorable men he has ever known.

No words are spoken between them as they step out of the past and into the future; however, they share an equal amount of tears rolling from the corners of their eyes. They reach the entrance of the chapel after strolling down a rosy red path. Zuri turns and faces his daughter and gently wipes away the tears and mascara streaming down her face restoring her to beauty and luster. Pastor Jamal is told of their arrival at the entrance. He motions for all to rise to their feet and on cue, the music that has launched thousands of brides down the aisle towards a new future begins to play, the doors of the chapel slowly open, all eyes turn towards the opening doors and the chapel is filled with oohs and awes as the congregation gets its first glimpse of the bride and future Queen of Malawi. Marcus' view is obstructed, he cannot see what everyone else is admiring.

Zephora's dress is a chiffon, sleeveless with hemline spaghetti straps, with a beaded bodice embellished with sparkling Swarovski crystals and deep blue sapphires. Its sweetheart neckline is embroidered with crystals and sapphires in a triangle shaped motif at the point of cleavage. The skirt of her frabjous dress is adorned with a flowing chapel train; and, Zephora's elegant dress is finished with a full length chiffon cape that drapes softly over her shoulders and flows gracefully down her back matching the length of her dresses' chapel train and is fashioned with a two inch beaded collar that is embellished with Swarovski crystals and enhanced with the deepest blue marquise cut sapphires speckled throughout it.

Zephora and Zuri's path to Marcus and the front of the chapel is decked with white and blue rose petals that are cushioning every step they take. Halfway down the aisle, Zephora is finally in view of Marcus and his eyes increase to the size of large brown marbles and his mouth is wide open and trying to form words. She is far more beautiful than Marcus could have ever imagined. Angelo nudges Marcus, "Close your mouth man you're embarrassing me." Marcus regains his composure and his open mouth is replaced with an ear to ear smile as his eyes meet hers as she reaches the front of the chapel.

"Who gives this woman to be joined to this man," are the words spoken by Pastor Jamal, as the doors of the chapel close and the congregation take their seats once more.

Zuri stands tall, glances at Zephora and proudly declares, "I, her father do." And with that, Marcus steps forward, takes Zephora's hand to assist her up the steps as her father simultaneously releases her to his stead and the bride and groom are finally standing face to face.

"Dearly beloved," Pastor Jamal begins, "ladies and gentlemen, royal and noble guests, special friends and dignitaries from around the world, we are gathered here today to join this man, Prince Marcus Howard, ancestor of the Noble Sakara Family from The Great Zimbabwe Tribe and Princess Zephora Sherman, ancestor of the Noble Netumba Family from the Mapungubwe Tribe. Ages ago, people from both these great tribes migrated northeast to form what is now our great country, Malawi. In order to create peace in a new land between these two great and proud peoples, Tribal Laws were written and one of those laws is the marriage between nobles from both tribes to consecrate lasting peace and unity.

Because of treachery, betrayal, greed and a lust for power, the Sakara and Netumba families were exiled and hunted by tribal assassins in an attempt to end their bloodlines and hide the deceit of the treacherous families who conceived such a diabolical scheme. However, the hand of God protected these families and their bloodlines continue despite all the efforts of evil men. Separated from their history by a great ocean and two continents, these two people standing before you today found each other and fell in love without any knowledge of their ancestral duty for their country and their people.

Still hampered by the betrayal of the disgraceful families who held power over the Tribal Council, Prince Marcus and Princess Zephora have been fighting for their lives, overcoming dark forces that imprisoned Marcus and almost had Zephora marrying the architect of yet another hideous plan to betray our way of life and our sacred Tribal Laws. Marcus, showing the courage of his noble family and, at the time, without any knowledge that he is the one who should be King, was able to thwart the plan, rescue Zephora and restore his family and his bride's family to honor, as well as reclaim their rightful places on the Tribal Council.

Now, I bet you didn't expect all of this when you came here today; all you expected was to see these two be wed. However, there is no way I could marry them without you all knowing the challenges they both overcame to be standing here today. And though they did not grow up in Malawi or know the history of their royal families, they are Malawians to their core and amazing examples of our people's strength and courage and the essence of our ancestors. Now that you know their past, it is time to start their present and their future and the future of our people.

Marriage is a promise of lifelong commitment between two people who understand the finality of their choice. It is an institution that should never be entered into lightly. Marriage is a commitment contract that enlists the mind, body and soul in working together to build a life of friendship, love, sharing, devotion and selflessness. Marriage is deeply rooted in communication, trust and compromise. This union will be called upon to persevere through good and bad times, through sickness and health, through agreements and disagreements and through the stresses of the world around it.

Marriage calls upon two people to look to each other first through whatever victory or tragedy that may come. It calls for a constant desire for one another, an ability and a necessity to forgive and it calls for the realization that marriage, especially this one, has a purpose beyond love and companionship. A successful marriage stands for something more than the two individuals joined by it and is applied with a prospective that promotes fruitfulness.

Marcus and Zephora, I implore you to put God first in everything you do, pray together consistently and approach your union with a system for success; I promote a system called the "I DARE" system. I dare you Marcus and you Zephora to approach your marriage with Integrity - never lie to one another, with Dedication - be loyal to one another first before anyone else, with Accountability to one another, with Responsibility to and for each other and finally, with Excellence - never give one another anything less than your absolute best. If the two of you can commit to this, you will celebrate everything marriage is meant to be every day of your lives – Heaven.

Marcus and Zephora understand the seriousness of this ceremony and have written their own vows to recite. However, before we go any further, it is my duty to ask, if there is anyone here today that has any just cause as to why Marcus and Zephora should not be joined here today, speak now or forever hold your peace."

Those last words from Pastor Jamal ring out loud in the chapel. Marcus and Zephora turn and look out over the room that is quiet enough to hear a pin drop, before turning back and looking at each other. Pastor Jamal gives the congregation one minute, sixty long seconds, during which Marcus and Zephora are locked in a loving gaze with one another. Right as the pastor is about to break the silence, it is instead broken by the creaking of the chapel door opening. In walks Charlie with her and Marcus' great aunt, Madame Zigumba, whom Marcus has not met but only heard of through his sister. Marcus smiles at his sister as she and Madame Zigumba slowly and quietly make their way to the front row opposite Zuri and Saphera. This is an unexpected but extremely welcomed surprise for Marcus and Zephora.

Madame Zigumba looks up at Pastor Jamal and speaks, "Okay young man, you can continue now." A low level giggle rumbles through the crowded chapel.

"Now that we have that out of the way, we can continue," Pastor Jamal proudly and gladly states. "Marcus you may read your vows."

Marcus clears his throat and stares at his bride, his eyes darting back and forth between her eyes and her lips as he begins. "When I first laid eyes on you, I said to myself that's my dream. You inspired me to change my attitude toward life and that transformed my world. Our friendship grew and my perspective about love changed and it became my reality. Standing here today, I tell you the truth with all my heart, that as your husband and King, my desire is to be one with you for all times. To live my life fulfilling your wants and needs as best I can, to comfort you in times of sorrow and pain, to laugh with you in times of happiness and joy, to listen to you when your heart is pouring out words and sentences about your past, present, future, and about your cares. To care for you in times of sickness, to eliminate worry and doubt from your mind set, and to sit quietly with you when there are no words left to say. But mostly, my desire is to love you with pureness, with passion and vigor, unconditionally and respectfully, compassionately and completely. My desire is to make every day the same no matter what challenges may come. I will shield you from the world and its evil ways, and make our lives mentally, physically, emotionally, and spiritually complete just as you are making my life complete by joining with me today."

Pastor Jamal turns to Zephora and softly says, "My dear, you may recite your vows."

Zephora raises her eyes to meet Marcus' eyes, smiles at him without the seal breaking on her lips and then slowly blinks her eyes twice and then starts her vows. "Marcus, the first time I saw you I desired you. Maybe just your body at first but, I took the time to get to know you; and now, what I desire is your heart, your friendship, your love and your strength. I have wanted to be your queen for a long time now, but I didn't know I would be the Queen too, WOW. I promise to give you the best of all that I am, I promise to love you with all the love God created me to give only to you. I promise to be the wife and Queen you want me and need me to be every day of our incredible life together. I promise to love you fiercely, victoriously, just the way you like it, the way you need me to be and want me to be for all the days of my life when you join with me today."

"Do you have the rings," Pastor Jamal asks. Angelo reaches in his pocket and hands Marcus a velvet navy blue ring box. Marcus opens the box, takes out the ring, hands the box back to Angelo and then turns and prepares to put the ring on Zephora's finger. Zephora looks down seeing this new ring for the first time. The ring boasts a four carat marquise cut, flawless, diamond center stone, flanked by a one carat round cut blue sapphire, and two rows of baguettes on each side.

Pastor Jamal speaks, "Repeat after me Marcus; with this ring, I do thee wed."

Marcus places the ring on Zephora's finger and says while looking at his bride, "with this ring, I do thee wed."

Pastor Jamal turns to Zephora and asks, "Do you have the ring?"

Zephora turns and takes the ring out of the box that Veronica is holding and then turns back towards Marcus and prepares to place it on his finger. Marcus looks down to see the ring and is surprised at what he sees. It is a platinum five stone ring. The center stone is a one carat round flanked by a three quarter carat and half carat round on each side.

"Zephora, repeat after me please. With this ring I do thee wed," requests Pastor Jamal.

Without hesitation, Zephora places the ring on Marcus' finger and smiling the whole time says, "With this ring, I do thee wed."

Pastor Jamal places Marcus' hand on top of Zephora's hand and finally says, "By the power granted unto me by the country of Malawi and the Tribal Laws Council, I pronounce you man and wife; you may kiss the bride."

Marcus clutches Zephora, pulls her close, never letting his eyes leave hers until their lips touch. They both close their eyes, slightly tilt their heads in opposite directions and in what seems like slow motion, kiss with passion and vigor for at least ten to fifteen seconds amid claps and cheers from all in attendance. Zephora now has her dream wedding.

Pastor Jamal then instructs Marcus and Zephora to take a seat in the two velvet blue chairs with white gold arms and legs. He then takes a three strand velvet rope, and with their hands still clasp together, he wraps the rope around their adjoined hands and then states, "This three strand rope represents the bond between God and the two of you in this union. God is the CEO of this merger, Marcus, you are President and Zephora you are Vice-President or in this case King and Queen. Though Marcus you are the lead, you are not the boss of your wife, nor is she your boss; you both answer to God for the positions you hold in this marriage and should work to please Him first and then one another.

This union has also produced our Tribal King and Queen and at this time, you shall be crowned." First the pastor is handed the King's crown by Bengono, which he takes from a velvet blue pillow. He walks behind Marcus and places the crown on his head. The crown is white gold and has three triangle prongs that extend upward and is endowed with a plethora of marquise cut diamonds and sapphires throughout. He then walks behind Zephora and places her crown upon her head. Zephora's crown has one triangle extension but is also endowed with diamonds and sapphires.

Pastor Jamal then stands in front of them and pronounces, "Let us pray. *Father God bless this union and as it honors You, let it be fruitful and prosperous. Give them the strength and courage to take on challenges before them justly and with integrity. Bless them from the top of their heads to the bottom of their feet, help them to rule as their ancestors have before them by remembering the duty of a King and Queen is to serve the people honorably. Guide their every step Lord, and open all doors and windows necessary to affect change. I pray Lord that they love you first and then each other and let that love extend to the people. It is in Jesus Christ Holy name we pray. Amen, amen and amen again.* Ladies and gentlemen, it gives me great pleasure to introduce to you our Tribal King Marcus and his Queen, Zephora also known as Mr. and Mrs. Marcus Howard Sakara!"

Everyone in the chapel stands to their feet and let out resounding cheers and continuous claps. Madame Zigumba gets down on one knee and bows her head to the King and Queen and the rest of the people follow her lead. Marcus and Zephora stand to their feet, they bow to the people and Marcus then instructs them all to rise to their feet and he hurries to help his great aunt to her feet, and then gives Charlie a hug and whispers, "I have missed you."

The King and Queen walk down the aisle and exit the chapel. Now in the chapel foyer, Marcus stops and faces Zephora. He gently grabs her face with both his hands, pulls her in close to himself, slowly and passionately lets his lips touch her soft lips before taking his time to kiss her. His eyes closed, her eyes closed and for the next few minutes, no one else exists in the world as they take the time to indulge themselves in the bliss that is and always has been their love. When Marcus opens his eyes and comes up for air, he smiles at his Queen and shouts, "We did it, so now let's party like a rock star baby!"

Unbeknown to them, the wedding crowd had been ushered out the front doors of the chapel. When Marcus and Zephora are let into what they thought was going to be an empty grand ball room, they are met by flying rice and rose petals as well as falling confetti and cheers abound. They make their way to the front giving kisses and shaking hands along way. When they reach the front, at the podium is Marcus' great aunt and she is tapping her champagne glass with a knife.

"Someone give our Tribal King and Queen a couple of glasses please." They receive their glasses filled with fine bubbly and Madame Zigumba continues. "As the residing Elder here, I reserve the right to make policy this night; if the King allows it." Marcus smiles and nods in approval and she begins again. "It has taken a long time to restore our family to its rightful place in the Tribal Council after years of being hunted and assassinated. I am honored that it is my great nephew who was courageous enough to see such a difficult task to this glorious end, or I should say beginning. This will be the only toast of the night. After this, we are going to dance and party like only our people can do. Long live the Tribal King and Queen, and may they serve our people with love and honor, because our ancestors are watching." Sips are taken by all and then Madame Zigumba says, "Now turn the music on so we can start dancing in here!"

The celebrating goes on for hours and everyone is seemingly having a grand time. Marcus approaches Angelo and taps him on the shoulder and says, "Brother, its time." Angelo locates Oliver and requests that he instruct the first born of the Tribal Council leaders' children to be escorted to the conference room. Oliver complies and when it is done, reports back to Angelo who gives Marcus a nod and heads to the conference room himself. Marcus, as respectfully as possible, takes Zephora's hand and gently pulls her away from the boring conversation she is having and whispers in her ear, " it's time my love," and the two of them head to the conference room as inconspicuous as possible, if that is even possible.

CHAPTER XXIII

When Marcus and Zephora enter the conference room, the nine men and women in the room rise to their feet and clap. Marcus sits at the head of the table, Zephora to his right, Angelo and Veronica to his left and Zuri is sitting in the corner to his right. Marcus looks around the room slowly and then gets right to it.

"Thank you all for coming, and I will be brief. Effective immediately, you who are around this table, are the Tribal Council leaders. You will be replacing your parents. Mr. Netumba will be overseeing the transition to insure that your parents know this and that they pass their family rings over to you, as their successors. With the young minds in this room, I know we have what it takes to change the outlook of our people and the poverty that they are suffering in. We all inherited fortunes that have just been stock piled; now it is time we use our fortunes and the education and training we have all acquired for the betterment of our beloved country and our people. If we are as smart as I know we are, it will take less of our money and more of our brains and our service. If you are not with me in this, leave this room now." Marcus pauses and waits for anyone who wants to leave; when no one does, he continues. "I don't have all the answers; however, I know we

274

have all the answers and the resources, and the motivation we need. While my cousin and I are on our respective honeymoons, please dig in and be ready to let me know where you want to serve, where you believe you can make a real difference, and how you plan to do it. I promise you, when we get back, we will be ready to join in, roll up our sleeves and make it happen. Oh, and one more thing, please do not call me anything but Marcus and my wife Zephora because we are a team that has mutual respect for one another, okay? Now let's toast to the new Malawi and long live this Tribal Council."

Everyone raises their glasses with excitement. Zuri stands up from the corner and whispers in Marcus' ear. "Well, you did well again son, you made me proud." Marcus turns, shakes his hand and says, "Thank you Dad."

Zuri responds, "And don't worry, I will be extremely diplomatic with the former council leaders, especially Bengono.

Marcus smiles and replies, "I would expect nothing less."

Not planning on hanging around and celebrating too long, Marcus and Zephora take the time to get to know all of their new fellow council members. The two are on different sides of the room conversing with various people, when the beautiful Tamrin approaches Marcus. Next to Zephora, there is none more beautiful in the room or that Marcus has ever known or seen; not to mention, she is highly educated, intelligent, and has proven herself to be an ally though Marcus is not sure why since her father has been trying to make things difficult for him.

"Sire," she says in her deep sultry voice, "I must inform you that one of your guards is loyal to my father and I do not know if you can trust him. If I were you I would have Mr. Netumba remove him and appoint another. I can suggest one for you, I know the men who are loyal to my father and the ones who are ready for a fresh start serving you."

With a bewildered look on his face and an eye on his wife, Marcus turns his attention towards Tamrin, smiles somewhat, looks into her beautiful grayish brown eyes and carefully responds. "Well you know Tamrin," he says, "I would appreciate that. If you would put a list together for Zuri, I mean Mr. Netumba, which would be extremely helpful." Marcus, trying not to be taken back by her extreme frankness and trying to remember his train of thought, comes back with a follow-up question. "Why are you helping me and turning your back on your father?"

"To tell the truth Sire," She replies, "I have watched the way my father has done business for years, and the close ties he had with Kwazan who was more treacherous than most, and swore I would not support his behavior or what he stands for ever. Not to mention, you represent promise for our country."

"I will do my very best for our country and I am impressed with your honesty and hopeful outlook," Marcus replies. Just as he finishes his sentence, Zephora taps Marcus on the shoulder and says, "What are you two talking about over here?"

Marcus reaches around and places his arm around Zephora and kisses her before answering her question. "We were discussing guards and integrity."

"Well," Zephora replies, "Let's cut this short because we have family to entertain before leaving for our honeymoon Sweetie."

Marcus reminds Tamrin to speak to Zuri immediately and he and Zephora promptly leave and reunite with their family to commune and celebrate. Marcus and Zephora spend time with Charlie and get to know his great aunt Madame Zigumba. Zuri joins the family after conversing with Tamrin and replacing Marcus' wayward guard. The party goes way into the early morning with no one thinking or considering leaving.

The sun comes up and the eight members of the new royal family make their way to the kitchen where they smell fresh coffee brewing. When they arrive downstairs still laughing and enjoying themselves, they are welcomed by Oliver and his staff with coffee, mimosa, and a breakfast spread fit for, well, a king. They dine, swap more stories, share more laughs and afterwards return to their suites to shower, pack and prepare for their various trips. Charlie and Madame Zigumba head back to the Bahamas, Angelo and Veronica prepare for their honeymoon in Hawaii, Marcus and Zephora pack for their honeymoon in the Maldives, while Zuri and Saphera, climb back into bed with plans of sleeping all day having already said their goodbyes and placing Oliver in charge of the palace for the day. Oliver, of course knows, he is in charge of the palace every day but holds no bitterness for the oversight.

Finally, things are looking up for Marcus and Zephora now that they have completed the stipulations of the Tribal Laws; although, they are unaware of the pages Bengono conveniently left out. As Marcus and Zephora set out to enjoy their honeymoon, Bengono believes he is still holding all the cards.

CHAPTER XXIV

Marcus uses his index finger to slowly and gently trace the curves of Zephora's beautiful faces while he watches her sleep. He leans in towards her and is compelled to kiss her lovely soft lips and tries to do so without waking her. His attempt fails and Zephora slowly opens her eyes and smiles.

"Good morning my King, what can I do for you this morning," Zephora utters in a soft sexy voice.

Marcus hesitates a moment, cracks a smile and whispers, "You're doing it already. I just want to lay here a little longer and take in the beauty that is you, my Queen."

They returned from their honeymoon three months ago and they make sure to find time to live in honeymoon bliss every day. Marcus is jumping head first into his new position, a new venture and the collaborative work with his fellow council members. He has successfully inserted each member into high ranking Malawi government positions; including having Tamrin run for President in the upcoming election. She has always been popular with the people of Malawi and she is primed to be the first female president of the country.

Zephora has been invisible since they got back; not even her mother and father have seen much of her. Occasionally she tours the country from the back of the palace limo, but she never gets out of the car until it arrives back at the palace. Angelo and Veronica have taken residence in Blantyre, the commercial center of Malawi. They live in the Livingston Mansion, an extension of the Royal Palace, and Angelo is running a branch of he and Marcus' import-export business there, as well as founding and heading the Malawian Business Chamber and helping to create 500 jobs there and 2500 jobs across the country.

Zuri and Saphera moved to Malawi's old capital Zomba, and Zuri is the Director of the Malawian Bureau of Investigators. With everyone busy with their new careers in their new country, it has been difficult for any of them to see one another; however, that is about to change.

Bengono, the former head of the Tribal Council, has been waiting for this day. It is three months after the royal wedding and time for the first official council meeting. Although Bengono is no longer a part of the council, he has been planning on being there for a while. Bengono willfully and with malicious intent withheld Tribal Law pages from Marcus in order to lawfully dethrone him at this meeting, or at least have his daughter become the new queen.

Tribal Law states that if the Queen is not with child within the first three months after the wedding, the King and Queen must step down or the King must take the daughter of the next tribal family as his new wife. These laws were written centuries ago and procreation was vital to the survival of their tribes. No matter how old or asinine the laws, they have always been adhered to and Bengono has plans to make sure this remains true.

Bengono gathers all the old pages of the Tribal Laws, including the ones he did not disclose to Marcus, puts on his favorite suit and waits for his daughter to pick him up. Tamrin arrives at her father's home to retrieve the Tribal Laws and head to the palace for the scheduled meeting not expecting her father to be going.

"Father, do you have a meeting to attend today?"

"Oh my daughter, I am going to the palace for the council meeting as I have always done."

"But you are no longer a part of the council father, and you know you and the King do not exactly get along. So why are you attempting to infuriate the King with your presence?"

"Because this is the day you, my daughter, will become Queen, and the interlopers can leave our country and go back to their own."

"What have you done father, what have you done?"

"I withheld some of the Tribal Laws from your King and because he doesn't know about them, we can oust them by law. It is his weakness that causes me to dislike him. He should have known that Kwazan was my friend. But instead he trusted me; something a King has little time for. So a King who is too weak to recognize his enemies, is unfit to lead and it is my Malawian duty to use every skill I have to betray him and insure our Tribal Leader is strong and wise enough to understand these things."

"Father, King Marcus has been working tirelessly for the last three months to help make our country's economy grow. All my life I have witnessed the poverty of our country while I was privileged. I worked hard in school to gain the knowledge necessary to help rid our country of this stain. I watched you and the other council members hoard your wealth and allow the people to suffer. What you and your cohorts did was commit genocide. I am ashamed of you and what you stand for."

"Because of what we did child, you have had the best of everything. And today, when you become Queen because of my actions, you will thank me for it all."

"Give me the Tribal Laws father, I'm leaving and I will apparently see you later. Just know that I am extremely ashamed of you and I will have nothing further to do with you." Tamrin takes the laws and slams the door behind her as she leaves; however, before she can make it to her car, her father covers her nose and mouth with a chloroform cloth until she is unconscious.

"Sorry my daughter, I cannot have you ruining my plans. You will thank me later when you are Queen. But until then, rest my darling daughter until I return with your crown."

Oliver and his staff prepare for the first Tribal Council Conference under the newly crowned King and Queen. The first three months have been good for the kingdom and there are great many successes to celebrate. King Marcus has thus far, orchestrated an incredible revitalization plan for his new adopted country but it has not come without some opposition. The old council leaders responded with outrage towards being abruptly ousted and replaced by their very own children; nevertheless, it is the right of the King to select his council. Marcus wisely understood that the old council had no intention of releasing their children's inheritance to them so soon and officially decreed it to be so, and under Tribal Law, they had no choice but to comply no matter how reluctantly they opposed it.

Marcus, with his new council, has sought out to change the selfish greed of his predecessors and in the process, made enemies of them all and their followers. This conference will be to lay out the plans for the next quarter, review all reports of the campaigns already in progress and to ensure that the King has complied with the last of the Tribal Laws that could threaten his reign. It is up to Oliver and his staff to prepare the palace to receive the council and conference stenographer. Only certain areas of the palace were necessary to be prepared for the council to enter; the rest of the palace is to be ready to receive the Royal family who will all be attending.

Marcus and Zephora reluctantly must end their lover's embrace and slowly climb out of bed and prepare for their big day. On the way to the bathroom Zephora reaches out and slaps Marcus on the butt and remarks, "Your Majesty," and curtsies. Marcus smiles and with love firmly assures, "Don't start something you know we can't finish."

"It may not be finished right now, but it will be finished my love, I mean your Majesty."

"Good point gorgeous; now come over here and let me give you a thing or two to think about." Marcus gently grabs his wife's hand and swings her around twirling her into his arms. His lips softly touch hers as if to say to her lips, "You're mine," and his tongue confirms this truth. Simultaneously, his hands follow a well-conceived plan to caress her sexy caramel tanned body in all the right places and all the business finishing places too. Zephora secretly doesn't want him stop but knows he should yield; however, his three pronged attack has defeated her will to resist.

Marcus has her right where he wants her and seemingly to her, he shows no signs of stopping. Without warning, he stops and walks away leaving Zephora stunned and standing there with every part of her body longing, waiting and wanting more. Marcus grabs his razor and shaving gel and commences to prepare for his day. Zephora is in shock, wet and annoyed. *"How can he have the audacity to take me there and then just walk away; you just wait dear husband, your time is coming, and when you least expect it too,"* she thinks to herself as she smirks at him, turns her back on him and washes her face. As the two newlyweds shower and playfully get ready for a day worthy of celebrating for so many reasons, they are unaware of the trouble brewing just miles away from the palace.

With his daughter knocked out on his couch, Bengono jumps in her car, instructs her driver to get out and replaces her driver with his own driver who makes a b-line for the palace while Bengono takes the time to bring his plan into fruition. Bengono calls the rest of the old regime and offers them retribution if they meet him outside the palace in two hours. They are ready and willing to comply with his request, if he can assure them it will work. He reminds them of their long ago oath and reassures them the Tribal Laws will be on their side.

Concurrently, both Angelo and Veronica's and Zuri and Saphera's helicopters land on the back lawn of the palace. They all make their way to the lavish palace patio and greet one another with the hugs and kisses of a family's love; and, Angelo and Veronica share their sensational surprise with their uncle and aunt as they all approach the rear guard of the palace's back door. They are again showered with even bigger loving hugs and kisses as well as tears of joy.

"Does Marcus and Zephora know yet," Zuri questions Angelo, "and why did you wait so long to let us know this great news?"

"Well Uncle Zuri," Angelo begins, "We didn't want to unnecessarily alarm anyone until we were absolutely sure everything was going to work out; plus good uncle, we knew we would see you all here today and it just felt right that we tell you now."

"I could not be happier for the two of you and I know your cousins will be as well," Saphera chimes in.

"I for one cannot wait to see my girl," Veronica establishes, "it has been far too long since we've talked, and I haven't had a chance to see her since we got back from our honeymoons."

Saphera shakes her head and insists, "I know what you mean; this is the longest time I have ever gone without talking to my Zephora. Those two went into seclusion as soon as they got back. I'm not used to this and I'm going to let her know it and Marcus too," Saphera asserts.

"Alright Ladies break it up, we have all been busy and I am sure those two have had their hands full these last few months. Being Tribal King and Queen comes with a boat load of responsibilities," Zuri explains. "Plus Marcus is working on something important and life changing. So let's stop standing out here fussing and complaining and get in there and see them. I for one have missed the heck out of my daughter; I talk to Marcus all the time, but I need to see my baby. So come on, let's get in there." The rear guard opens the back door to the palace to receive the Royal family.

CHAPTER XXV

Oliver greets the royal family at the rear of the palace and escorts them to the second floor parlor as instructed by Marcus. He informs Zuri that all the other guests except one have called in, should be arriving shortly and that the conference room is ready to receive them. Oliver makes his way downstairs and as he does, the new Tribal Council is arriving on time and he escorts them to the conference room. He phones Marcus and Zuri and informs them of the council's arrival. No sooner than they hang up, he has to call Zuri back to let him know they have uninvited guests who want to be heard. Zuri asks Oliver to escort them to the downstairs parlor and asks Oliver if he has informed Marcus.

Oliver answers with a resounding, "No, the King asked only to be informed when you and the council arrive; otherwise, he wishes not to be disturbed," Oliver adds.

Zuri demands that Oliver keep them in the parlor and that he place armed guards at the door. As soon as Zuri hangs up, Marcus and Zephora enter the parlor and on cue, their family kneels down and simultaneously shout, "Good day your Majesty, good day my Queen!" They all laugh and the room is filled with joy, laughter, hugs, kisses and handshakes. It is the best family reunion any of them could ask for and that all of them need. Zephora and Veronica drift to a corner, look each other over and laugh hysterically at their coincidental circumstances. Marcus clears his throat and gets everyone's attention and shouts, "We have an announcement to make." They all turn and face Marcus. Zephora walks over and stands next to her husband.

"Zephora and I would like to tell you," Marcus pauses and looks at Zephora before starting again, "For the past few months I have been studying intensely and I am proud to announce to you that I have completed Seminary School and I am officially an ordained minister."

All mouths are open and bottom lips on the floor; and then Marcus finishes with, "And oh yeah, we're pregnant!" Without hesitation, Angelo shouts, "I'm not a minister but we're pregnant too!" The royal family celebrates at the double fisted gifts that heaven has bestowed upon them but the day is still young.

It's time for the Tribal Council Conference and the royal family must get back to the other business of the day. Marcus asks the ladies to stay in the parlor and he will call for them when it's time for them to make an entrance. Zephora is pleased by this, she has much to catch up on with her mother and Veronica. The three of them have smiles on their faces that will be hard to erase. Marcus orders his personal guard to stay outside the door and watch over them as he, Angelo and Zuri head down to the conference prepared to celebrate more. However, on the way down, Zuri informs him of his uninvited guests brooding in the downstairs parlor. Marcus chooses to deal with them after the meeting.

Tamrin grabs her throbbing head and attempts to shake off the effects of the chloroform attack from her father with the help of her driver and trusted friend. While she was out, he secured them a car from her father's garage. After some water on her face and some down her throat, Tamrin is pissed and determined to see her father severely punished for his actions. Still a little wobbly from the drugs, her legs cross one in front of the other, as she slowly walks towards the car, falling onto it just as her hands reach its top, she is still stinging from the unabashed assault by her callous and cruel father. Her driver jumps out of the driver's seat, runs around the car and helps Tamrin get into car. She touches his hand and thoughtfully bows her head towards him in thanks for his help. Once she is settled in the car, he reaches under his jacket in the small of his back, pulls out a .357 nickel plated snub nose and checks to insure it is still loaded with hollow point bullets, spins the cylinder, 'click' and reestablishes it in the small of his back.

Tamrin's phone rings; its Zuri telling her he has been trying to reach her and asking her if she's okay. She gives him a summary of the recent events, articulates to him that she will be there in ten minutes, asks if her father is there and expresses for him to be careful, which he always is anyway. Zuri reaches inside his coat, pulls the slide back on his nine 'click', turns off the safety and informs Marcus of the situation.

The climate in the palace has changed from festive to aggressive entanglement. Marcus and Angelo continue to the conference and take care of business as if nothing is going on, and Zuri turns right to the security office and then makes his way to the downstairs parlor.

The front entrance guards allow Bengono's driver to enter the palace to go the restroom; one of Oliver's staff escort him to the main floor men's room. Marcus, Angelo and Zuri's minds are on high alert; however, they feel they have all the bases covered and there should be no need to call for a support platoon. Tamrin and her driver arrive at the palace. The front entrance guards allow her and her driver, who is now her body guard, to enter. They enter the conference room and Marcus hugs her, "Thank God you're okay," and she takes her seat acknowledging the other members with her driver seated in the corner facing her and in position to watch the door.

Zuri makes another detour to the security office; he radios the guards who are with his wife, daughter and niece and conveys to them how important it is to stay alert. He has eyes on the men in the parlor and they present no threat at the moment. Zuri emphatically stresses to security that they must have eyes on everyone and then drills them on the importance of it, and the consequences of failing to do so.

While Marcus confers with his council members, Zuri chooses to confront Bengono in the parlor in order to end this threat. Bengono is cool, calm and collected. He has a plan and a right to be there challenging the new Tribal King; however, his reasoning for attacking his daughter, a presidential candidate is puzzling and a felony punishable by death and as the former council leader, he knows this which makes him dangerous. He expresses to Zuri that he merely wants to exercise his right to oppose the new King, based on Tribal Law.

"If my claims are discredited, I will accept my fate and be put to death," demands Bengono.

"Bengono," Zuri retorts, "you are scum; I know you were the ring leader of that Kwazan fiasco, and I also know the whole council here is guilty as well. Based on the evidence I have on you, I don't have to let you speak to the King or his council at all; however, I will humor you and allow it."

Sweat begins to run down Bengono's face and his hands are shaking. This is a wrinkle he did not plan for; from this point forward, he will be improvising in order to achieve his goal and survive the fallout.

Zuri grabs the little menace by his arm and walks him down the hall to the conference room, sits him in the corner across from Marcus, takes his position standing behind and to the left of Marcus and whispers something in Marcus' ear. Marcus stands up abruptly and addresses the council members.

"My fellow council members, Bengono, the former council leader, would like to speak at this conference with the intent to remove me as King and council leader based on what he says is a disparity on my part in compliance with all the Tribal Laws outlined by our ancestors long ago. Bengono is the very person who provided me with the laws. I have to adhere to them in order to be in compliance with these ancient laws of our people. It will be very interesting to hear what he has to say and I vote we allow it."

The rest of the council agrees with Marcus and a grinning Bengono stands up and prepares to address the council. His daughter holds her head down in shame for the disgraceful actions of her father and has no desire to hear any more but has no choice. Marcus taps his gavel on the table, sits back down and gives Bengono the floor and five minutes to state his claims against Marcus.

"My fellow council members, I posit that our new King has failed to comply with all the statues of our beloved Tribal Laws. Up to this point, it would seem that he is in compliance; however, I will substantiate my claims. I purposely and willfully withheld pages of our Tribal Laws from him. Admittedly, I confess to being Kwazan's partner in attempting to have him killed; nevertheless, none of this matters now; and in my defense, I did all of this for my daughter because it is my family's time to lead, it's her turn to be queen and I will do whatever it takes to see it through. What I have done is now academic and does not matter. If this King from a foreign land can be tricked by me, betrayed by me, he is not worthy to be your King. On the pages of our laws that I withheld is the final thing this foreigner must complete in his first three months as King; if he does not complete it, he must forfcit his crown or divorce his Queen and take the hand of the daughter of the next noble family, which just happens to be my daughter. The law states that if the Queen is not pregnant within the first 100 days of their reign, he must comply with one of the two terms I mentioned. This is what I withheld. Now, King Marcus, give up your crown or marry my daughter; either way, my daughter is the new tribal Queen of Malawi. I did this all for you baby, all for you my daughter. You can hate me forever, but do it while being Queen."

The council members are stunned at the lengths Bengono went through just to make his daughter Queen. Tamrin is in tears, tears of shame and apologizing and begging Marcus for forgiveness, sincerely confessing she had nothing to do with this nonsense and vowing not to be Queen or attempt to take the thrown this way. Marcus slams his gavel on the table twice to quiet the room. He hands Tamrin a box of tissues and stands up to address the council and his accuser.

"My fellow council members and friends," Marcus proclaims, "I stand accused of not complying with a law that I apparently knew nothing about by a treacherous and vile man who is consumed by a lust for power and riches. The Holy Bible states that the love of money is the root of all evil and it would seem, the Word is proving true through his actions. However, he is right about one thing he says, if he can so easily betray me, so effortlessly deceive me, I should not be King. I came here to this country, my country, not seeking to be King but seeking answers and help in freeing my beloved from the madman who had kidnapped her and was attempting to force her to marry him. We knew nothing of Malawi, of our ancestors, or of the Tribal Laws that judge us now; however,

God opened our hearts to where we belong, to our destiny and to our purpose.

I was captured here, stripped naked and thrown into a dungeon here. I have accepted my birthright and someone whom I allowed to remain as part of the council, even though he or his family has no claim, is going to remove me because he believes he has me over a barrel. You see Bengono I never trusted you for one minute that you would give me everything I needed. I am King and did not then and do not now need you to get me anything. I had the right to hold and go through the original scrolls, which I did with a translator and a historian. The test was for you, I was testing you, testing your loyalty, testing your honor, testing your integrity and not having my so called incompetence be tested by you. I have known of your treachery from the beginning. You are the one who had me kidnapped, the one who tried to have me killed. But I forgave you and gave you another chance and this is what you did with the opportunity I gave you. You sadden me; however, as King, I will deal with you and your cohorts as our beloved Tribal Laws require."

"Wait just a moment," Bengono shouts, "you have not yet disproved my claims; and if you cannot, your reign is over."

Zuri stands up, places his hand on Marcus' shoulder and states proudly, "He's right Marcus." The other council members nod their heads in agreement. Marcus sits down, shakes his head, reaches into the inside chest pocket of his jacket, pulls out an envelope and opens it.

"Well, we hadn't gotten to this part of our meeting yet, but what I have here is the ultrasound of me and Zephora's first babies, twins actually."

The conference room erupts in claps and congratulations, and one brooding man in the corner. Bengono reaches down to pull a .22 caliber pistol from his ankle holster, pushes his way through the joyous council members and fires at Marcus. Instantaneously Zuri, whose eyes have been trained on Bengono the whole time, pulls his 9mm from his chest holster, pushes Marcus aside firing two shots simultaneously into Bengono. The council members dive for the floor, Bengono's chest caves in, his head flips back and his body flies violently into the corner. Zuri is the only person standing when Marcus gets up from being pushed by him. The two men stand there face to face staring at each other. Marcus looks down to see blood trickling down Zuri's shirt. At the same time, Zuri smiles at Marcus, drops his weapon and falls forward into Marcus' arms who catches him and slowly lays him on the floor, resting Zuri's head on his knees, while refusing to let go of his hand.

Angelo is now on the other side of Zuri, who looks at Marcus and then Angelo with his eyes blinking slowly still with a smile on his face when he asks, "Did I get him?"

Marcus continues grasping his hand tightly and responds, "You know you did, that's why you're smiling; one in the chest and one dead center, in his forehead."

Out of nowhere, they hear a shot followed by two quick shots and then three shots which sound like they came from upstairs. Marcus releases Zuri's hand, lays it across his chest, glances at Angelo and calmly says, "take care of him," as he reaches down, picks up Zuri's weapon and darts toward the conference room doors forcing them open in stride as he motors his way up the stairs.

Security lost sight of Bengono's driver who had gone to the restroom earlier. When he heard the first shot in the conference room, it was his cue to head upstairs to shoot the newly crowned Queen as his mission demanded. When Marcus arrives upstairs, he proceeds cautiously but with purpose. As he reaches the parlor, he first notices one of his guards on the floor dead. He pushes the door open and with his finger on the trigger of the weapon, he slowly enters the parlor. The driver is crawling in an attempt to reach a gun on the floor in front of him and Marcus kicks it away from him as he makes his way towards the women who are in a corner behind a coffee table that the second guard is sitting in front of bleeding from a wound to his right shoulder and another to the left side of his torso. He is barely alive.

He looks up at Marcus, a tear slides out of the corner of his eye and his head slowly leans forward, his chin touching his chest and blood dripping from his mouth. Marcus checks for a pulse as he reaches him, but feels nothing. When he reaches the ladies, Veronica is kneeling beside Zephora who is also kneeling with her mother's head in her lap. Saphera turns her head to look at Marcus, smiles and slowly claims, "I stopped one of those bullets from hitting my baby and her babies," with her eyes blinking slowly like the eyes of her husband downstairs. Marcus kisses Zephora on the forehead as she continues to gently stroke her mother's face, sniffling with tears streaming down her face; neither she nor Veronica have spoken a word. Marcus gets Veronica to put pressure on Saphera's wound. The driver is still attempting to crawl his way to them and Marcus walks over and finishes him.

Oliver comes running in with a doctor and two nurses and begins to tell Marcus what's going on downstairs. Marcus shakes his head no as he picks his wife up, squeezes her tight and moves her out of the way to allow the medical professionals to enter the room to do their job. Angelo runs around the dead man on the floor and Veronica runs into his arms. No one speaks, they just hold on to one another with tears trekking down the weary faces of Zephora and Veronica and from the sad, angry watery eyes of Marcus and Angelo.

Saphera is on a rolling bed headed for the sanatorium with Marcus and Zephora on one side and Angelo and Veronica on the other. When they arrive downstairs, Zuri is already in surgery and they begin prepping Saphera for surgery as well. In order to stabilize him, the doctors place Zuri in a medically induced coma to give him the best chance of healing from his wombs.

The bullet is being removed from Saphera; her injuries are not life threatening unlike Zuri's; they are serious, but thank God, not life threatening. She has not been told about Zuri's condition yet, but she will be forcefully asking for and about him when she wakes up from anesthesia, and someone better have answers for her.

Marcus and Angelo head back to the conference room to make a report to the council members and on the way he is briefed by Oliver and the security chief on the cleanup of the palace and the lapse in security that allowed two armed men access into the palace in the first place. By the time they reach the conference room, all evidence of the shooting has been removed and the men in the parlor have joined the council members. Marcus adjourns the conference and sends all except Angelo, Tamrin and the old council members away. Marcus offers Tamrin condolences but she assures him that it is not necessary and assures him that her allegiances are with him, with the Tribal Council and the Tribal Laws.

Tamrin asks to be excused and Marcus hugs her, gives her a kiss on the cheek and tells her she will have two of the Royal guard with her at all times from now on. Marcus must now deal with the conspirers of Bengono swiftly and definitively. He gives the new chief of security his instructions and commands that the old chief of security suffer their fate as well, because he is responsible for this debacle that could cost them the life of the patriarch of the royal family and Marcus' mentor. After giving his commands, Marcus and Angelo head to the Chapel to pray and as they kneel at the altar, their wives enter the Chapel and without saying a word kneel down beside them. Marcus leads his family in prayer for the recovery of Zuri and Saphera, for peace, for healing, for grace, for mercy, for family, for protection, for strength, for courage, for knowledge, for understanding, for wisdom, for love and for an anointing of the Holy Spirit for all his people. And the Lord impresses upon Marcus to spare the lives of the condemned, enough blood has been shed. His reign cannot begin with needless death and expect to be blessed with abundance of and for life. Marcus assures God he will obey and thanks God for His unfailing love, Amen.

CHAPTER XXVI

Prayer and supplication has worked. After three months in a doctor induced coma, Zuri blinks his eyes for the first time and squeezes Saphera's hand who has been at his bed side day and night since she recovered from her surgery. When she awoke in the recovery room from her surgery, she looked around the room and didn't see Zuri. After getting some water to restore her dry, parched throat, her first words were, "where is my husband?" Zephora, who had been parked at her bed, with tears in her eyes, slowly and quietly responded to her mother with the explanation of what happened to Zuri. Being the strong woman she is Saphera did not panic, she did not cry; she held her daughter's hand tight and with the strength of her faith, told her everything would be alright.

Now, it is Saphera who is parked at the side of her husband when he awakes. Zuri gradually opens his eyes and when the blurriness fades and clearness appears, it is Saphera's face, more importantly her eyes that are staring back at him and he has the presence of mind to muster a smile. Saphera kisses him on the forehead and says, "Hello husband," She then presses the button for the nurse and when the nurse replies, she proudly retorts, "He's awake." Immediately the doctor and nurses come in and attend to Zuri who has not yet attempted to speak. Saphera steps back, sits in the corner, pulls out her phone and texts Zephora and Angelo in all caps:

HE'S AWAKE!

Zephora calls Marcus who is working in his office and gives him the news. Marcus is ecstatic and runs up the stairs to his wife and they hug jubilant about the news. Marcus helps his six month pregnant wife to the elevator and they ride it down to the sanatorium to see her mother and newly, awakened father. In one day of terror, she nearly lost both her mother and father; her mother was protecting her, and her father was protecting her beloved Marcus. Inside, Zephora is beginning to feel insecure about herself and her relationship to everyone close to her; however, she has thus far been able to keep these feelings of insecurity a secret from her husband who has been preoccupied with his new position and transforming the atmosphere of Malawi, as well as taking on the duties of a minster to the people.

With his family around him, Zuri utters his first words, "W a t e r, please get me some water." Saphera quickly sticks a straw in his mouth and Zuri slowly sips on it and apparently not slow enough as he starts coughing from nearly getting choked. Everyone braces with fear hoping he hasn't triggered one of his violent coughing spells. The doctor steps in and checks his heart rate and monitors his blood pressure which both go back to normal after Zuri's brief cough.

After the incident at the last Tribal Council Conference, Marcus decreed that all his family members remain at the palace at least for a while until peace and tranquility have been restored. Now that Zuri seems to be recovering from his injuries, the spirit of the royal family are beginning to calm and be more at ease. The family rallies around Zuri and with all that support, his spirit is lifted, he heals faster and after a couple of weeks, he is released from the sanatorium into the care of his beloved wife. The doctor shares important information about Zuri to Saphera and she has chosen to bare the weight of it alone and not share it with Zuri, Zephora, Angelo or Marcus; she chooses to rely on her own prayers and her faith alone, which is never a good idea. Together in prayer a family can withstand the enemy; however, standing alone the enemy can pick them off one by one.

Zephora and Veronica have been able to bond through their shared experience of pregnancy and it has deepened their friendship even though Zephora possesses a secret. As a team, Marcus and Angelo are carving out a brand new history for the country of their ancestors, together with their fellow Tribal Law council members. Each member has secured critical positions within the government including Tamrin winning overwhelmingly, the Presidency over her opponents which is a victory for both the country and the council. Marcus' plan to transform the country is working and he has proven to the council that he is an effective leader and a devoted and loyal friend, as well as a loving husband and wise spiritual leader.

Marcus and Angelo are adapting to their new lives as friends and brothers as they have done at every phase of their lives together, helping each other, having each other's back; and now on the brink of fatherhood together, the circumstances and situations will be no different. Together they embrace the challenge with joy and infinite possibility for the future.

Saphera lovingly takes care of Zuri and with each passing day, he is mounting a full recovery from being shot like he has many times before. His job as a government agent has nearly cost him his life several times before. This time, as an agent for a new government that he is helping to transform, he is not alone. Before he was fighting to stay alive to get back to his family; this time he is teaching and training others with his family and it gives him a sense of pride that he has such a fantastic family and a sense of relief that he isn't alone through this process. Day becomes night and with Saphera in his arms, Zuri thinks to himself, *"All my efforts for the past thirty plus years have not been in vain. I made it back to a life with my family and it is beautiful and growing, and my new role as patriarch is exciting but still scary, it's exscared."* He laughs to himself and marvels at the creation of his new word to describe his current emotional state.

CHAPTER XXVII

For the last two and a half months Zephora has been on edge and Marcus has had enough and chooses this moment right before bed to question her about it.

"Ze, what's wrong with you, why are you snapping at me all the time, what have I done to you?"

"If you haven't noticed King Marcus," she retorts, "I am pregnant and my hormones are raging."

"Ze, you know I know you better than that. And I did notice; and you calling me that; is so not necessary woman. So please tell me what's going on with you."

"Fine Marcus. I don't feel like I'm good enough."

"Good enough for what Zephora, what are you talking about?"

"If you would be quiet and listen I will tell you." Marcus wants to lash back at her but chooses to listen in an effort to find out the truth. He sits on the bed and gives Zephora his undivided attention. Zephora continues, "I don't feel like I'm good enough for you. You have so much going on for yourself with being King and a minister and council leader. And I feel I am stuck in your shadow and that soon you will leave me because I cannot keep up or compete with everything else going on in your life."

Marcus takes a deep breath, rises off the bed and gently sits his beloved Zephora in the very spot he previously occupied. He kneels down in front of her, takes hold of both her hands in his and peers into her eyes. "My love, there is no way on earth or in heaven above that I would ever leave you, forget about you or replace you. You are the earth, the moon, the stars and the sun to me, as well as my center of gravity. Without you I am not whole, I am not complete and I am definitely not the man I am today. You are more than just good enough for me, you eclipse me, you outshine me, and it is I who works so hard every day of my life to prove that I am worthy for a wife such as you, for a Queen such as you and that I have what it takes to be the kind of husband and father you will always want beside you. I am nothing without you my love and everything with you. You are my very best friend, my confidant, and more than my dream of my Queen. You exceed my hopes and dreams by leaps and bounds; and, I am indebted to you for saving me. I like you, I love you, and with the beginning of every new day, I fall more and deeper in love with you. You never cease to surprise me or excite me; even now I am excited by your innocence and earnestness. We are forever my love; you were created for me and me for you, and we shall be together always and forever, in this life and the next."

Zephora has tears pouring out of her eyes, her faith in their marriage restored and her love elucidated beyond her imagination. Her eyes are open and her heart is overflowing with a fresh understanding of true love. She places Marcus' hands on her stomach to allow him to feel the kicks she feels before responding to his outpouring of love and understanding. "Marcus baby, please forgive me. I suppose I'm just a little scared with everything going on right now." She gets up and wraps her arms around him and embraces him. Still stunned by Marcus' words, all she can say to rebut him is, "Marcus, Sweetheart, I loved you yesterday, I love you now and I will love you always; until we meet God on judgment day and every day after that."

"Baby, we are in this together," Marcus replies, "and it scares me too; being parents, being a father. But I know, together we can accomplish anything. Think about all we have been through: marriage interrupted and stopped by a mad man, the same mad man attempts to kill me and marry you and when I stopped him, he tries to kill you and in doing so, almost kills me again. We've both been kidnapped, it took three times for us to finally get married and then we had to come here and get married all over again. And here we still stand, together, and I would go through it all again if I knew it would lead me right here, about to embark on this brand new chapter of our journey. Together, you and I, and with God as our foundation, we can overcome anything, any challenge, any endeavor. Now come lay here in my arms and let's talk some more, you know the way we used to talk until the sun came up; let's talk tonight, let's catch up for all these months we were unable to make time, let's make time and tonight talk all night long, into the early morning."

Zephora cuddles up next to Marcus and whispers, "Let's get it on my love, because I have missed talking with you too."

Marcus dims the lights, turns the smooth jazz down low and within ten minutes, before any words are spoken, they are both fast asleep; Zephora in Marcus' arms, and Marcus with one hand on her stomach feeling the tiny kicks in her swollen belly.

On the west wing of the palace, Angelo is trying to keep Veronica calm as she is having what seems like a contraction. She is panicking because the baby isn't due for another two weeks.

"Calm down baby and breathe; whew, whew breathe; whew, whew breathe. You're okay, you're okay, just breathe baby, just breathe."

"I'm okay Angelo, I'm okay. It stopped, it stopped; I'm okay now." Veronica takes a deep breath and tells Angelo again, "I'm okay honey, I'm okay. I just need to walk around for a bit."

Angelo helps her to her feet and they begin walking around the room one slow step after another. Veronica stops walking and just stands there for a moment; and then, she looks down and water is gushing down her legs. "Oh my God Angelo, my water just broke, my water just broke! You got to get me to the sanatorium now!"

"I got you baby, I got you Roni; now aren't you glad I brought that wheel chair up here?"

"Well, stop patting yourself on the back and just get me down there now. Call Zephora and then I'll be glad crazy man!"

"Stop yelling at me woman and breathe! I'll call Ze and Marcus when we get there. Now breathe; whew, whew breathe, whew, whew breathe."

Oliver is taking his nightly stroll around the palace and hears the commotion above him and screams out in his proper voice, "Might I be of any assistance?"

Angelo yells down to him, "Veronica is going into labor, have everyone meets us in the sanatorium please!" Angelo makes it to the elevator still telling Veronica to breathe and she in turn is telling him to shut up and she goes back to breathing.

Oliver makes the calls waking Marcus and Ze up first and then Zuri and Saphera who are on the first floor already and are able to make it to the sanatorium right behind Angelo and Veronica. Marcus and Zephora are moving slower and when they get there, Veronica's contractions are five minutes apart and she is dilated 7 centimeters; then three minutes, then two, now one minute apart.

Angelo is doing his best to comfort Veronica but her screams are drowning out his comforting words. He holds her hand and she squeezes it tight. The nurse tells Veronica to push and Angelo goes into coaching mode and gives Veronica the order again, "Let's go baby, let's go; now pushhhhhh!"

Veronica squeezes his hand tighter, bears down and pushes as hard as she can. The nurse tells her to stop and Angelo tells her to breathe, "You're doing great baby, you're doing great. Rest and breathe because the next one is going to be it. Breathe, breathe, breathe; now pushhhhhh!"

Veronica bears down and pushes as hard as she can with Angelo whispering in her ear, "You can do it baby, you got it baby, she's almost here baby, she's almost here, she's out."

Veronica stops pushing and breathes in deep and then releases it slowly; then, she and Angelo's ears are flooded with the loud screams of their new baby girl. Angelo kisses

Veronica and then calmly announces, "You did it baby, you did it." Veronica is overcome with emotion and the tears begin to flow down her face. She rests her head on Angelo's forearm and looks up at him with huge oval shaped tears dropping off her eyelashes and onto his arm. Veronica whispers a quiet personal prayer, "I wish you were here mom and dad; but I know you are watching me, watching us from above. Bless my new family Lord, its perfect; thank You for blessing us Lord, with a perfect and healthy daughter. I love you mom and dad, rest in peace.

After a few minutes in the care of the nurses getting wiped down and wrapped up, the lead nurse turns to an exhausted Veronica and an excited Angelo and presents them with their new five pound and eleven ounce baby girl, asking if they have a name picked out yet.

Veronica looks at Angelo and nods yes. Angelo stands up tall holding his new baby girl and proudly declares, "Her name is Angel Naria Henson Netumba." He hands his little Angel back to Veronica and when their eyes meet, he mouths to her, "I love you," without the words actually being heard and she mouths, "I love you back," in the same manner. The two of them are filled with joy at the new beautiful life they have brought into the world. Angel is in her mother's arms and with her father standing next to them, she has her first pictures taken with her parents by the lead nurse. She is laid in a rolling clear plastic and sterile crib next to her mother and the rest of her family comes in to meet her.

Marcus and Zephora are astounded at the beauty of the newest addition to the royal family. Zuri walks over to the crib and picks little Angel up, smiles at the marvelous miracle he is holding in his arms and asks Angelo her name. "Her name is Angel Naria Henson Netumba," Angelo proudly announces.

Zuri smiles at Angelo and now directs his attention towards the new baby he is holding and speaks to her, "Hello little Angel Naria Henson Netumba and welcome to our family. Know that you are loved unconditionally."

Zuri hands Angel to Saphera, takes a seat in the corner and watches his family with great pride and adoration. He watches his daughter, loves her smile and cannot wait to watch her bring a new life into the world; the thought of it fills him with a sense of great pride, joy and love.

Mother and child are exhausted. The family is ushered out to allow them to get some much needed rest. Marcus and Zephora walk hand in hand to the elevator and back to their suite, neither one of them saying a word. The jazz is still playing as they climb back into bed and resume their previous position and fall back to sleep as if nothing had happened; after all, it is 2:45a.m.

Zuri and Saphera on the other hand cannot stop talking about the beautiful new baby all the way back to their room. Saphera is extremely excited and cannot wait to go shopping. She is oozing with joy and doesn't see Zuri in his recliner laboring to breathe until she turns around because he hasn't responded to her chatter. She immediately runs to his side. "Zuri, honey are you alright?"

Only able to get a word out every other second between breaths. "I'll be okay in a minute precious, just trying to catch my breath; it feels like my lungs are on fire." Saphera runs to the bathroom and retrieves Zuri's medication, pours it in the provided cup and helps him drink it down. Within a couple of minutes, Zuri's breathing eases and the burning begins to subside. Saphera helps Zuri in to bed and curls up behind him spooning and rubbing his chest in an attempt to help him breathe. Zuri hasn't had the heart to tell his beloved Saphera that he has Stage 4 lung cancer, and their second chance at happiness will soon be cut short. Unbeknownst to Zuri, Saphera is aware of his terminal condition, and she also doesn't have the heart to broach the conversation with him.

CHAPTER XXVIII

Angelo and Veronica have been enjoying parenthood for about a month now. Angel is proving to be a good baby, she sleeps all night and hardly cries. She is the joy of the palace and awaiting the arrival of her cousins, as is everyone else, especially Marcus and Zephora. Zuri and Saphera have made the palace into a baby boutique with gifts for Angel Naria and with presents awaiting their royal grandbaby.

Its 8:15a.m. and Marcus is awakened to Zephora screaming his name from the bathroom. He runs in frantic wondering the problem when he looks on the floor under Zephora and notices the puddle of water. Zephora's eyes are the size of marbles and Marcus's eyes match the size of hers. Fortunately, Marcus listened to the advice of Angelo and has a wheel chair in the suite ready for Zephora. He brings it to her and they are on their way to the sanatorium.

Simultaneously, Zuri begins a violent coughing spell. Saphera tries to get him to take his medicine, but his coughing doesn't stop to give her a chance to get him to take it. She quickly calls Oliver for his assistance. Oliver is there within minutes and he helps Zuri to the sanatorium. Out of the corner of his eye, Zuri notices Marcus pushing his daughter her toward the sanatorium too. His chest is on fire, he can hardly breathe and his daughter is about to have a baby and he can't be there for her. Zuri is officially in hell.

Father and daughter are both in the sanatorium on opposite sides; one about to give life and the other fighting for his life. The doctor quickly orders an IV for Zuri in an effort to get medication in him. On the other side of the sanatorium, Zephora's contractions are getting closer together. Marcus calls Saphera to tell her Sephora is in labor. Saphera informs Marcus that Zuri's condition is worsening and they too are in the sanatorium. Marcus meets Saphera in the hall to discuss both situations and does his best to comfort Saphera without success.

Zephora is calling for you Saphera. So she and Marcus switch places and as they pass each other in the hall Marcus yells, "You just need to let me know when her contractions get closer together please!"

"Okay Marcus, but you must know that Zuri is…."

"It's ok Saphera, you needn't say anymore, I already know. I will sit with him and won't leave his side until you call me."

"Thank you Marcus; call Angelo please and get him down here."

"I'll take care of it; now you get in there and see your daughter."

Marcus calls Angelo and he is there within minutes. The two friends sit with Zuri and discuss the dire nature of his health, Zephora giving birth and how Veronica and Angel Naria are doing. Marcus prays and Angelo paces back and forth. Zuri open his eyes and sees Marcus and Angelo watching over him and make an effort to talk to them. With a raspy voice, he conveys to them what could be his last instructions and tells them how much he loves them. Marcus lets Zuri know that Zephora is still in labor and Zuri's demeanor changes and he closes his eyes again. Marcus' phone rings and he runs out of the room to his wife's room, whose contractions are now a minute apart. He and Saphera change places and she runs down the hall to her husband's side.

Zuri expresses to Saphera that he isn't going anywhere and she should go be with Zephora. Angelo remains with Zuri and Saphera runs back down the hall to be with Marcus and Zephora. Her emotions are erratic, her husband could be dying and her daughter is about to give birth to her first grandchild. On the other end of the sanatorium, Zuri opens his eyes and signals to Angelo to come closer. Angelo approaches, leans in and Zuri whispers something in his ear. Angelo listens attentively, occasionally saying, "Yes sir" and "I will." When Zuri finishes passing on information to Angelo, Angelo stands tall, shakes Zuri's hand and doesn't release it until he falls back asleep. Angelo sits beside Zuri's bed still refusing to release his hand.

Down the hall Marcus and Saphera are doing their best to comfort Zephora who is pushing, panting and breathing hard waiting for the next time to push. She pulls Marcus close by his collar and whispers in his ear gritting her teeth the whole time, "I know something is wrong with my father or he would be here; I can feel it." Marcus shakes his head no. "Don't shake your head no Marcus just listen to me. When our babies are born, let my mother take them to him so he can see his grandchildren." Marcus complies with fear in his eyes.

Saphera is eaves dropping and hears the word grandchildren. "My God Zephora, why didn't you tell me you are having twins? I should have known it, because you were a twin."

At that moment, one of the nurses yells, "Okay Your Majesty push!" Zephora squeezes Marcus' hand as tight as possible and stares at her mother with a look of disdain on her face and pushes. Saphera is crying and holding Zephora's other hand, and she leans in close and attempts to talks to Zephora while she is enduring the pain of child birth. "Your twin died as I gave birth to him and that is why I never told you."

Zephora is crying and pushing. Marcus is enraged and expresses his contempt to Saphera. "You picked this moment to tell her this? Please step back until this is over." In that moment, Zephora pushes one more time and one of the nurses shouts "It's a girl," and the cries of their new baby fills the room. Their new babygirl is taken to the baby table in the corner, measured, weighed, cleaned and wrapped in a blanket and adorned with a pink little hat and placed in the cradle. Saphera watches over her new granddaughter, as the doctor and his nurses prepared for baby number two.

They look at each other in despair as they notice that the second baby is breached, which immediately causes concern which they attempt to hide from Marcus and Zephora. "Your Majesty do not push until I tell you to and when you do, give me all you got until I say stop."

"Is everything okay Doc," Marcus asks.

"It will be as long as she follows my directions," he replies.

Saphera is holding her granddaughter in the corner with love and pride exuding from her. Attempting to distract her daughter she yells, "Zephora, Marcus, what is her name?"

Marcus leans in, kisses Zephora on the forehead, smiles at her and says, "We have a daughter my love, a beautiful daughter." Zephora is exhausted but looks up at Marcus and says, "I love you Marcus." Marcus looks over to Saphera and proudly states, "Her name is Zeza Eurika Howard Sakara."

Then he looks at Zephora, wipes the sweat from her brow and speaks truth to her, "My love do not worry, we are in God's loving hands and all will be well. Now ready yourself for the next big push. Breathe, breathe, breathe."

The doctor checks her uterus, notices a little more blood than usual, but steadies Zephora with his hand on her knee. "Okay, now push!" Zephora pushes with all she has; she pushes for what seems to be forever before the doctor yells, "Stop pushing." He checks her uterus and says, "Now get ready to push again." Zephora takes a deep breath, Marcus gives her kiss and the doctor again yells, "Push Zephora push!"

Zephora bares down and pushes with all her might. The doctor yells, "I have the feet, keep pushing, keep pushing, keep pushing, he's out." The doctor cuts the cord, but no cry is heard. He hands the baby to his nurse and together they begin working on the infant. Saphera is watching and crying; she has been here before. Marcus has never felt helpless in his life, until right now; he is in an abyss, lost trying to find his way out. He wants to run and take over but he knows he wouldn't know what to do; so helpless, he stands there holding his wife's hand with a huge lump in his throat too afraid to swallow.

Zephora is past the point of exhaustion, her bleeding goes unnoticed while they are trying to revive her baby and she is nearly unconscious when she hears it, the cry of her new born son. His cry is loud and a sweet sound to her ears. Marcus looks down at his wife, she smiles at him through her exhaustion and then he notices she has stopped breathing. Marcus shouts, "Doc get over here, she's not breathing!" The doctor leaves the baby in his nurse's capable hands to finish prepping the baby and she places him next to his sister in the cradle with a blue hat on.

The doctor notices Zephora's bleeding and calls for a code blue. The room is immediately filled with more nurses and more equipment. His team works to stop the bleeding and attempts to restart her heart, manually at first. Marcus refuses to let go of her hand. He leans in and whispers in her ear, "You hold on baby, I love you, I need you and our children need you. You hold on Ze, don't you dare think about leaving me."

The doctor yells, "Clear," and Marcus releases her hand and they hit her with defibrillator charged at 200.

While they are working on Zephora, Saphera, with tears streaming down her face, rolls the cradle down the hall and into Zuri's room. To her surprise, Veronica is there with Angelo and Angel. Zuri finds the strength to sit up in the bed with the help of Angelo. Saphera brings the babies close so Zuri can see them. Zuri is overcome with joy at the sight of his grandchildren. "My God Saphera, look at our grandbabies, a boy and a girl. How is Zephora doing, I know she must be beaming with joy."

Saphera shakes her head and says, "They are working on her Zuri, her heart stopped and I am scared to death."

Zuri reaches to hold his wife's hand and whispers to her, "She is strong and has a lot to live for, and she will be alright." For the next few minutes, the room is quiet, until Zuri says, "Let me hold my grandson and what is his name?" Saphera is unable to tell him; however, Angelo speaks up.

"Marcus told me if he has a son, his name will be Zikomo Xavier Howard Sakara in honor of your father."

There is not a dry eye in the room at this gesture from Marcus. Zuri, who is beginning to feel worse, asks Angelo, as he begins to feel himself fading, to take some pictures of him and Saphera with all the babies including Angel. Angelo is able to take three pictured of them before Zuri, says, "That's enough, I'm tired," and begins to slump down in his bed. Saphera places the babies back in their cradle, runs to her husband's side and presses the button for the nurse. Before the nurse gets there, Zuri whispers to Saphera, "Tell my daughter I love her." The nurse arrives, Zuri isn't conscious and she calls for a code blue. When the doctor arrives, Zuri is barely breathing and his pulse is weakening.

Meanwhile, down the hall, the defibrillator is again charged, this time to 300, in an effort to revive Zephora with Marcus looking on in distress, helpless again, the void closing in on him. He begins to pray out loud, *"God, You told me that she is the woman You made for me, don't take her away from me now. I need her Lord, please don't take her away from me. Father, I am pleading, I'm begging; Lord, no, please Lord no, don't take my beloved away. In Jesus Holy name, please Lord, please."*

Simultaneously down the hall, Zuri's fight is ending. The doctor calls his time of death, "Time, 3:27p.m." Zuri Netumba's life has expired. At that precise time on the other end of the hall, Zephora's doctor and nurses are able to resuscitate her for a few minutes before she takes a deep breath and her heart has stopped again.

In Zuri's room, Angelo is beyond words, Veronica has tears running down her face, all three babies are crying and Saphera is overcome with grief, nearly fainting but remembering her daughter is still fighting for her life on the other end of the hall. She kisses his forehead and hugs Zuri's lifeless body; she rubs his head and kisses his lips one last time. She pulls the sheet up to cover his body and hurriedly pushes her crying grandchildren down the hall to be with her daughter. Angelo and Veronica follow her to be there for

Marcus and Zephora in their time of need but still reeling from Zuri's death.

They enter the room, Marcus' eyes are red, swollen and overrun with tears creeping out of the corners. Marcus looks up at Saphera, she shakes her head to make him aware that Zuri has passed on, and more tears begin to flow from his eyes. The doctor and nurses have finally stopped Zephora's bleeding and they are continuing to attempt to revive her. Saphera is on the brink of an emotional breakdown and the newborn infants are crying as though they can sense the trauma happening.

Marcus runs to his children, pushes them over to Zephora's bedside. He kneels down between them and her; he draws strength from his faith, and over the cries of the babies calmly says to Zephora, "I know you can hear your children crying my love, fight to live, we need you. Zephora, Ze, wake up baby, we need you, I need you, don't leave me woman, wake up now, don't leave us alone!"

It's 3:30p.m., and even though the room is filled with the voices of the doctor and nurses working to save Zephora, they are only able to maintain a heartbeat for minutes at a time before she crashes again. And even though their children are crying uncontrollably, and even though Saphera is screaming Zephora's name with Angelo trying to restrain her, Marcus is numb to it all. He has tuned it all out and hears none of it; he only hears dead silence. And in that silence, he is searching for the heartbeat of his beloved Zephora. He places his hand on her chest searching in the silence for her heartbeat. He searches in hope, he searches in faith, he searches in the name of love; he searches in the name of their love.

It's 3:40p.m., and with his hand on her chest, Marcus feels a beat, then nothing. "Not yet God, not yet," he silently declares. The doctor tries to pull him back, to let her go and Marcus shrugs him off. His family is watching in disbelief. Marcus places both hands on Zephora's chest and he pumps; 1 2 3 4 5, he breathes into her mouth and her chest rises. He pumps, 1 2 3 4 5 and breathes into her mouth and her chest rises. He pumps her chest again 1 2 3 4 5, and again breathes into her mouth and again her chest rises. The doctor has given up, but Marcus refuses to stop, refuses to give up. As he starts to pump her chest again, Angelo stops him, "you blow, and I'll pump." Together Marcus and Angelo feverishly attempt to do what the doctor has given up on. "1 2 3 4 5, breathe Zephora breathe," Angelo shouts as Marcus blows air into her lungs.

"1 2 3 4 5 breathe Zephora breathe, 1 2 3 4 5. . . . ." Marcus feels his dream slipping away from him. His heart is beating twice as fast as it should be. The light at the end of the tunnel is getting farther and farther away. Angelo has stopped pumping but Marcus is still blowing air into her lungs and her chest rises again and again. He turns and looks at his crying children, and turns back towards Zephora. Marcus blows into her mouth one last time, then raises his left fist high in the air, and with the force of the love he carries deep in his heart and soul for Zephora, he plunges it onto her chest simultaneously yelling "BREATHE ZEPHORA….. BREATHE!"

Made in the USA
Charleston, SC
01 October 2015